The
Maximilian
Emancipation

Charles A. Conyers, Jr.

ISBN-10: 0-9991499-0-3
ISBN-13: 978-0-9991499-0-4

For Pops.

Hi, folks—

This is a work of science fiction. While there are elements of the story based on fact, the characters and situations are merely speculative.

I would also like to point out that some of the language used in this book may be objectionable to some. While I tend to use naughty words from time to time, there is some language and a few conversations presented here that some may find difficult or offensive. Frankly, the entire book deals with triggerable issues that cause distress, anger, frustration, and anxiousness in some. All I ask is that you power through it and give the story a chance.

The worse thing that could happen is that you experience something new.

N-Joy,

Charles

PART I
MAAFA

1

August 8th, 2041
10:13 am
Jersey Shore

Jake Townsend has absolutely no idea where he is. He had his suspicions about that turn he took a few miles back. That was when the GPS app froze. Should have done what he thought was right, instead of listening to *"her,"* otherwise known as his wife, Candice Townsend.

Candice is not speaking to Jake at the moment, not after he used that tone of his. *Nasty,* she thinks to herself, *and now we're lost in this shitty neighborhood- we'll probably get car jacked.*

The car slows to a stop at the red light. Jake reaches out and pokes the NAVICOM[1] screen on the dashboard. He cycles through a series of windows, hoping that he can find some option he hasn't noticed before that will finally get this thing to work right. Of course, he could just read the instruction manual; he never reads the manuals. Candice sucks her teeth and rolls her eyes.

The kids slump in the backseat isolated in their self-imposed techno bubbles of portable entertainment. Jolene, 14 years-old, is 'glyphing' with her 'boo'. In English, that means she and her best friend are exchanging picture messages with her NAVI. For a brief moment, she manages to look up and 'peep' her 'area.'

They are at an intersection in a dilapidated urban neighborhood. Jolene watches five hard-looking black

---

[1] *Media Navigation and Communication Device, other wise know as the NAVICOM (nicknamed NAVI), has replaced the smartphone and tablets as the portable media and communication device of choice.*

boys standing outside a bodega on the corner. They look to be about her age, engaged in an animated conversation that at first appears to be heated until they all burst into laughter. She smiles.

"Where are we?" Jolene asks.

"Ask your father," spits Candice.

The 11-year-old, Brett, looks up from the video game on his NAVI, and out the window. He also notices the boys at the bodega wearing basketball jerseys and expensive sneakers. That's the kind of gear that he keeps bugging the 'rents for, but they refuse to buy. "You'd look like a thug," is what his mother says. It didn't matter to her that most of his friends had the same stuff.

"I told you not to by that cheap piece of crap," Candice sneers. "There are so many new ones on sale, and you had to buy it used? It makes no sense."

Jake shrugs. "It's not used, it's pre-owned. I saved $200, plus I got a deal on the installation. So really, I saved $300. I just need to reboot the system."

He taps the screen a few more time, and the travel map pops up. "Calculating route, Jake," announces his NAVI's silky female voice.

Jake clenches his fist in victory. "Got it!"

"Great, let's go," sneers Candice.

"Can I wait for the light to change?"

Candice rolls her eyes. Jake grips the wheel with his sweaty hands, releasing a great big sigh. He notices a black family of five-and-a-half using the crosswalk in front of him. The woman is pregnant, slightly overweight, with tired, faded bitterness and frustration etched in her eyes. She turns to her three screeching kids.

"Hey! Stop fuckin' around and let's go!"

Trailing behind is the daddy, skinny, beaten and worn down.

"Would you hurry the fuck up? You look like a beaten dog!"

As the man crosses in front of the car, he looks up at Jake. The two make eye-contact. Awkwardness and discomfort spray through Jake's body like acid. He hates that. It's that involuntary rush of embarrassment and shame that he feels when he enters a neighborhood like this. Intellectually, he knows this is foolish. His liberal sensibilities tend to trump good old-fashioned common sense. *At what point*, he wonders, *do they just give up on trying? What is their end game in their life's pursuit? Do they know there is more than this? Are they raised believing that this is it?*

"Go!" barks Candice.

"Turn right at Martin Luther King Boulevard," instructs his NAVI.

10:45am

Jake is losing his grip on the beach umbrella as his folded beach chair begins slipping through his sweaty arm. His other hand grips the fully-packed cooler he is dragging through a maze of people.

"I see a spot!" shouts Brett. He bounds through the slim aisles of blankets and flops down onto an unoccupied patch a beach.

As Candice struggles with her packed tote bags towards Brett, she notices another family moving in. She doesn't like the looks of the situation. The woman leading the other family, that *other mother* looks like the combative type, with her cornrows and her long Freddy Kruger fingernails. *No way are you going to squat your fat ass in this spot, 'sista,'* Candice yells in her mind.

Brett also notices the other family approaching, so he lies back, spreading his arms and legs, and makes a sand angel.

Candice reaches the spot and drops her bags down before the other family moves in.

"Let's get the blanket set up," she says to Jolene. Candice never looks up at the woman. The sound of ol' 'cornrows' sucking her teeth as she leads her family away is satisfaction enough.

Jolene drops her bag and strips down to her bikini. As she pulls off her t-shirt, she notices 'cornrows' 15-year-old son looking at her. She likes it. He smiles.

"Come on, Jolene," demands Candice, fully aware of the way Jolene is looking at that boy; she knew that bikini was going to be trouble.

As soon as Jake reaches the spot, he gets to work. He unpacks and plants the wind proof beach umbrella. He sets up his beach chair, digs through the cooler and pulls out a beer, and finally plants his ass down for what he hopes to be a very, very long time.

"What are you doing?" Candice complains. "You should put the umbrella over here. Why are you drinking a beer before noon?"

Jake pops off the cap and takes a nice, long swig. *Mmmmm, cold, sharp and bitter...just like her*, he says in his mind, followed by a comedy drum fill and a laugh track. He sets his beer in the beach chair's cup holder and reaches into his backpack. He pulls out a pair of noise-canceling headphones. Jake puts them on and taps a few buttons on the side.

"Don't just sit there, help us with this bla-"...silence.

Jake taps another button, and now the only sound he hears is the ocean. Candice is still talking, but he only sees her lips moving. He wishes those lips were doing something else instead of berating him. For now, he'll take mute. He lays back in his chair and continues drinking.

Candice stops talking and looks around. "Wait, where is Brett?"

No sooner do those words leave her mouth does Brett appear, carrying a bucket of water. When he pours the water down Jolene's back, she lets out an ear-splitting screech that could break glass. Brett laughs and runs away.

Jolene darts after him. "You little shit!"

"Hey, mouth!" Candice calls out to Jolene as she chases Brett to the water. At least now she can get some peace. With no nagging kids and a temporarily incapacitated husband, she is finally going to relax. She only wishes that the fat baldy on the blanket next to them would turn down his NAVI streaming a vidcast from who she calls "that annoying asshat," Gerry Baines; the self-proclaimed "Dark Fury" of Neo-Progressive thought.

"God, to me, is love," Baines begins. "She can also be harsh and cruel, seemingly unjust and unkind. But She is not without Her reasons--Her will. Even with all we face in our country today: corruption, recession, socialism, racism, atheism, the death of our values as a nation--as a people! America has lost its way, my friends. It's these pro-Anglo, pro-European, anti-American attitudes that take us further and further away from being one nation...under God! We cannot be under God when we are constantly running away from Her."

If he was white, he wouldn't have that show. He'd be driving a bus or cleaning shitters, is what Candice thinks. At that moment she notices that there aren't that many white faces on the beach at all. She hadn't been to this beach in a while. It wasn't like this when she was a kid. *It was better back then.*

Baines continues. "We are constantly getting interrupted and disrupted by know-nothings and malcontents who want everyone to feel and think the way they do. The racists, the bigots, the anti-government socialist fascists-- proud, uneducated, and they say they believe in God. But do they? Anti-intellectualism is the gateway to Hell, people-- and from the looks of things, there's a waiting list! Do you think God wants you to be stupid? Do you think God expects you to have absolutely no curiosity about the world around you? God gives you a brain and, what...you don't want to use it? While you're wrapped up in huffing your own flatulence, She's got plans for you- for all of us, in fact!

7

"We are about to be tested, America. And it will happen soon-- hell, it could happen today! What if today was the day? What would have to happen, what would it take? What's that wake-up call sound like? Will you even notice it? Many of you won't. I've got news for you sunshine...you're in for a rude awakening."

Meanwhile, Brett stomps through the water trying to get away from Jolene. Brett can't move as fast in the water, allowing Jolene to grab his arm and pull him towards her.

"Wait, wait! I'm sorry!" he yells.

"Beg me to stop," she demands.

"Please, please, please Super Sis!" That's good enough. She releases him.

"I bet I can hold my breath underwater longer than you," Brett challenges.

"Oh yeah? Go ahead."

Brett takes a deep breath and dunks himself under water.

As Jolene counts out loud, she turns towards the beach and almost immediately spots 'cornrows' son walking into the water several feet away from her. She watches him dive into the water, and stand back up. She likes the way the sunlight glistens on his wet, bronze skin. His chest is strong. His hair is knotted and textured. He's hot.

"How long was that? Hey!"

Jolene whips her attention back to Brett, who has resurfaced. "What? Eleven seconds."

"No way, more like 35."

"Okay," she says, looking back at the boy. Brett sees him, too.

"Your turn," he says.

"Maybe later." The boy looks at her now and smiles.

"Are you coal-mining, Sis?"

Jolene smacks him in the arm. "Brett! Where did you hear that from?"

"That's what Bobby calls it when a girl dates a black boy."

Jolene rolls her eyes. "You're getting this from Bobby, no wonder-- he's an idiot."

"You know how Mom feels about that stuff," warns Brett.

"Alright, my turn," she says. Jolene takes a few breaths and drops underwater. She counts out thirty-eight seconds before she resurfaces, wiping water away from her face and back through her hair. She opens her eyes to find Brett moving towards the beach.

"Hey," she yells at him, "where are you going?"

Brett looks back at Jolene. "Getting Dad's goggles," he yells back and points to the horizon. "There's something out there!" She turns and sees it immediately; there are three large dots sitting close to each other on the horizon.

"What is that?" she asks.

Brett bounds from the water and sprints through the sand to Jake.

"Dad," Brett yells, grabbing Jakes arm, and scaring the shit out of him.

"What the shit!" Jake yells, removing the noise-canceling head gear.

"Jesus, Brett," says Candice, looking up from her NAVI. She doesn't read ebooks or any other books often, but she will read anything about the 45th president-- *God rest his soul*, she believes.

"Dad, I need your binoculars!"

"They're in my bag," Jake says, sliding his equipment back on. "Maniac..."

Brett rummages through Jakes duffle bag, finds the binoculars, and runs back to the water. He runs by Jolene, who's now talking to the boy.

"Hey," she yells after him. "What are you doing now?"

Using the binoculars, Brett looks out at the objects in the distance.

Jolene and her new friend wade out to Brett. "What do you see?"

"They're ships. Three ships."

"What kind of ships?" Jolene asks.

"They're old. Like pirate ships."

Jolene grabs the binoculars and looks out. "It must be a boat show or something. Wanna see, James?" She hands the binoculars to her new friend.

"Only if your brother says it's okay," James says, looking at Brett.

"Brett, do you mind if James looks through the binoculars," she asks her brother with a 'please-do-not-be-a-jerk' look on her face.

"Yeah, sure," says Brett, handing them to James. As he looks out, Brett sticks out his tongue playfully.

"They look like cutter ships," James says.

"What's a cutter ship?" Brett asks.

"They're cargo ships," James answers. "Before airplanes and FedEx, that's how they used to ship things. They could ship all kinds of stuff from one end of the world to the other. Took weeks, sometimes months."

James hands the binoculars back to Brett.

"How do you know about all of that?" asks Jolene.

James smiles at Jolene. "I know some stuff." She smiles back, unconsciously biting her lip.

Brett sees this and rolls his eyes. He looks back out at the ships.

"They're getting closer," he says, and suddenly turns up his nose. "What's that? Do you smell that?"

Jolene slaps Brett in the arm. "Did you freaking fart, you pig?"

"That's not me!"

A woman covering her nose several feet away catches Jolene's eye. She notices others reacting.

"I don't think that's a fart," James says, covering his nose. "It's different."

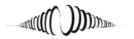

11:21am
Lower Bay, New York

Eight years ago today, Jim Stockton became a captain in the New York City Harbor Patrol. As a young boy, there were two things that Jim loved: police cars, and boats. Now, as a man of 42 years, he has almost everything he's ever wanted. Except for kids. It wasn't for lack of trying. He had been married and divorced twice in fifteen years. At this point, he's so jaded in love that the prospect of having kids was slim to none in his mind. There's a small part of him that's still hopeful, but that part is dry and bitter.

In the middle of these unpleasant thoughts, a voice squawks over his radio from dispatch.

"5-13, Dispatch," Jim answers.

"5-13, we have calls of possible unauthorized traffic in your vicinity."

Unauthorized, he thinks. *Probably some asshole rappers on a rented yacht.*

"Finally," cheers Officer Scott Bolicki, fumbling forward from the back of the boat. "We finally get some action!"

"Yeah, right," says Jim. "Taking shit from some overpaid, talentless cunt is not my idea of action."

"Hey, man. Maybe they'll hook us up. A couple of beers, maybe a bottle of Dom— you know, whatever those guys drink. Maybe it's one of those Gen-Z billionaires- they drink craft beers and organic wine and shit."

Jim shakes his head. "Don't get your hopes up. It's probably some retired couple that took a wrong turn. Maybe they'll give us a few of their multivitamins."

"Three o'clock." Officer Bolicki looks out at the black dots on the horizon with his binoculars.

Jim sees them, too. He steers the boat in their direction and picks up speed. He looks over at Bolicki, wondering why he's not reporting what he sees.

"What, are there naked girls out there or something?" Jim asks.

"They're like pirate ships," says Bolicki.

"What?"

"They're old-looking ships, with sails. Three of 'em."

The wind gets stronger as Jim accelerates.

"Is there a boat show?" Bolicki has to shout a bit over the wind noise. "They look like 18th or early 19th century? Have to be replicas."

Jim picks up the radio. "Dispatch, we have a visual. Looks like we've got three sailing ships, historical replicas, possibly from a nearby boat show?"

"There are no a boat shows going on today, 5-13," says the dispatch voice.

"Wait, I see something!" Bolicki adjusts the zoom on the binoculars. "Looks like two men..." Bolicki lowers the binoculars. "Whoa!" He turns up his nose and covers it with his hand.

Jim smells it, too. The wind reeks of it. "What the hell is that?"

Bolicki shakes his head, pinching his nose hard. "Jesus! It's like fifty homeless guys takin' a dump on sixty homeless guys!"

They are close enough to the ships that Jim can read the back of the vessel closest to them: Leusden.

Bolicki tilts his head. "Loose-den?"

Jim slows the patrol boat. Aside from its engine, things are very quiet. And that smell…Bolicki's gag reflex flares up.

"Tell me about it," says Jim, trying to muscle through it. "You said you saw two men?" Jim asks, squinting and turning up his nose. It's a putrid, sour, earthen stench that touches the back of their throats. "This is almost too much to-"

"Shit!" Bolicki raises the binoculars, looking out at the ships. "Men overboard!"

At least ten dark-skinned bodies leap from one of the ships and splash down flailing into the water. As Jim picks up the radio to call dispatch, he hears motor sounds coming from behind their boat. He turns to see a group of three kids on jet skis heading for them.

"Mayday Mayday, we have about twenty men overboard—require immediate assistance."

Bolicki grabs a lifesaver as the jet skiers get closer. A boy and two girls, no older than 15. One of the girls is holding a video camera.

"Hey!" the boy shouts, " Did you see that light?"

"What?" Bolicki shouts back.

"That flash!" the boy opens his arms mimicking an explosion. "They came out after that flash!"

"You kids get out of here," Jim commands over the loudspeaker.

As Jim moves the boat towards the jumpers in the water, more people-- men and women-- jump from the ships. This time, it's hard to tell how many there are—could be twenty, could be forty.

"What the fuck is going on," shouts Bolicki. "These people are naked!"

Jim throws the boat into reverse to slow down and stop near a cluster of the jumpers who look as if they are drowning. Bolicki throws out a few of the life preservers they have on board, but the jumpers are yelling and freaking out, and trying to move away from the boat.

"Come this way!" Bolicki yells. "What are you doing? We're trying to save you! This way!"

BANG! POP!

A shot is fired into the hull of the patrol boat. Jim and Bolicki hit the deck.

"Who's shooting at us?" yells Bolicki.

Jim draws his weapon. "It came from one of the ships!" Jim grabs the radio handset. "Dispatch we have shots fired, shots fired from one of the vessels and about 30 people overboard-- request immediate assistance!"

Bolicki takes cover behind the cabin of the patrol boat with his gun drawn and ready as he peers up at the ships, looking for the shooter. He looks down at the flailing people in the water, three to five to each one of the six life preservers Bolicki threw into the water.

"They look life refugees, are they refugees?" he asks.

"From where, Newark?" Jim says this just as he can hear the so-called refugees shouting and yelling amongst themselves. Whatever they're speaking, it's not English.

"Jim!" Bolicki shouts. Bolicki points out at about 2 o'clock. Jim spots the shooter. At first, they see a head of messy blonde hair peek up, followed by the barrel of what looks like a rifle. Then, the shooter jumps into position to shoot. Bolicki and Jim fire multiple shots. The shooter falls out of sight.

"Did we get him?" Jim shouts.

"There's no way I missed," says Bolicki, just as the shooter pops up and fires a shot, shattering the windshield of the harbor boat cabin. They both duck down.

Jim watches the glass rain onto the deck. "Fuckers!"

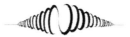

12:08 pm

Detective Chris Stellman stares at the three wooden ships as his boarding party approaches. Two additional harbor patrol boats and three ships from the United States Coast Guard have formed a perimeter around the wooden ships.

Stellman hates the water and always has. He's a very tall, strong-looking dark-skinned man whose presence induces intimidation and demands respect. When it comes to being on boats or flying over large bodies of water, he'd rather do something far less stressful, like getting a bikini wax.

He is a bit more at ease once he boards the first of the three ships; The Fredensborg. The ship is big and sturdy and doesn't move around as much as the schooners. Once he is on board and feeling somewhat secure, his attention shifts from the ocean to the scene on board this ship.

The deck is full of activity. Personnel from the NYPD and Homeland Security are on board, some milling around, a few examining the ship. A few of the officers were wearing face masks, for the smell.

As Stellman walks, the boards in the deck creak. The ship is worn and weathered- like it had been used for hard work over several years and many journeys.

Sergeant Walker steps up, also wearing a face mask. He hands one to Stellman. "Detective," he says.

"Sergeant," Stellman answers, waving away the mask. The smell was bad but didn't bother him that much. He was a first responder years ago on 9/11, helping sort through "the pile" as it burned with fuel, chemicals, bodies...he's smelled worse. "What's the story?"

"We're working our way around the ship," Walker explains and points to the cargo hatch in the middle of the deck. "We're about to bust this lock-- look at this thing. It's old as fuck."

Stellman looks down at what appears to be an antique metal padlock.

"Anyone on board?" asks Stellman.

Walker points to a ragged-looking group of men lined up against the rail of the deck, cuffed and seated, and flanked by a pair of police officers. They look like extras from a pirate movie, sunburned, dirty, and unshaven. All except for one of them, who is tanned, clean-shaven and healthy-looking. He's also smiling, leaning over to a stoic crewman next to him and whispering something in his ear.

"Almost none of these guys speaks English," Walker says.

Stellman looks at Walker. "What do they speak?"

"I dunno," shrugs Walker. "It sounds like Dutch or German or something."

"Which one speaks English?" he asks. Walker points to the tanned smiler, who looks up at the Sergeant, then to Stellman, then back to the Sergeant. His smile disappears.

"He says his name is Jacob Morgan," says Walker, consulting his notebook. "Gimme that piece," he calls off to an officer.

The officer hands Walker a pistol that looks like another antique. Walker hands it to Stellman. "He was armed with this."

Stellman takes the pistol, and examines it. "What the hell is this?" he asks.

"Looks like a musket or something," says Walker. "There's black powder all over it; I'm assuming it's gun powder. I guess that means it works."

Holding the gun, Stellman steps up to the Jacob. "Do you speak English?"

"Yes," Jacob answers, with a bit of a quiver in his voice.

"Good," Stellman says. "Well, Jacob, is it? Quite a boat show you have goin' on here." He holds up the pistol. "This is yours, right?"

"It's for protection," says Jacob.

"Protection from what? Dinosaurs?" asks Stellman. He looks at the handle and sees a small brass panel with an inscription:

Jonathan Morgan
1735

"Who is Jonathan?" asks Stellman.

"My father," says Jacob. "I'm sorry, who are you?"

"I'm Detective Stellman."

Jacob looks confused. "Detective?"

"That's right," Stellman answers. "You're telling me that this is your father's gun?"

"Yes," answers Jacob. "He gave it to me on my sixteenth birthday."

Stellman looks at the date on the gun; 1735. "I'm no good at math, Jacob," he says, "But I'm having a hard time believing that story. So, do you want to tell me what you and your friends are doing here?"

"I don't know," says Jacob. "I don't know where we are. We were on route back to Virginia, and we met with a lightning storm. All of a sudden, we were here."

"Virginia? You're a long way from Virginia. Where were you coming from?"

Jacob looks up at the noise that he hears in the sky. Stellman looks up and sees a police helicopter. The crew members stir, reacting as if they are either confused or frightened or both.

"What is that thing?" asks Jacob, his voice shaking.

"The detective asked you a question, buddy," says Walker. "Show some respect and answer the question."

Jacob looks back at Stellman, then looks back up at the helicopter.

"I have to tell you Jacob, whatever community theater foolishness you're pulling right now is getting on my nerves. I want to know where you were coming from and why you are here."

"We left port three says ago, out of the Bight."

"The bite?" Stellman asks. "What's the bite?"

"The Bight," Jacob says, waiting for a hint of recognition from Stellman. There is none.

"The Bight of Benin," Jacob tries again. Nothing. He doesn't understand how this man could not know this. He even sings the limerick: "*Beware, beware, the Bight of Benin/Once you go out, you won't come back in...*"

"I have no idea what you're talking about," Stellman says. "I don't know anything about a bite of Beneen. All I know is that you and this boat show are in New York Harbor, and you are not authorized to be here."

"New York?" Jacob says, confused. "We're in New York? But that is not possible...!"

"Oh, it's possible," Stellman says, as he looks around. Something is bothering the detective. This ship, these men...this is not a boat show. Just then, he gets another whiff of that smell, but this time it's so intense that it makes him cover his nose and mouth.

"What the <u>hell</u> is that smell?!"

THUD!

Everyone looks down. The sound came from underneath them.

"What was that?" Stellman asked Jacob.

"It's nothing," Jacob fumbles, "some of the cargo fell…"

"Cargo? What kind of Cargo?"

Jacob's mouth moves to answer, but no sound comes out.

"Sergeant," Stellman gestures towards the cargo door, "We need this open right now."

Walker and two other officers lower their weapons to concentrate on breaking the lock. "What the hell kinda lock is this?" one of them says.

"What am I going to find down there, Jacob?" Stellman asks.

"Look," Jacob begins, with panic in his voice, "I don't know what is going on. I don't know who you are—"

"I told you who I was, Mr. Morgan," says Stellman while watching the officers work on the lock. "Now we need to know who you are."

"You said you were a detective."

"Very good, you remembered."

"<u>You</u> are a detective? Or is your master…" Jacob trails off as he sees the way Stellman and Officer Walker are staring at him.

"Did he just say 'master'?" asks Walker.

"Look, I don't know what's going on! I don't know why we have you people on my ship! I'm just trying to make a living," pleads Jacob, "we all are!"

Stellman listens to Jacob and looks around at the ship. This ship does not look like something that is brought out for tourists for show; this ship looks like it's in working condition, and has been that way for a long time. The ragged crew looks terrified; one of them is crying, and another produces a puddle of piss on the deck.

"Consider what would happen to them anyway!" continued Jacob. "If the wars don't kill them, they'd probably starve! We are giving them a chance at a normal life! We're helping them!"

Snap! The lock breaks into pieces. Stellman watches Jacob look down frantically at the floor, then back up to him.

Walker and the two officers lift open the cargo door but drop it immediately as the smell surges from below. The men scatter to catch their breath and gag; the masks do nothing to block the smell. The others fan at the air, turning their faces away.

The officers return to the cargo door, hold their breath, count to three, and LIFT! The back of the door slams against the deck. As the heat and smell radiate away, the men step closer to the door but stop suddenly. A cluster of dark-skinned hands reach out.

Detective Stellman steps to the cargo door, his jaw dangling as he peers down into the hole and sees a sea of black faces staring back at him. Women and little girls. Filthy. Naked. Weak. Crying. Pleading. Chained and shackled.

Stellman stares back at them, forgetting to breathe for a few moments. His palms break into a rapid sweat.

"Jesus Christ," says Walker.

Stellman turns to Jacob, who looks as if he knows what's coming. The detective steps to him, hovering like a beast about to devour its prey.

"What is this?" asks Stellman through gritting teeth.

Jacob is paralyzed and says nothing.

Stellman reaches down, grabs Jacob by his throat, squeezes it tightly, and picks him up from the ground. Since Jacob's hands are bound, he has no defense.

As the other officers try to pry the detective's hands from around Jacob's neck, Stellman continues to yell over and over again, "WHAT...IS...THIS?!"

CHARLES A. CONYERS, JR.

2

The first images of what comes to be known as the "African Refugees" were shot from a local news channel's traffic helicopter. From the sky, the three ships were in a triangle-shaped cluster, towed by tugboats, with a circle of police and Coast Guard vessels surrounding them. When the camera zooms in on one of the ships, the images are graphic and horrific.

African men and women huddled on the deck, shivering, and scared, barely clothed, if at all. Most are still chained and shackled. They look up at the swarms of helicopters hovering over them. Some are pointing, some are screaming. Some are jumping overboard, forgetting they are chained to others; they either dangle over the edge or pull a few down into the water with them.

The officers on board move in cautiously to try to help them, but the Africans cringe away, or fight back. The officers are advised to hold their ground and not make any aggressive moves until the ships are docked.

A few more news choppers show up in time to capture an incident involving a group Africans advancing towards a cluster of officers, that ends in the tasing of at least four of the Africans. The others see this and cringe away; between the flying beasts overhead and the frightening men with their magic pointing fingers, they are too scared to do anything else.

2:03 pm

Programming on all major networks is interrupted by graphics announcing "BREAKING NEWS" or "SPECIAL REPORT." Media reporters appear with images of the three ships receiving an escort up the Hudson River towards the dock at 37th Street.

Hundreds of New Yorkers gather along the Westside Highway. Amateur and professional photographers armed with any and everything capable of capturing an image aims at the flotilla. These images are plastered media wide. It is a local story that, within less than 2 minutes, becomes international news.

By the time the ships reach the dock, it is packed with first-responders and on-lookers. The police set up barricades to keep pedestrians and media people as far back as possible, allowing FEMA, EMS crews, the Coast Guard, NYPD and Port Authority as much room as they need. In addition to the standard medical equipment, shower facilities are set up. All personnel are also provided with masks and gloves. Those boarding the ships are required to wear HAZMAT suits. Clothing and shoes provided by the Red Cross are also on site for the refugees.

A series of ramps connect the ships to the docks. The first refugees to disembark brings audible gasps from the onlookers. Even the clicking and flashes of the media cameras pause. The looks in the eyes of the men and women as they step onto the dock is heartbreaking; their faces convey all of the confusion, pain, discomfort, distrust in everything they see around them.

The refugees are led to a large shower tent. FEMA personnel stand in an assembly-line fashion but are emotionally unprepared for the encounter. Some are so mesmerized by the sickly, filthy state of the Africans that they almost forget that they are not spectators of a catastrophe, but are here to help these people. As the refugees approach the showers, they are given bars of soap, which some mistake for food, and take big and multiple bites out of the bars. The workers immediately snatch them away and try to get these people to spit out whatever they tried to eat.

They assist the refugees with their bathing, using sponges and low-power water jets to scrub their skin. The water is cold, and met with many shrieks of shock. But considering that it is nearly 90 degrees on this day, the cold water quickly becomes soothing. They help the refugees scrub the soap on their skin and hair. Some of the refugees' hair is caked with fecal matter, lice and other filth; the only thing to do is shave the hair. A hair shaving station is set up to accommodate this unenviable task. This is particularly dreadful for the African women. The situation is so painful; it is hard to tell who is crying the most and the hardest-- the refugees or those there to help them.

Onorede Madaki takes the bar of soap from the FEMA worker's hand. He looks at the big, light brown-skinned man, speaking that strange dialect that the pale-skinned "ghosts," as he calls them, were speaking. He wonders what tribe he could be from, as he looks like no one he has seen before. This man is standing next to a tent-like stall with water spraying down from the inside.

He doesn't know what this bar is at first and looks around at the others for clues. Some smell it, some eat it and vomit immediately. The worker in front of him resorts to mimicking soap-bathing directions.

Onorede put the bar up to his nose and sniffs it. The smell triggers with such familiarity that he feels like he briefly flashed back in time, to when he was a little boy, running through a field of white and purple flowers that gave off an odor that is very similar to the white bar in his hands. This strikes him with a somewhat disturbing sense of calm. It is then that he begins to think about how to escape. Before he does that, he needs to find Fakih, the only surviving member of his party.

He steps into the cold spray of water, which sends chills throughout his body, causing his skin to tense and spread with goose pimples. The worker hands Onorede a sponge, and stands outside the shower stall, continuing to mime out the use of the items, pretending to rub it all over his body. Onorede mimics the movements, producing a bubbly lather with the bar and sponge as he rubs it over his chest and arms. He watches the worker bob his head up and down as he continues to mimic. Onorede watches the filth slide from his skin and down the drain of the stall. For the first time in over a week, he feels clean.

The worker hands him a towel as he waves him out of the shower, and points him to the left. The next aid worker gives Onorede immediate pause. It's one of the white "ghosts," handing him a clear plastic package containing a blue, cotton tunic and pants, and white boxer shorts. Onorede refuses to take it at first, staring at this "ghost" and wondering whether or not he should grab him by the throat and strangle him to death. He wants to, but this man's eyes did not have the fire and blood-lust that his captors did. Onorede snatches the package of clothes, continuing to watch this "ghost" cautiously as he is led into another stall by a dark-skinned aid worker, who helps him put on this strange clothing.

Onorede is very confused. The "ghosts" that put them on the big boat were not like these people. Why the savage treatment on departure, and then the wave of compassion at the destination? He is beginning to think that he may have slipped into the afterlife.

Once his clothes are on, he is escorted to an area at the end of the dock, and led to a queue of African refugees standing in front of what to him look like large, shiny caterpillars with windows and wheels. He looks at all of the black faces around him; they too appear very confused. Calm, but confused. Some can find others that speak a similar dialect. Others are left in silence to either stare at the ground, or crane their necks to and fro taking in the suroundings. Huge structures of stone and shimmering glass, standing tall, reaching to the heavens. The sounds, and the noise, the smells…it is enough to overload the senses.

"Onorede!"

He looks up, scanning the faces in the crowd until he spots a man looking right at him, waving his hand in the air. His boyish face and beaming smile indicate he is clearly happy to see him. It is Fakih.

Fakih pushes his way through the crowd to meet up with Onorede, whom he greets with a hug.

"Onorede!" he exclaims happily.

"*We made it, old friend*," says Onorede, in the dialect of their people, the Krou[2]. "*How do you feel?*"

Fakih rubs his hands against his freshly showered skin. "*I am just thankful for that cleansing! I have never been or felt so filthy in my entire life. Where are we now? What is this place?*"

"*I do not know*," says Onorede. "*Our trials are getting more and more complicated, it would seem.*"

"*I hear some of the others around us. They think that we are in the afterlife. Or that we are going to be eaten by the white ghosts.*"

Onorede shakes his head. "*We are most definitely not in the afterlife. And I don't think they mean to eat us. There are many among them that look like us, even though they are not one of us. They speak, act and dress the way ghosts do.*"

"*What about the ghosts in this place? They are most unusual. Not like our original captors.*"

"*You are right,*" says Onorede. "*They are very different. They seem peaceful. I still do not trust them. It is as if they are preparing us for something. It is not making any sense to me right now.*"

---

[2] Pronounced as "crew."

They notice the group is being led towards the wheeled-caterpillar-type structures. When the doors pop open, many of them jump and react horrifically. They move away, huddling into mass groups. They remember the last time they were led into a similar structure.

"*Do they expect us to get into those things?*" asks Fakih.

"*Come,*" Onorede says to Fakih.

"*Where are we going?*" he asks.

Onorede moves through the crowd and steps up to the front of the queue to the doors of the structure. He looks at one of the aid workers who is trying to assist the Africans. The worker says something in that ghost language that he does not understand; it sounds like she is saying "pleez genadabuss", whatever that means. It is such an ugly language—so much of the tongue involved that it sounds to him as if they are speaking with their mouths full. Onorede ignores her and immediately steps up into the structure. The others look on in quiet anticipation and a bit of amazement.

The first thing that Onorede notices is the smell. He inhales deeply. There is nothing offensive; it is not filthy. There are soft seats, with some fabric over them. The aid worker steps into the bus behind him, watching him examine the bus. She says something, but Onorede ignores her. He sits down on one of the seats. Comfortable. Fakih steps inside, moving past the aid worker.

"*What do you think?*" he asks.

"*They want to take us somewhere,*" says Onorede. "*And I say we let them.*"

"*What if they kill us?*"

Onorede looks up at the aid worker, who looks back earnestly and says something that he cannot understand.

"*They are harmless,*" he says.

3

3:23pm
Manhattan

Professor Joseph Healy stares out of the window of his cab as it makes its way toward City Hall. Like every other person in the world, his attention was drawn to the broadcasted images of the mysterious wooden ships, and their human cargo. Unlike most people who would simply see images brought to them on their televisions and media devices, he will see it all first hand. In fact, not only will he see them, he will attempt to communicate with the African refugees themselves.

He snaps his attention away from the window and down to his NAVI. He flips open the device like a brochure, converting it into tablet mode. Tapping a few icons, he brings up his notes. It's been a long time since he's had to try to speak any of the African languages that he studied over the years. He has no idea what languages he'll need. Information is sparse at best. He's been told that the only English-speaking person involved in the incident had mentioned something about the Bight of Benin and the African Congo, so he figures he should focus on languages from that region: Yoruba, Bantu, Mandé, Igbo, Fulani. It feels a little bit like he's back in school chasing after his Master's degree.

As the cab approaches City Hall, he watches the throng of media staking out the building. He figures that word must have spread out about the meeting. New York Mayor David Jú called him personally with an invitation to this meeting. They had met previously at a function honoring Louis Armstrong, and the two became casual acquaintances.

Even with this connection, and at the Mayor's request, Joseph is not sure of what he could contribute to this situation. *This is a hoax*, he's been saying to himself. *This is a sick joke some sick bastard threw money at.* In fact, that's what he believes the meeting is about; how to deal with the hoax. *Besides*, he thinks to himself, *if this were a real situation, they would've called Max, not me.* Joseph has known Maximilian Oroko for over 20 years, and this sort of thing is what he lives for. Apparently, he wasn't available, and Joseph hasn't seen or talked to him in a few years.

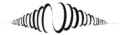

3:56pm

The briefing room is tense when Joseph walks in. As he finds a seat, he scans the room. He seess Mayor Jú and his aide Patricia, along with Governor Diane Steele, various Badges and Medals, including retired General George Hiller, and Secretary of State Lucy Fender, who just happened to be in town for a much-publicized and equally demonized "Global Poverty Initiative" conference at the United Nations.

Patricia outlines the official initial status and assessment of what has been dubbed "The Event."

According to FEMA's reports, there are between 300-400 refugees on each of the three ships; the overall total is estimated to be a little over 1100 people. Almost every one of them was covered, head to toe, in sweat, feces, urine, saliva, vomit, and bacteria found in the sea water they were doused with during cleanings. Of the total number of people, about half of them were malnourished. At the time of the tally, nearly 300 were diagnosed with dysentery and various other diseases.

Eighty-nine people were found dead, some still chained to the living. 115 people are seriously ill or dying.

"Upon removal from the ships," she sighs, taking a moment to collect herself, "the refugees were taken to the Jacob Javits Center for processing and further care. Emergency medical teams are treating the ill at Javits, through a triage center we have set up there. The remaining group was moved into a few of the large conference halls, where they are getting food and water."

There is an ear-ringing silence in the room, with faces that range from shock to anger to utter shame. Joseph's jaw has been agape for so long that he doesn't notice the drop of saliva falling from his bottom lip.

Mayor Jú clears his throat. "Thank you, Patricia. I am uh…" he stops, looking at the faces in the room. "I'm sorry, I don't…I don't know what to say."

"Well," says Secretary of State Fender, standing up to address the room. "This is certainly horrible, to say the very least. We should try to get beyond that for the time being, and focus on what the hell is going on. Has anyone been talking? What about the crews from the ships?"

At the end of the conference table, a man that looks to Joseph like an actor from an old 1990s sitcom raises his finger in the air.

"Madam Secretary," he says. "Brad Spencer. I've been working with the crews, trying to communicate with them. Unfortunately, most of them don't speak English; it was Dutch, and either Portuguese or Spanish, we're working that out now. The only English speaker was a Jacob Morgan, on board the Fredensborg."

"He was the one assaulted by the detective?" Fender asks.

"Correct," Brad says. "He has quite a story to tell. The most interesting part is that he says he believes it's the year 1768."

"You're kidding," Joseph blurts out.

"I am not," Brad replies, consulting his notes, "He says he bought the ship 13 years ago, which by his calendar would be 1755, yes? He also says that he left port from Virginia over a month ago to uh..." Brad looks up and scans the room for a moment, "Excuse me, he said he was going to, I'm quoting here, 'pick up his new crop of niggers in time for the harvest' end quote."

The room erupts in disapproving outbursts.

"He said that?" Secretary Fender asks in disbelief.

"That's an exact quote, Madam Secretary," Brad answers. "And he claims he left port from the Bight of Benin eight days ago."

"Did you say The Bight of Benin?" asks Joseph.

"What is the Bight of Benin?" asks Mayor Jú.

"Benin is located under the horn of Africa," says Joseph, "From the 1600s to the 1800s, it was one of the busiest slaving ports in Africa."

The cacophony of disapproving sounds gets louder and more intense.

"Ladies and gentlemen, please," bellows Secretary Fender. "This is not the 17th Century. Are you telling me that human trafficking of this magnitude is still going on? In wind-powered ships, no less?"

Dead silence from perplexed faces struggling to make sense of the senseless.

"It's the goddamn Chinese," growls General Hiller. "They've been pissed at us ever since we placed those sanctions on them— it's retaliation, clearly. Probably working with the Russians, too."

"We placed sanctions on them for their inhumane treatment of workers," says Mayor Jú.

The general points to the Mayor, "Yes, exactly! This sick little stunt is a comment on our history, to make us look like hypocrites on the world stage!"

"In this case, General, we are," says Secretary Fender. "It's true that we are hypocrites when you consider this country's history. My people, my ancestors, were enslaved by your ancestors George. That's a history that we can't deny."

"My family got here in the early 1900s, Madam Secretary," say the general, holding up his hands disavowing.

"My point is that nothing is off the table right now. We don't need to jump to conclusions; we just need answers."

"We need to talk to the refugees," Joseph interjects. "Once I talk to them, and once we get the rest of the crew talking, we'll have more answers. There has to be something more to this."

"I agree, Professor Healy," nods Secretary Fender. "Let's get to the bottom of this as soon as possible. The news is spreading fast, and we need to catch up."

CHARLES A. CONYERS, JR.

4

4:24pm

There is a frenzy of media and spectators outside the Jacob Javits Convention Center. Joseph looks out the window of the SUV like a deer in headlights. He would normally feel anxious, but he's distracted by the smell of cinnamon buns that fills the car. The smell is coming from his car-buddy, staring at her NAVI over horn-rimmed glasses. He noticed her at the briefing. She is gorgeous, and the array of mathematical equations she's manipulating on her NAVI proves that her intelligence is as breathtaking as her beauty.

She looks up at Joseph and smiles.

"Joseph Healey," he says, offering his hand.

"I know, I remember you from the briefing. Kiki Bishop," she says, shaking his hand. "What a situation, huh?"

"Never seen anything like it," he says.

"So, what do you think? Do you think this whole thing is a hoax?"

Joseph smiles. "You mean, do I think that China is involved?"

"Well?"

"I don't know if it's a hoax. If it is, it's a sick one."

"The Chinese are many things, but we are not sociopaths," Kiki says.

"You're Chinese as well?"

"It's the melanin," she smiles, rubbing her skin. "I get Filipino a lot, too-- there aren't many bronze-skinned Chinese folks walking around."

"True that," he nods, laughing.

"My dad is West Indian," she continues. "Mom is Chinese. How about you?"

"Black, born in Philly. My DNA links me primarily to the Moors."

Kiki nods, "I have Moors in my DNA as well!"

"Look at that- we're practically cousins. Beyond the DNA, it's difficult to trace my family's records before the late 1800s. For obvious reasons."

"So how does all of this feel for you?"

Joseph shrugs, "Surreal. It's something that we've all read about, we know about, but we have the luxury of time and distance, so we don't have to think too much about it, if at all. To be honest, part of me doesn't even want to be here. It makes me feel...I don't know, I don't like it. I can't miss this, though- I have to be here. Does that make sense?"

"Yes, sir-- you nailed it. My dad used to always say 'know your history,'" deepening her voice to sound like her dad. "He would tell me how Jamaica was the first destination for millions of African slaves. He'd tell me crazy stories. He told me stories about 'seasoning' camps where they would break the Africans into servitude."

"Damn, your dad's hardcore."

"I know," Kiki laughs. "He'd say 'I know it's harsh. You know what else is harsh? Real life.'"

"He's right," Joseph nods. "Especially for these folks to go through that ordeal, as if the Middle Passage didn't break them enough."

"If they even lived through that," she says, shaking her head. "which makes all of this so remarkable. To see what these people went through..."

"So you don't think this is a hoax?"

"No, it's not a hoax," she says. "It's a lot more complicated than that. Over the last few weeks, my team and I have been picking up odd electrical anomalies all around the world. The latest one occurred at approximately 10:51 am this morning, at the exact location of the appearance of the ships. I happened to be in town today, so, here I am. I'm usually in town, I live here, but I travel a lot. You know how it is."

"What is it that you do, exactly?" asks Joseph.

"I do a lot of stuff. I lecture, run research groups, write books and papers no one reads…long story short, I'm a quantum physicist."

Joseph's eyes widen a bit. "All right, wow, okay, that's cool. So what do you do?"

Kiki laughs. "Basically, I sit in a room and try to figure shit out. It's a lot of math, a lot of theory, a lot of headaches, and I love it. It's my thing, it always spoke to me."

Joseph nods, impressed, "All right then, brainiac."

"Ha, yes!" she laughs, "I don't mess around."

"Fair enough," says Joseph. "So, I guess you have a theory about all of this."

"I do, yes. It all begins with these storms we've been tracking. 'Storm' is not the best word. They're more like bursts of electrical energy, and they've been popping up over the last week."

She taps on her NAVI and pulls up a world map. She touches the map in four spots, leaving a glowing marker behind; one in the middle of the Atlantic Ocean, one off the coast of Angola, Africa, the third off the southeastern coast of Florida, and the fourth in the Lower Bay, New York, north of Sandy Hook, New Jersey.

"It started on the 1st of this month. We started picking up these faint readings of these three energy bursts. They were weak, and they also varied in intensity-- the one in the middle of the Atlantic was the weakest of the three, followed by Angola. Seven days later, we have this new event, same pattern and far more intense." Kiki draws a circle with her finger around the four dots. "I think these bursts and this new event are connected."

"What's causing the energy bursts?"

"I have no idea. I won't know until I analyze more sample data."

"What do you think?"

Kiki sighs. This will be the first time she is saying these words out loud to someone. In the last hour, she's heard every theory from a Chinese conspiracy plot to an act of God. At least this theory, according to her research, has teeth. "I think those ships traveled through time."

Joseph laughs. She does not. *Time travel*, he repeats to himself. *Time travel?* "You're serious?" he asks.

"If my theory is correct, we're going to find out that these energy bursts are the opening and closing of wormholes. That's the only way the ships just appeared out of nowhere-- nothing detected by NORAD, nothing on satellite, just <u>poof</u>! Nineteenth-century ships arrive carrying African slaves."

"Okay, look," Joseph protests, "I don't know if I'd call them slaves. We don't know what's going on yet, but I can't say they're slaves. In 2041?"

"That's the point, Professor— they're not from 2041. You already have a crew member from one of the ships who believes it's the year 1768! He was carrying a flintlock pistol! What, do you think he's cosplaying Pirates of the Caribbean?"

"It's just that 'time travel' sounds kind of crazy. It just doesn't seem possible. The idea that this could be some anti-colonial demonstration by the Chinese and the Russians sounds a bit more feasible than time-travel."

"Okay, so let's say that it's the Chinese, and the Russians. How do they get over a thousand people to humiliate and sacrifice themselves?"

"Threats. Blackmail. Brainwashing. I don't know. If someone said 'Do this, or we'll kill your kids' or 'We'll kill your family' or 'Kill you,' when you have no power, wouldn't you just do it?"

"Honestly," she says, "I'd rather die than lose my right to choose. Nothing is worth that. And who's to say 'they' still wouldn't kill you or anyone else?"

Joseph shakes his head slowly. "It's a sick world."

"Indeed," she says, as their SUV pulls into the parking garage. "Indeed it is."

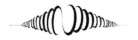

4:42pm
Jacob Javits Convention Center, New York

Joseph spots the Mayor's aide Patricia standing with an officer outside the doors of Exhibition Hall 1C, waving him towards her. As exhausted and haggard as she looks, she puts on a pleasant face as Joseph approaches. The closed doors behind her muffle a blaring concert of frightened voices. "Professor Healy, welcome sir," she smiles.

"Hi Patricia," greets Joseph. "How are you feeling?"

Patricia rolls her eyes while holding back tears, "I don't know how to handle this, Professor. I look at some of those faces; I see cousins, I see aunts and uncles…This is horrible; it's worse than I thought it would be."

She takes a deep breath to pull herself together. "We've had CERT teams separate those who are in critical need from those who have treatable conditions."

The officer opens the door to the loud and anxious sounds blasting from inside. The hectic hive of bodies in the room is overwhelming. The arrangement of curtained-off cots is not enough to mask the screaming, yelling, shouting, moaning, crying, squealing, begging, all mixed in with sounds of machinery beeping, equipment moving, doctors and nurses giving and taking orders. It's an all-out assault on the senses.

The motion in the room guides Joseph's eyes to take in a collage of snapshots filled with tragic moments happening all at once. There are faces soaked with tears, strained from yelling, blank with anguish. Some are receiving fluids. Others are expelling them. When Patricia said that she could see familiar faces, Joseph is shocked to see a woman that looks just like his grandmother in an old picture he remembers seeing when he was a kid.

I'm done, Joseph says to himself. *I'm done, I can't do this.* When he turns to Patricia to excuse himself, he sees Mayor Jú approaching with Police Commissioner Walter Wilson, and a few other aides and officers. The peppy older fellow leading the group is Dr. Paul Ellis, a general practitioner who five hours ago answered the call for doctors that could be of assistance in this situation. He is one of the few Black doctors in the triage center, which makes him one of the few people that the Africans would allow getting near them for treatment.

"Professor Healey," calls Mayor Jú, "Dr. Ellis, this is Professor Joseph Healey, he's our translator."

"Oh, thank God! My man!" claps Dr. Ellis, extending his hand and shaking Josephs. "I'm flying blind here- I could use your help. This way."

Dr. Ellis leads Joseph and the others through a maze of wailing and misery. *This is getting worse, and I haven't even started yet.* Joseph opens his NAVI and loads the *Tongue* translator app.

"I've heard of that app," says Dr. Ellis. "One of my colleagues uses it, and she loves it. Expensive!"

"Ain't that the truth," says Joseph. "But I don't think it will work in here. It's too noisy."

Dr. Ellis pats him on the shoulder. "Anything is better than nothing. Let's do this."

The first patient the doctor brings Joseph to is a young woman sitting on a cot, swaying back and forth, moaning and wailing. Next to her is another young woman trying to hold her, speaking to her.

A nurse hands Dr. Ellis a needle. "Okay, Joseph. We have to give her this shot immediately. Whenever we go near her with it, she explodes."

Joseph activates the recorder on the app and holds the NAVI's mic to his mouth. "My name is Joseph. This is Dr. Ellis. He is here to help you."

The app takes a few seconds to process before it responds with a red window with the words UNABLE TO PROCESS.

"Too bad," mutters Joseph. He opens up a text window and uses his finger to trace shorthand gestures in

the window to type: My Name is Joseph, This Is Dr.
Ellis. He Will Help You.

"Okay, here we go." Joseph holds the NAVI facing
the sick young woman. He selects "Swahili" and taps the
"speak" icon. The young woman looks up at Joseph, then
at Dr. Ellis, who looks at the young woman nodding.

"This will help you," he says, showing the needle
to the woman. Joseph traces out the words quickly, and
taps "speak." She listens to the words, looks at Dr. Ellis
and that needle. She calms a little, but still breathing
heavily. Making eye contact with the doctor, she nods.
The doctor and nurse move in to administer the shot.

"My man," Dr. Ellis nods to Joseph.
Unfortunately, the rest of patients did not work out as
smoothly. After several frustrating attempts in conditions
that got louder and noisier, Joseph puts the NAVI away.
He has a difficult time relying solely on his memory.
He's able to pick up a few simple words, like "pain," and
"help." He also hears "family," and "child" or "baby," the
latter coming primarily from the women. He tries to
respond, but he gets only blank and confusing looks from
them. Some even turn their backs on him, or turn away,
or flag their hands at him in frustration

This is depressing. Joseph takes a deep breath, but
it doesn't feel deep enough.

After making the rounds in this hall, Joseph moves
with the mayor's group to the next holding area in
Exhibition Hall 1A.

5:52pm
Exhibition Hall 1A

Onorede and Fahki have been very busy. After being escorted to the largest hall in the convention center, the two set out to lay the groundwork for their escape.

Onorede makes the rounds, speaking to as many people as possible, with Fakih's help in translating whenever he can. Fakih has always had a proclivity for language. He was very valuable to the Krou tribe, being their communication chief, of sorts. He is well versed in eight regional dialects, a skill fostered over years of study.

Onorede, through Fakih, moves around the room, speaking to groups and individuals, making the case that their current detainment is nothing more than the calm before the storm. *"We think that there will soon be a time when we will have to make a move against our captors,"* Fakih translates. *"Our current conditions are better than the journey that brought us here, but the savage ghosts and their stooges may be preparing us for more horrors. Don't be fooled— their chains are gone, but they and these ghosts are now unguarded and weak. We could make an escape easily."*

Word spreads fast in this small community. Those who could understand passed the information on to others, so that by the time Joseph Healey, Mayor Jú, and the others show up, the Africans know the plan, and they are ready.

Joseph notices the immediate hush of silence that overcomes the mass of refugees once he and his group enter the hall. By an act of fate, he happens to lock eyes with Onorede as he steps further inside. One of the ten officers in the room approach the group.

"How are things here?" asks Police Commissioner Wilson.

"I dunno," said the officer, "Seems like they're up to somethin'." He points at Onorede. "That one's been goin'

THE MAXIMILIAN EMANCIPATION

around from group to group talkin' to people. He's like the leader or something. Or he's acting like it."

"Leader of over a thousand people? This quickly?" scoffs Wilson, "I doubt that."

"Who's been talking to them?" asks Joseph.

The officer points once again to Onorede.

"*Who do you think they are?*" asks Fakih.

Onorede says nothing, only watches them approach, focusing on Joseph. He stands at the ready, chest forward, face stoic, eyes hard as steel.

"*Be ready,*" Onorede says to Fakih, who turns to a man standing behind him and nods. The man walks away.

Joseph breaks into the routine that he's been practicing on the sick Africans for the previous hour. He starts simple.

"*Hello,*" Joseph says in Swahili. Neither Onorede or the others respond.

"*Can you understand me?*" Joseph says in Yoruba. Still nothing. Onorede and the others just stare at him. Joseph tries three other languages before he hits his question in Zulu: "*Do you know where you are?*"

Fakih's eyes widen. "*I understood him…!*" he says in Krou, trying hard not to sound too excited. Onorede turns to Fakih, surprised. "*He asked if we knew where we were.*"

"*Are you sure?*" asks Onorede.

"*I believe so. His way of speaking is so ugly—his tongue is getting in the way. But I think he said 'do you know where you are?'*"

Onorede is surprised that one of these people, particularly a stooge of the ghosts, could speak any language recognizable to his people. He thinks, for a moment, that this might be useful.

"*Answer him,*" Onorede says.

Fakih turns to Joseph, and in Zulu says "*We do not know where we are. We do not recognize this place. Where are we?*"

"What did he say," asks Mayor Jú excitedly.

Joseph doesn't know. Fakih speaks so fast he didn't catch it at all. Fakih sees him struggling, and repeats himself slowly, as if he is talking to a small child.

Joseph picks up "We know…not…where we are…" He pauses for a moment. "I think it's quiet enough in here."

Onorede watches Joseph remove a glass sheet from a bag and tap it with his fingers. He then raises the glass to his mouth and speaks at it in that strange ghost dialect. Joseph taps it a few more times. Fahki looks at Onorede, confused.

"Why does he speak at that glass?" Fakih asks.

Joseph raises the NAVI. Onorede, Fahki, and a few of the others flinch. Then, the plank speaks in their language: *"My name is Professor Joseph Healey. You are in New York City, in the United States of America. What is your name, and where do you come from?"*

Fakih repeats this to Onorede in Krou.

"What is the New City of York?" Onorede asks.

"That is what that thing said," replies Fahki. *"The New City of York, in some place called 'America.'"*

That word, 'America' triggers an image in Onorede's mind. It is after a battle. There is blood all over the leaves, huge palms of green, dripping with red. An injured prisoner, a young boy, says his village made a pact with pale-faced men from a place called…'America.'

Fakih watches Onorede's face light up as he turns to him. *"Are you sure? You heard him say 'America,'"* Onorede asks.

"That is what it sounded like," Fakih answers. He is surprised when he sees Onorede smile.

"We're here! This is it; this is the place! This is where our people were taken!"

"The York City?"

"No, you fool! America! It's the name of the place of the pale-faces—the ghosts! This place…these are the ones that have been stealing our children."

Onorede looks up at Joseph, *"And this **stooge** is working for them!"*

He slaps the NAVI to the floor. Joseph and the others flinch. The officers step forward.

"Okay, everyone take it easy," says Police Commissioner Wilson. But it is too late. They watch Onorede shout something. Then, a mass of about 50 African men gather quickly, standing in what looks like a battle formation, ready to attack.

"Oh shit," says Mayor Jú.

The officers pull out their tasers and move in front of Joseph, the Mayor, and the others.

"Get back!" One of the officers says.

"All right, everyone needs to take it easy—" says Police Commissioner Wilson. "Professor Healey, say something!"

The only thing that Joseph could think to say was "*Please!*" and "*No!*", which he repeats in Zulu, over and over.

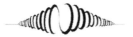

6:17pm

Jerry Ramirez is reporting live from outside the convention center, for People's News Network (PNN). He's been on the ground covering this story for 4 hours, but the intensity of the day has not calmed. It's been non-stop insanity since the news first broke. Officials investigating "The Event" were warned against talking to the media.

"Mayor Jú's office is not returning calls, neither is Governor Steele's office, and the White House refuses to comment until they have 'all the details," Jerry says on camera. "This is amidst the persistent rumors that Beijing has claimed responsibility for what is being called an 'elaborate stunt'. The Chinese government denies any and all responsibility, calling this event shocking and baffling."

For several hours now, Jerry has been telling the PNN viewers the same thing, over and over again, each time it's his turn to give his analysis. It gets to where he is daydreaming while he is speaking on-air. He imagines it's two weeks from now, and he's on a beach in Barbados, with his sexy model girlfriend.

"The crowds here around the convention center are still anxiously awaiting any word or sign from inside to explain the day's events," he says to the camera. "One thing is for sure, the sights that we have seen today have—"

Someone shouts, another voice yells. Still live on camera, Jerry looks to his right and says, "What the hell was that?"

An explosive crash of shattering glass startles the crowd as the African refugees burst through the doors, plowing down the police barricades as they stampede towards the crowd of police, media, and on-lookers.

"Look out! Move!" Jerry yells as he sprints past the camera. The camera captures glimpses of the mass of Africans, all dressed in matching blue outfits, charging out of the convention center.

Onorede, Fakih, and nearly 75 Africans, sprint for their lives across the West Side Highway, unaware of the oncoming traffic. The first 20 to cross the highway are lucky. Several others are hit and hit hard when drivers don't see or expect anyone to be crossing the highway against the traffic lights.

One after another, 23 Africans are hit by cars. And even after the remaining cars hit their brakes, they still slide and crash into other cars and other Africans, resulting in a massive pile-up of cars and bodies on the north and southbound lanes of the highway. The remaining mass of Africans see the carnage in front of them and fade back towards the convention center.

Meanwhile, Fakih and Onorede lead several others sprinting down 38th street.

"*Where are we going?*" Fakih barks out between pants.

"*I don't know.*" Says Onorede, in between swift, steady breaths.

As they reach 8th Avenue, Onorede slows his pace; he notices the red traffic light shining at him.

"*Stop here!*" he says.

Fakih and the others slow to a stop.

"*What are we doing?*" asks Fakih, still trying to catch his breath.

Onorede has to stop. He finds it extremely painful and difficult to run on the concrete that seems to cover every inch of ground. He looks around, and doesn't recognize anything. The tall structures of stone, metal, and glass are intimidating and cold-looking. The shiny metal machines on wheels that move faster than any man. The strange people with their full-mouth style of talking— is this the America that he's heard so much about? It is more terrifying than he ever imagined.

"*Onorede, what do we do?*" asks Fakih.

Onorede turns to Fakih, then looks at the others. "*I don't know, old friend. I don't know what we are going to do.*"

They notice a small crowd forming around them; people in cars, people on the street, people in the buildings, everyone is staring at them through their NAVIs as they record, photograph and live stream. Black faces, yellow faces, olive faces, white faces. Black, wooly hair. Blonde, straight hair. Red, straight hair. White, curly hair. Brown hair, with blonde tips. Their clothes are so different. Their faces are so very different.

Fakih puts his hand on Onoredes' shoulder. "*Why are they all looking at us through those glass things? Are we just animals on a safari? They are aggravating to me!*"

"*Fakih,*" says Onorede, trying to calm his friend's tone. "*These people are different somehow. Something is wrong.*"

"*What are you thinking?*" asks Fakih.

45

"We need to go back."

"What?"

"We need to go back. Something is wrong— something is not in its right place."

"Yes, it's us! And we need to get home!"

"I don't know if we can go back home," says Onorede.

"Don't say that," begs Fakih.

"There was always a chance we would never go back home. But...I cannot explain it."

Just as Fakih is about to offer a stern protest of his friends' decision, they are surrounded by the people in the blue uniforms and their magic stinging fingers. The other Africans are getting restless and scared, but Onorede holds up his hand to his people. They cease.

From behind, the swarm of officers move in to surround them as Joseph appears. He is dusty and bruised, his lip bleeding. He stands in front of Onorede and Fakih, with an earnest but stern look on his face. Onorede is not interested in fighting, neither are Fakih or the others.

As the officers stand prepared to attack, if necessary, Joseph taps on his NAVI, but the screen is cracked and not responding. He throws it to the ground, then begins to speak to the Africans in the best Zulu he can muster.

"What is he saying?" asks Onorede.

"I have no idea," answers Fakih. *"He is speaking too fast, and his accent is terrible. He sounds upset, though— like he is about to cry."*

Joseph pauses. Then begins to cry, and drops to his knees, still trying to speak in a language that he thinks the Africans can understand.

"Told you so," says Fakih.

Onorede does not know what to do, except laugh.

5

9:23pm
O'Malley's Bar and Grill, New York

Joseph takes the last swig of his fourth beer. He has the internal argument over whether or not he should have another. *I've had enough*, he thinks, *haven't I*? Maybe not. Maybe not, because it still stings. He is still embarrassed. More than embarrassed, he is totally mortified. On every news show, in every media stream, all over social media, it's everywhere: video of himself, Professor Joseph Healey, with the lower third graphic announcing his name and title, down on his knees, in tears, babbling and begging. To him, this is worse than being seen naked, after soaking in a pool of cold water.

"Just what the doctor ordered," says Brad Spencer as he sits down at the table with two beers.

"I don't have my doctorate yet," says Joseph, licking his lips drunkenly. "Haven't gotten around to it yet."

"We can pretend," says Brad, sliding a beer in front of Joseph. "It'll be all right, man. You know how people are, they'll forget about this crap in a week!"

"Are you kidding?" asks Joseph. "No one's gonna forget about this—are you kidding me? I looked like an idiot out there! I'm the laughing stock of the city."

"My ass. Look, none of this makes sense. Do you know I've been working with the ship's crews for hours, and I'm still nowhere! I've got Dutch and Portuguese translators that can't figure out the dialect these sailors are using; it's like they're speaking an older version of the language. What the hell is that?"

Joeseph takes a swig of beer #5. "This is a goddamn nightmare."

"Don't keep beating yourself up, man— it's not like you have an easy job. How many languages and dialects are there in Africa, anyway?"

"Over 2000," Joseph says.

"And how many did you use today?"

"Four. Maybe five. I fucked up about four or five."

"And you'll fuck 'em up tomorrow, too. That's what we're here for. Jesus, look at the cops! They lost control of the refugees. Look at all of those deaths on the West Side Highway. You think you've got it that bad? Compared to them, you're a goddamn hero! It doesn't matter that you can't speak the right dialect— the way the world sees it, you stopped a potential riot!"

"I didn't stop anything—it already stopped."

"It doesn't matter, dip-shit! It's all about the optics. People with their faces in their screens saw you engage with the refugees, and they complied. A picture's worth a thousand words, buddy. It doesn't matter if the words are wrong. You're a media star because of this! If I were you, I'd concentrate on how I could make that work. Maybe even involve a friend, you know…someone who was close to you, was there for you in the rough times…"

"Yeah, yeah, all right, all right," laughs Joseph. "So if I'm the star, who are you?"

"Your loyal sidekick," Brad says, toasting his glass to Joseph's.

As Brad swallows, he looks down at the tall, thin gin and tonic sitting in front of an empty seat.

"Where'd she go this time?" asks Brad.

"Phone call," says Joseph.

Brad nods. "She single?"

"I don't know," says Joseph. "Never came up."

Brad nods. "Aren't you curious?"

Joseph holds up his hand, wiggling his wedding ring with his thumb. "Never noticed. She's super smart- the work she's doing seems interesting. I don't understand any of it, but…"

"Oh, I'm sorry, man," Brad smirks, "I didn't know you were gay."

"You are such a dick," says Joseph.

Brad smiles and raises his glass. "Come on, tell me it doesn't look so good!"

"What's so good?" says Kiki, returning to the table.

"Life," says Brad. "Life is good."

"Life is pretty damn good, that's true," Kiki concurs as she picks up her drink with one hand, and motioning to Joseph with the other, "Especially for our hero friend over here."

"Ha-ha," says Joseph.

"And I hear all the networks are dying to talk to you…" chides Kiki.

"Right? He'll be on The Gerry Baines Exchange in no time!" laughs Brad.

"Yeah, that's the first place I'll go. On that idiot's show."

"He says that you're a hero," says Kiki.

Joseph takes a big swig. "Wonderful."

"He did predict 'The Event,' though," says Brad.

"Oh my God, can you believe that?" exclaims Kiki.

"What are you talking about?"

"Baines went on this ridiculous rant about how God will test America." says Kiki.

"Now his dopey fans think he's the messiah," says Brad.

"Maybe he knows about the time-travelers, too," says Joseph.

"Oh Dr. Healey," says Kiki, with a biting, but playful tone of "suck it" in her voice. "What have you seen today?"

"The bottom of 1000 Africans feet," says Brad, making Kiki laugh.

"You guys are such dicks," Joseph says.

"Okay, okay—" Kiki manages to say through her oddly goofy laugh, which sounds like a tiny goblin revving up the engine of its motorcycle. "Seriously, Professor. What did you see today? You saw history!"

"This was historic," Joseph says, "I completely agree with that."

"Not just historic in that romanticized sense. I'm talking about real history! These people are the direct link to the past!"

"What the hell are you talking about?" asks Brad.

"She thinks these Africans traveled through time," says Joseph, pointing at her with his glass right before taking a long pull.

Brad looks at her, twisting his mouth slightly. "What do you mean? Like McFly?"

"Yeah, like McFly," she says, mocking him. "Not exactly."

"There were these energy storms that happened seven days ago," says Joseph, "and then happened again this morning, when the ships showed up."

Brad pauses for a moment. "Like 'The Final Countdown'?"

Joseph looks at Brad. "What the hell does that song have to do with time travel?"

"No, jackass, the movie!" says Brad.

"It's a good comparison, though. I think that these ships traveled through a wormhole in their own time, and they've reappeared here."

Brad lets that roll around in his head. "Like 'Stargate'?"

Kiki laughs. "Yes, actually, that too! I'm impressed, Brad, you know your sci-fi!"

"I have my moments," he says.

"So I think each of these ships went through three separate worm holes and all three converged into the same one."

"But how could they come through the same hole?" asks Joseph.

"The same way two or three or four different subway tracks can end up in one station. Or lighting strikes have multiple stems. It's like the 'All Good Things' episode of *Star Trek*, with those three ships converging on the same place from different times."

"Yeah, but they made that happen," says Brad. "They shot lasers or something into this cloud thing, and made that wormhole happen. And Doc Brown built the Delorean. And that guy from 'Time Machine.' They all made those things."

"That's right," says Joseph. "I mean, what are the chances that a naturally-occurring wormhole just happened to grab three slave ships from different times. Someone must've made it happen."

"That's true," says Kiki.

"So, how can time travel happen without someone making it happen?" asks Brad.

"I'm not sure," Kiki admits. "That's part of the problem. Whatever it is, it's extremely powerful. Almost too powerful."

"How can it be too powerful?" asks Brad.

"To create a wormhole, you'd need the power of 10 quintillion stars."

"What the hell is a quintillion?" asks Brad.

Kiki busts out a huge laugh.

"It's like two past a billion," says Joseph. "You know, billion, trillion, quadrillion, quintillion."

"And there were four energy bursts, four wormholes, created with the power of 10 quintillion stars, each," says Kiki.

"No way that's possible," says Brad.

"Well, that's why you guys are here," says Kiki, "To talk to these people, and find out who they are."

"Oh Jesus, don't remind me," says Joseph. "I've got to get up tomorrow morning and start this shit all over again." He looks up at Brad. "I've had enough. I'm gonna get him here."

"No you're not," says Brad. "He'll never do it; they'll never go for it."

"Who?" asks Kiki.

"I can't do this without him," says Joseph. "I won't, not again. We need him—there's no one else, and you know it."

"He doesn't play nice," says Brad.

"Who are you talking about?" asks Kiki.

"Max Oroko," says Brad.

"Oroko," says Kiki, "Why does that sound familiar?"

"Remember when they were breaking ground for the Saxon Hotel ten years ago?" asks Brad. "They found an old slave graveyard…"

"Oh right!" says Kiki. "I remember that! He was trying to save it, to make it a national monument, right? He chained himself to a tree or something?"

"He went nuts, that's what happened," says Brad.

"That's not fair," says Joseph. "He's passionate about what he believes in. With this one thing he just…he went over-the-top. Unfortunately, he upset a lot of the wrong people."

"That's the thing," says Brad. "He didn't just burn bridges, he burned the towns and the people in them. This thing is way too high profile for the likes of Maximilian Oroko," says Brad. "He went ballistic over an old graveyard, imagine what would happen with this."

"That was ten years ago—twelve, actually," says Joseph.

"He called the Secretary of State a 'condescending asshole' during a live stream," says Brad, looking at Kiki, his smirk asking for affirmation.

"No!" blasts Kiki.

"She wasn't the Secretary of State then," insists Joseph. "Back then she was the CEO of Dancorp."

"Why did he call her a 'condescending asshole'?" asks Kiki.

"It's a long story, and I'm too drunk to tell it."

"I think they were fucking," says Brad.

"And you would be wrong," says Joseph.

"Seriously, though," says Brad, "I think he's a mess. He doesn't play well with others, and he's a pain-in-the-ass. He'd be going to the media, calling people names, start cursing at press conferences—you know how he is."

"I need him," says Joseph. And that settles it. He decides to finish this beer, then have one other, and then he will go home and look at train schedules to West Chester.

It's been a while since he's seen his friend. Two years in fact. Just dropping in out of nowhere might seem a bit rude. But Joseph knows that a phone call would be fruitless. Just showing up unexpectedly would be the only way he had any chance of convincing him to come back.

9:00pm
Furious Studios, New York City

Four-and-a-half years ago, Gerry Baines, the self-proclaimed "Dark Fury" of progressive thought, handed over the ideas for the opening sequence of what was to be his extremely successful television news program; *The Gerry Baines Exchange.*

He was very specific about what he wanted. He described seeing the sun rising in time lapse photography, over the Washington monument. Cue majestic music. Then we see various shots of the sun rising from all over the country, from the midwest, to Midtown Manhattan. Then, cue the hard driving 'Rock & Rap' music. It's quick cuts of images of police in a violent confrontation, cut to in a fistfight on the floor of the Senate. Then cut to troops in a gunfight in Ukraine, then cut to shots of a gay couple kissing at their wedding. Finally cutting to a diverse group of college kids in a dorm room sharing a bong. That's when the voice-over begins, booming over images of himself-- tall, dark-skinned, confident and attractive man of 56-- saluting the American flag:

"If you are like me," he pontificates, "you love this country, and you'll fight like hell to protect it. Let's win that fight together!"

After a dramatic, fire-licking explosion, and a musical shift to a piece more reminiscent of a cavalry charge mixed with a Southern Baptist church song. The title, in red, white and blue type, emerges from the flame: "THE GERRY BAINES EXCHANGE." That was the show intro that Gerry wanted, and that's exactly what he got. It has aired every evening before every broadcast, until tonight.

Tonight's episode opens with footage from the 37th Street dock, as the African refugees are liberated from their floating dungeons. Only the ambient sound of the video is heard; the gasps, the clicks and flashes of cameras, the crying and moaning.

Fade up to Gerry Baines, standing in front a giant touch screen display. He taps the screen, and a window of video appears; a close-up one of an African woman, no more than 22 years old, her face is dirty, her deep, dark eyes stare back with the soul-stinging intensity of someone who's lived a thousand lives. Gerry taps the window, pausing the video to absorb the heart-melting feels. He scales it down, moves it to the side, and taps the screen to produce another video window, this time of an African man, skinny, sick, on a hospital gurney, with tubes in his nose and his arms. After a few moments, he scales it down, moves it to the side.

Next is the now-iconic video of the sobbing police officer carrying a naked refugee, her neck, wrists and ankles still shackled and chained. She is wilted in his arms, though clings on with her hand over his shoulder. His hands grip her through latex gloves, powering through his tears as lifts her into his arms.

"What do you say?" he asks. "What could anyone possibly say? I mean, it's unreal. It's barbaric. You look at this savagery, and you think, 'what kind of monsters— what kind of animals would do this to human beings?' In this day, in this age— in any day or any age, how could this happen?

"Let's be blunt. Let's point out the elephant in the room, okay? You see these images, you think…wow, yeah, this all looks familiar…and you know exactly where it's from. We've all studied it in school. We all know about slavery, the Middle Passage, and the African slave trade- it's a part of our history. Hearing about it, and reading about it, is one thing. It's not in front of us, we never saw it, so we don't think about it. Then we get this. This all happens. We think it can't be real; there's no way this can be real. But here it is."

Gerry takes a few steps towards the camera.

"When I found out about 'The Event' this morning, I got on my knees, and I prayed to God—I said 'Why?! Why this, why now?' I know, it sounds dramatic, but I was humbled, truly and sincerely. In retrospect, it felt a little like what happened to this man today." He points to the display, then approaches it as it plays footage of Professor Joseph Healey dropping to his knees in front of the Africans, weeping.

"I know how this man feels. I understand how lost this man is. This is Professor Joseph Healey; he was brought in as a language specialist to communicate with the refugees. When all else failed, he dropped to his knees. He humbled himself, gave in to the situation, sacrificed himself! Why happened? The refugees stopped their riotous rampage, and they surrendered. This man, this Professor Healey, is a hero. We should all be thankful for him. We tried to get him on the show tonight, but he declined. I don't blame him. He's had a rough day, and there's no reason for him to talk to a schlub like me!"

Gerry walks away from the display, but in full view of the studio's graphics walls, showing a collage of footage of the refugees being helped off the ships. He shakes his head in disgust at what he sees.

"A lot of people are probably saying, 'Hey, Gerry, we don't really know everything! This could be a hoax!' A hoax? Yes, I thought about it, And I'm not going to be popular for saying this: I don't think this is a hoax. I believe these people are the real deal. There's nothing fake about it-- you've seen the footage! That's as real as it gets. No, this wasn't a hoax. This was an act of God. They were brought here by God. Make no mistake, don't get it twisted, God made this happen. God brought them here!

That's right, oh no, I said it! This will be all over the news tomorrow—'oh, Baines has lost it now!' Have I?"

Gerry points at the display. "Ask yourself. Do you really think the Chinese did this? The Russians? What reason would they have to do something like this? Because we've criticized their immoral labor practices? Maybe it's because one of our Senators called them a name? Some of you may remember on this show when Senator Edward Tunney had a slip of the tongue, some would say," referring to an incident seven months ago when the Senator, while discussing the US relationship with China, said the following:

"This is a problem! These people are a problem, and they must be DEALT with. The chinks- uh, no. The China-Chinese...government is abusive, and I believe outright evil. They operate behind a shadows of communism and socialism. They torture their own people, for god's sake! Look at all of their human rights violations! The chin-Chinese are a threat to the American way of life!"

As Gerry continues, the graphics walls show images representing a communist Chinese regime. "Now I know, it was a horrible name...but come on. That was seven months ago! Do you think they could put together something this elaborate in seven months? Seven years, maybe, but NOT seven months! No way, people."

With suppressed urgency, he points his finger up. The image behind him washes away to a white screen. "This is how God works; this is the work of God. You can't deny it at this point. Right now we are, all of us, being judged. All of you feel it, can't you? The harsh, judgmental eye of righteousness."

Gerry glances at the timer mounted to his A camera just as it hits the 90-second mark. He moves his pointing finger from the sky to the camera for his final dramatic statement before the tease. "You see what washed up on our shores, and you are full of shame! It doesn't matter if you're Black, Hispanic, white, Asian...America's Shame is very real for all of us, isn't it?

"We're going to spend the whole show tonight talking about this and more, so stay with us. We'll get through this."

Gerry waits for the all clear from the floor director before stepping over to his desk. "We're back in two minutes," he announces.

"That was a great opening, Gerry," he hears through his ear piece. "I don't know about the God angle, but otherwise it was powerful stuff."

"Let me worry about the words, Tom. You concentrate on the producing," Gerry says.

"What do you think I'm dong, wise-ass?"

"Annoying me at the moment," says Gerry with a smile.

"Just trying to help," says Tom. "The God stuff can be a real bitch, especially with a fluid story like this."

Gerry knows he risks looking like a fool if the Chinese and Russians are connected to this event. But, like his mother and grandmother would always say: "When you don't know, the only answer is God." That's good enough for him.

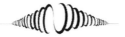

10:18pm
The White House, Washington D.C.

President Matthew Lopez turns off his NAVI and flops it down onto the President's desk. He takes a deep enough breath to let out a sigh that tussles the pages of the daily briefing in front of him. No matter what anyone thinks about how antiquated or wasteful it is, one fact remains; paper can't be hacked.

Most of the day's briefing was more of the same; high poverty numbers, weak but stable economy, civil unrest, poor approval ratings. This morning brought something new; the arrival of African refugees in large wooden sailing ships. It was the piss glaze on the shit cake known as the first year of his administration. This was the one thing that no one could rationally blame him for, but will anyway. With an approval rating of 37%, he's lame before the duck is hatched.

Being the first Libertarian as well as the first Mexican American POTUS was supposed to be a proud moment for him and his family. Instead, as he suspected but wouldn't completely accept, his heritage has become a great hindrance. He narrowly won the election last year. Had it not been for the four other candidates running in the General Election, whittled down from 30 during the primaries, he would have lost.

So far the only shining beacon of his presidency was the veto of a Congressionally-approved bill to instate a nation wide chip implantation initiative, said to aid in maintaining an accurate population count while also being able to track an individual's location and biological profile, including vital signs and DNA analysis. The polling showed 87% voter opposition to this bill, so the veto was a no-brainer politically. It was also a reflection of how he felt about "chipping"— "This is not a dystopian science fiction world," he announced in his veto message, "We still have a free society, and I will take no part in removing our basic rights to privacy."

The shrill beep from his NAVI alerts him of an incoming call. He picks up the device and stands it in on top of a hockey puck-sized disc that holds it up in place almost magically but scientifically. He taps the phone alert icon, which reveals the face of Secretary of State Lucy Fender.

"It's that bad?" he asks.

"I've never seen anything like this, Mr. President," says Lucy. "We had a translator here; I'm not sure if you've seen the news…"

"The guy on his knees."

"That's right. He did what he could, and from what he could make out...these people were confused, they were scared, they were looking for their families and friends. They were just very confused, and in a lot of pain."

"Ay Dios Mio," he said, pausing for a moment. "What about the crews of those ships?"

"Well," she begins, with the faint sounds of long fingernails tapping her NAVI screen, "Matthew, I think these people have been brainwashed. I can't explain it any other way. Each of the crewmen has a very elaborate story. Everybody's got a history. There was hardly any crew on the Leusden- most of them were said to have abandoned ship, but we've found no trace of them. The captain is not saying much, a Jochem Outjes, Swedish. He thinks it's the year 1738."

Matthew has known Lucy long enough to read her face. She is sincerely perplexed, and that worries him.

"And they're not the only ones," she continues. "The Danish crew of the ship called The Fredensborg thinks it's 1768. 1741 for the crew of the Henrietta Marie."

The President sits up in his chair. "The Henrietta Marie. Why does that sound familiar?"

The Secretary of State taps on the screen keyboard *Henrietta Marie*. She scans the information quickly using a text-only graphical interface. She shifts through floating stacks of phrases and titles: "slave ship Henrietta Marie," "sunken slave ship Henrietta Marie discovered," "SCUBA team recovers artifacts from Henrietta Marie." She selects a few titles, and drags them over to a window labeled "POTUS."

A window opens up on President Lopez's screen. Three icons are inside each one representing different news stories.

As he opens them up, Lucy continues. "The Henrietta Marie was a slave ship, sunk in the Florida Keys in 1788. What a co-winkie-dink."

Matthew watches another window open up. This time there are ten icons. As he opens them up, he catches a glimpse of a few of the titles; "Sunken slave ship the Leusden claims nearly 700 deaths", "Fresdenborg sinks near Cuba."

"There something else, sir. There were eyewitnesses to the appearance of the ships."

A video overtakes Matthews NAVI screen. It's two teenage kids on jet skis having a great time when loud pop precedes a flash of intense light. "What was that?" the girl in the video frame asks. The camera pans to the horizon as a ball of light hovers over the water, growing larger by the second. "What is that?" asks the boy. "Oh my God," says the off-camera voice. Suddenly the ball of light vanishes. In its place, the three ships. The video pauses.

"Does that look like China to you?" asks the President.

The video disappears, exposing Lucy's expressionless face. "We have an expert looking into this. A quantum physicist. She's observed some other anomalies similar to this event. It may be something, maybe nothing."

"But you still want to blame China."

Lucy is exhausted. "I admit that this makes blaming China difficult. I would even say impossible."

"That's the thing, Lucy. There's no one to blame."

"What?"

"Let me explain. Yes, someone made this happen. There is some physical reason for this event, and someone is to blame for making it happen. I'm looking at what it represents. You saw the election last year- the vote split between four parties. We won by 50,000 votes. We narrowly edged out the Neo-Nationalist party. That's 32% of the voting population for a party that ran on a platform of secession."

"Yes, Mr. President, I am fully aware of-"

"Well, if you're fully aware then I don't need to explain that more than a third of this population has felt that it has been under siege for the last 40 years- no matter how irrational that seems. Caucasians are having a difficult time adjusting to a minority status. This event reinforces stereotypes that will only ignite more anxiety in that community. They're volatile as it is."

"That's racist sir, is it not?"

"Is it? There are 40 million Caucasians gradually migrating to the Northwest trying to form an ethnonationalist caliphate[3]. That's a pretty volatile move if you ask me."

"White folks have always been reactionary."

"That's not racist?"

"That's observant, Matthew. There's a difference."

President Lopez points at the screen. "You are 100% correct, Madam Secretary. It's a matter of perception and the recipient of that judgment. You and I look at today's events, and in addition to the sadness and disgust, we may feel vindication, or an affirmation of our feelings and beliefs, and everything we've been taught. To others, it's indictment. It's the cold, gnarly finger of accusation, blame, and shame pointing right in their faces. Technically, most of them have done nothing wrong. But the sins of the Founders run deep. And karma is coming to collect."

Lucy cracks a smile. "You sound like John Shaft."

"Don't you mean *Juan* Shaft? That's what they called me when I wore my leather jacket on the campaign trail, remember that? Preston made me promise not to wear it again, and I said 'Why? I like Juan Shaft!' I just needed a mustache, some sideburns, bigger hands…"

Lucy can't hold it anymore. She busts out laughing. *Finally,* he thinks to himself; *it's been a while.* "The

---

[3] *The mass migration to the greater northwestern states, from Oregon to Washington state, otherwise known as The Northern Alliance. The group calls themselves Neo Nationalist Confederates, a population of disenfranchised caucasians who have felt left behind by what they call "America's diversity sickness." The hashtag #CaucasianCaliphate is widely used to mock or "troll" the group.*

2040s are just starting and already are kicking our asses," he smiles. "But we'll get through this. Keep me posted on what the physicist says, what's his name again?"

"Her name," Lucy answers, "Kiki Bishop."

"Okay. What a name. British?"

"Filipino, I believe."

"Great, well keep me posted on her findings."

"How's the speech coming along?"

"Ay Dios Mio, don't bring that up," he says, rubbing his temples. "I only have to convince a nation with the attention span of a pack of wild puppies, who are on the brink of self-destruction, to not panic. Piece of cake."

6

August 9th, 2041
11:46 am
West Chester Academy, West Chester, PA

Maximilian Oroko looks out at the sea of young, predominately white faces as he sits on his desk, in front of a classroom full of forty-five 11th graders. In variations of interest and disinterest, they stare at a video monitor showing a wrap-up of the previous day's drama from PNN's perspective. It all seems so surreal. When the adrenaline subsides after the initial shock, it feels as if they are watching a short film with a huge budget.

When the clip ends, Maximilian taps his NAVI screen and switches to his presentation. On the video monitor, an outline of the day's prospectus:

History and Perspective 101
Dr. Maximilian Oroko
An examination of yesterday's events
and what they mean to today's world.

"This is bullshit," someone murmurs. Everyone stirs and reacts, turning and looking at a student in the second row.

"Relax, guys," Maximilian says in his thick, but easy to understand Nigerian accent. "Duncan, so tell me. What is bullshit?"

"This," rants Duncan, "All of this! Come on, bruh—this can't be real! They dressed a bunch of dudes up in costumes! It's staged!"

A young lady sitting next to Duncan shoots her hand into the air. "Didn't you see the vid that just came out? This girl shot a vid with her friends when the ships appeared!"

Duncan sucks his teeth. "Yeah, and that girl's dad is the head of a movie studio-- she got that vid made!"

"Why is everything a conspiracy to you?"

"You're livin' in an 8/7 world, booboo."

A portion of the class rouses at what they perceive to be a sick burn.

"Calm down, everyone!" Maximilian booms. The students' silence is almost immediately. "Let us suppose that this is a hoax," he begins. "It is certainly possible— anything is possible. Yes, and what of this video? That could be part of the conspiracy, but that is assuming there is a conspiracy. You see? What we have are a lot of questions and nothing but speculation with no solid answers. No answers period. So, let us suppose that this is a hoax. What would be the purpose? Why this? "

"It's a provocation," someone shouts out.

"There are a billion ways to provoke someone. Why this way?" asks Maximilian.

There is silence at first.

"To divide us," another student says.

"Okay," says Maximilian, "...so you want to stage an event using African slave labor to provoke and divide your enemy. For what purpose?"

"For war!" is the response of several students

"What war are you speaking of?"

"They want us to go to war with ourselves," says Duncan. "To make it look like slaves are here so that black people can blame us. The black—the black people will get angry. And they'll blame white people for slavery and racism, and they'll start rioting, and we'll have to go to war with them."

Shouts of "That's so stupid!" and "The 'black people'?" blast from many of the students.

"It's not stupid!" says Duncan. "We're always getting blamed for racism."

"Because white people <u>are</u> responsible for racism!" says the young lady sitting next to Duncan.

"Oh please, Joanie," says Duncan flagging his hand at her, "you're just saying that because you date black guys."

That line gets jeers from the entire class.

"That's exactly what we're talking about," smiles Joanie. "You're representing this old white view of the world that thinks that white is the center of everything. You don't realize how destructive and counterproductive that is. It's racist, and it's wrong."

"What are you talking about!" blasts Duncan. "I'm not a racist! I don't care about black people! It's all the time we have to hear about black shit or Mexican shit-- I don't care! I just don't want that shit in my face all the time! Live your life. I don't care! I don't care what you do! I don't know any black people, but that doesn't mean I don't like them! I just don't know any! I mean, other than you, Dr. Oroko…"

"Dr. Oroko's not like them," says a student behind Duncan. "He's from Africa. He's not an American Black."

"Really?" asks Maximilian. "There is a difference, Matthew?" As if Maximilian doesn't know where this is going. He knows all too well. He's heard, and had, this conversation more times than he can count.

Matthew shrugs. "American Blacks are different."

"What the hell?" says a black girl in the side row of the classroom. "I think the only thing different here is you! You people are always finding problems in everyone else, and you don't even see how messed up you are yourselves."

Many in the classroom applaud this line, as Duncan cuts in. "See? There's no place for us. We built this country, and now there's no place for us!"

"You didn't build this country," answers Joanie, "<u>You</u> didn't build anything!"

"Why don't you go move up north, whissy[4]!" a voice shouts out, with laughter erupting throughout the class.

Duncan pounds his fist on the desk, yelling "Don't call me a whissy- I'm not a whissy, asshole!"

"All right, people-" Maximilian's voice booms, "cut this off right now."

The period chime interrupts the discussion, and the kids gather their things but do not leave. They know well enough not to leave while Dr. Oroko is speaking.

"Saved by the bell," he says. "Do yourselves a favor, wink-wink, and write five pages about how you are feeling about this event—your personal feelings, not what you saw on some video stream somewhere. Let us see some of this passion on the page. Have a good day."

They rise from their seats and file out. As Maximilian gathers his things, there is a knock at the door. He turns to find a familiar face in the doorway of his classroom.

"I must be a psychic," says Maximilian. "I saw this coming from miles away."

"Well, everyone says you're too smart for your own good," says Joseph, "And you just keep proving them right. All hail Max Oroko."

They step to each other, shake hands and hug.

"You know," says Maximilian, "They have these futuristic devices called the NAVICOM. It is amazing; it does almost everything you need a portable media and communication device to do. It even does video conferencing, so you do not even have to travel 90 miles to have the conversation that I knew you would probably want to have."

"I also know, smart-ass, that there was no way in hell I was going to have a productive conversation with you by staring at a block of glass and titanium."

"Well, then," Maximilian smiles, "I guess we're doing an early lunch."

---

[4] "Whissy" is a derogatory term for a white supremacist, derived from either "whine supremacist," or "white wussy."

12:12 pm
Donnely's Bar and Grill

Maximilian takes Joseph to the after work place he and his colleagues visit frequently. They find a table in the back so Joseph can avoid his new-found fame. It's a little early for a beer, but since yesterday Joseph finds himself thirsty for a bit of numbness.

"What were you speaking," Maximilian asks, "Yoruba? Swahili?"

"Swahili's what I've been most comfortable with. I had the best results Swahili."

"Something tells me that you would have better luck with Basaa, or Kako. Even Benti. You cannot go wrong with the Atlantic-Congo languages."

Joseph shakes his head and takes a swig of his beer.

"It is a lot to process at one time. You should not be so hard on yourself."

"I don't think they want to talk, after what they've been through. I looked inside the ships, too. Jesus, Max, you should have seen it."

"Everyone thinks it is China," says Maximilian.

"You don't think it's China," says Joseph.

"Neither do you," he says. "I do not know who or what it is. But it has to be something. It has to be someone."

"I know someone who thinks it's time travel," says Joseph.

Maximilian shrugs. "That video from that young girl certainly supports that theory."

"Come on," Joseph sneers, "You don't seriously believe in time travel?"

"It would give Middle Passage a whole new meaning, eh?" Maximilian smiles. "I believe time travel

CHARLES A. CONYERS, JR.

as much as I believe that China or Russia has unprecedented technological and psyop capabilities. I feel the same about those who believe that this is the work of God. At this point, all three of those theories seem viable."

"What's viable would be talking to the refugees and getting their story. This is why I need you up there. We can get this all figured out, you and I. Who am I kidding, you and you alone can translate for these people."

Maximilian rolls his eyes and shakes his head. "Joseph..."

"Don't do that, Max—don't shun this before you've even heard me out. Come on-- this is more important than ego and stupid political crap."

"First of all, Joseph, there is nothing wrong with my ego. Secondly, I am not the one harboring the 'stupid political crap,' as you say."

"You are harboring it! You're still sore about something that happened 12 years ago!"

"Yes, you are right," nods Maximilian, "The same clowns in charge then are in charge now. I see Fender is there..."

"She happened to be in town for a UN conference."

"Right. For all we know, she has something to do with this."

"Oh come on!"

"She is a crooked opportunist who would step on her mother's throat if it would help her career. The thought of having to answer to her makes my bones ache."

"Twelve years ago, Max. People change, you've changed too. This is far more important than that- you can at least acknowledge that."

"Look Joseph, dear old friend—"

"Don't say it, Max. Please don't say what I think you're going to say. This is history! Happening right now! There will never, EVER be another event like this in our lifetime. You mean to tell me that you're not the least bit curious?"

"I am curious, I will give you that. I am very curious."

"Just think about how historic this is! Think about what it means to our people to hear the voices of their ancestors."

Maximilian smirks and shakes his head. "You almost had me with Fender. If you believe that 'our people' would appreciate any of this, my friend…I am afraid you are, what is that phrase…barking up the wrong hydrant."

"Tree, first of all," frowns Joseph. "Second, I don't think that's very fair, man. You can't say that Black folks aren't interested in this."

"They are not, Joseph," says Maximilian, shaking his head. "American Blacks know nothing of their roots in Africa."

"That's not fucking fair, Max," huffs Joseph. "What do you expect? Look at the state of education in this country!"

"That is a lazy excuse, Joseph. The piss-poor state of education in America has nothing to do with connecting with your ancestors. Africa is a brand to Americans, not a culture. It is up to the individual to take an interest. It is incredibly naïve to believe that the same people complicit in your oppression would educate you about your culture. When the white man told the American Black man that he had no culture, the American Black man believed him.

"You know what, Joseph?" Maximilian continues, "How many of those Black folks out there do you think have any idea of how many languages are spoken in Africa? How many tribes, how many traditions, how much do they know? They could not care less, other than for the image of their self-victimization. They know the Middle Passage. They know chains and shackles. They do not know a thing prior to their enslavement."

Joseph sighs, shaking his head. "You're still nursing those wounds from grade school. After all these years, you cannot get over it."

"This is not about grade school, Joseph. If you think that I am still affected by children calling me 'African booty scratcher,' I can assure you that I am not. Children are children; they say stupid things. When adults do it as well, you start to put these things into perspective. You can see how severe the brainwashing is- how they have been bred to mock and disregard their own history, while at the same fetishizing it. This will not empower them. It will only give them another reason to march and whine. It is bad enough to ask me for Fender. It is worse to believe that I owe those listless negroes anything."

Maximilian looks up at the waiter as he brings their food.

"Ah, good. I am starving!" he says.

"If you're finished with your screed, I need an answer, Max," demands Joseph impatiently.

Maximilian shakes his head. "I will not waste my time and energy helping people who do not deserve it, Joseph," he says, "Howev-" before he can add anything else, Joseph gets up. "Where are you going?"

"I'm going back," Joseph says. "I've wasted enough time on this trip. Goodbye, Max. See you in another few years."

"Joseph!" Maximilian calls out, but he walks away and doesn't turn back.

Maximilian slumps back in his chair, emotionally drained from his friend's visit. Joseph is right, though. Had he had this conversation over the phone, it would have been a quick 5-minute discussion. No need to think about anything. In Joseph's presence, he had to put some thought into it. It was sneaky because even though Maximilian *had* been thinking about it, he didn't want to have to confront it. Now that he has, the wheels are turning.

10:32pm

Maximilian packs the last of his week's worth of clothes into a travel bag. He called Joseph a few hours earlier to tell him that he would be on a train to New York City first thing in the morning.

"Thank you, Jesus!" Joseph shouts out loud. "This is great news! You were so hell-bent against this—what changed your mind?"

Earlier in the evening, Maximilian returned to Donnelly's to meet up with three of his colleagues for drinks. Bob the Algebra teacher, Megan the European Literature teacher, and the new Biology teacher whose name he always forgets. All in their 30s, white, married, although it's been rumored that Bob and Megan are having an affair. They were always excited to join him. They talked about work, and the food, and what beers they liked better than others. After a while, talk veered towards *the* topic.

"Yeah, I haven't had a chance to talk to you about this," Bob begins. "You're the doctor, what do you think? You think this is real? I mean, as real as being covered-in-real-shit real…"

"It's gotta be a stunt!" says Megan. "How the hell could it not be a stunt?"

"Seriously," says the Biology teacher. "It's so obvious. Otherwise, you're saying they traveled through time. That's Harry Potter shit."

"Supposedly," says Bob, "the Russians developed this radar blocking technology so that they could sneak up on us-- maybe they'll find that on the ships!"

"That's right!" exclaims Megan, pointing to accent her understanding. "Don't they have some oil deal going on?"

"Yup, oil, and technology! Right, Max?"

Maximilian sighs deeply. "A friend of mine came to see me today. He is the fellow in the media clips, dropping to his knees..."

"Holy shit, you know that guy?" asks Bob in an astonishment shared by the other two.

"Twenty-five years," says Maximilian.

"Wow!" says Megan.

"I have known him for a long time. He did not look good. Whatever this event is, it is very, very real. That is what is confusing me. I look at those people, and I don't just see a lot of 'African refugees.' I see the Koti, and Bensu, and Medi. Tribes, groups, some of them hundreds, thousands of miles apart. It's like the Maafa[5]."

"The what?" asks Megan.

"It's an old Swahili word. It means 'great tragedy,' or 'terrible occurrence.' In other words, 'holocaust.' The slave trade, including the Middle Passage, is considered a holocaust of the African people. Our people were kidnapped as well as sold and traded by our own. It is what happens to an empire at the end. You do anything to gain back your wealth and power."

"And I think that's why they're doing it," says Bob. "They're trying to divide us!"

"Divide us," asks Maximilian. "For what?"

"For war!" the three say in unison.

"What war are you talking about?"

"Another Civil War," says the Biology teacher. "RAHOWA."

"The only people interested in the Racial Holy War that you speak of are uneducated American whites," says Maximilian. "I think you are giving the Chinese and the Russians more credit than they deserve in this case. Now, are Americans being hypocritical when it comes to

---

[5] Pronounced *Mah-ah-fah.*

human rights? Yes. This country has a track record of dehumanizing its own people."

"You're talking about something that happened hundreds of years ago!" the Biology teacher says.

"Does that make any difference?" asks Maximilian.

"Yes," says Megan. "It makes a lot of difference! I never owned slaves. My parents never owned slaves—"

"But you benefit from a system that has always favored your people. You put yourselves on a pedestal, but unfortunately, that pedestal rests on the back, shoulders, and throats of a group of people that your ancestors, your countrymen enslaved, dehumanized, abused and murdered."

"See? That's what I'm saying," says the Biology teacher. "We're always gettin' blamed for all the problems in this country!"

"You only want to own all that is good about America and ignore all the bad," says Maximilian. "All in the name of abstract concepts like 'liberty' or 'freedom,' or 'white supremacy.' What does that mean, when during its foundation those things only really applied to one group of people? That is antithetical to the Constitution that you people claim to hold dear."

"That's bullshit," says the Biology teacher. "Everyone is free in this country. If you're not free, then it's your fault!"

"So," says Maximilian. "The incident that occurred yesterday. Seeing a part of your history played out, whether real or fake, you still believe that people are free in this country? You still believe that it is poor white folks who are the innocent victims?"

"At this point, we are victims! Give me a break— we've elected two Black presidents, and we just elected a Mexican! Every time you turn on the television, you see Blacks and Mexicans. This whole culture now is based on Blacks or Mexicans—and everyone is always dumping on Whites!"

"Are they dumping on whites?" asks Maximilian. "Or do you just feel threatened by equality?"

"Fuck that."

"Okay, Craig, take it easy," says Megan. *Craig*! thinks Maximilian—*that's his name*!

"No, he's fuckin' sittin' here sayin' stupid shit! I'm supposed to feel guilty because some Black kids don't want to get out of the ghetto? Or Black people don't want to be educated? That's my fault? That's white people's fault? Shit, you look at the news, and they're always talkin' about how they fixed up some Black ghetto, or they build new schools for them! They're givin' more to poor Blacks than poor Whites! It's nothin' more than reparations! It's all those government programs that benefit these poor Blacks that don't even want it! We built this country, and we get the shaft? Slavery is over!"

"Craig, Jesus man…" says Bob, who has been glancing at Maximilian the entire time, to gauge his reaction.

"What? He's not like them," says Craig, the Biology teacher, pointing at Maximilian. "He's not even from here—he's not the same as them! It's like, there are Black people, and then there's 'niggers.' But he's not Black or a nigger, he's not even from here!"

Megan's face is buried in her hands. "I can't believe you just said the N-word like that," she says.

Maximilian smiles. "You know the only difference between me and Black folks living in America?"

"What?"

"I came here of my free will. They did not have a choice. I have a history. I have a heritage. They have ambiguity and abstract notions. These people, these 'niggers' that you talk about…they are only 'niggers' because it makes you feel better about yourself. That is how a slaver mentality works. You suppress and demean to place yourself on a pedestal, keep the other down and reliant. Not so much these days, however. Now it is out of fear and anxiety over a loss of power and influence. It is out of pain and frustration, and blind ignorance."

It was after those words came from Maximilian's mouth that his decision is final. He does not want to see his fellow countrymen as refugees of the United States government. He does not want to see his people sick, desperate, and hurting. However they got here, they are alone and surrounded by strange people, both white and Black. He knows Joseph would not get anywhere with them. They don't trust him. Maximilian doesn't know if they would trust him, either. He does know that Joseph is right, as he often is; this is history.

CHARLES A. CONYERS, JR.

7

August 10th, 2041
10:09am
Manhattan

"How many people do you think are out here?" Maximilian asks the officer driving the unmarked vehicle.

"They say it's gonna be over a hundred thousand," says the officer.

The tension is palpable; you could feel it watching through the car window. The sidewalks are swarming with a synchronous mass of predominately Black and Brown men and women, young and old, moving towards the convention center. Many are waving their DIY protest signs or pumping their fists in the air in tandem with various call and response chants.

"'Let my people go,'" quotes the officer, reading from a poster illustrated with bonded Black wrists breaking the chain in between.

"'You degrade us, we degrade you,'" quotes Maximilian from a poster with a racist caricature of a Chinese face; huge slanted eyes, bucked teeth, bright yellow skin. "Great use of color," says Maximilian sarcastically.

"Not for nuthin', but…these people are retards," says the officer. "We're not supposed to use that word anymore, but I'm old school, you know?"

"Yes, that word can be misused, but I can appreciate the sentiment," says Maximilian.

"You're a smart guy, Professor. A good guy. Can I say something personal?"

"Absolutely."

"I don't know how many white folks you know…"

"Quite a few."

"Then you probably know what I'm about to say. Especially if they feel comfortable enough to say it. Anyone that says that racism is made-up or doesn't matter is a fool. Look at what's happened over the last 30 years. People thought we'd elect a Black president, and all of our race problems would go away. I don't know what they were thinking. It's like they didn't know shit about this country's history."

"History is always repeating itself, isn't it?" says Maximilian. "Time and time again. Besides that, it's easy for people to ignore racism when it doesn't directly affect them. "

"You're a young guy-- how old are you?"

"Thirty-eight." smiles Maximilian.

"I'm 68 years old, Professor. Been white my entire life, Italian first and foremost, you know what I mean? White folks hate talkin' about this stuff. They hate dealing with it, talking about it. Since the census came out last year, talking about how the population grew, and white folks weren't on top anymore. Lotta white folk see America as their country. It's delusional nonsense. A lot of 'em are moving up north to that all-white commune, whatever it is- my brother is moving up there! My own brother, moving his wife and kids, everything, just because the country got browner. And this event the other day, now there's a panic."

"It is not just white folks that are the problem," says Maximilian. "My parents moved to this country when I was eight years old. I always got along with the white kids, but the Black kids never liked me. They never really wanted to try to like me. They never called me by my name. Instead, they called me 'Jungle Book.' That was replaced by 'African Booty Scratcher.' Some others called me 'Midnight' because of my complexion. What is sad is that the adults are no different. They do not use the same words, but...they tend to mock what they do not understand."

The officer shakes his head. "Kids don't know anything, especially when they learn from ignorant adults. And that's our problem. Ignorance."

"This incident, this event, whatever it is...this may be the breaking point. Lots of people have talked about what it would take for tensions to boil over. We have been too volatile for too long. Centuries of racial animus are not going to evaporate overnight. I think that is what the expectation was-- free the slaves and let them sort it out for themselves. Write laws as you go to keep the white people in check. Foster a battle for civil rights, yet builds a segregationist capitalist economy."

"God Bless America, right?"

Maximilian nods. "My home sweet home."

"You know what," says the officer, "Honestly, and you'll think I'm insane or somethin', but honestly...I think it's a sign from God. I mean, there's no other way to explain it! You saw that video—these ships pop up out of nowhere—nuthin' on radar or satellite. And I don't care how advanced the Chinese are; they ain't makin' anything like that. Like they got a cloaking device or something on Star Trek or some shit? What else could've brought those ships there? With those people like that— with Black slaves on board? I don't think they're from here. The only way they coulda been brought here is an act of God. Period. That's what I think, anyway—call me crazy if you want, but that's what I believe."

"Well, that is not the craziest thing I have ever heard," says Maximilian. "Whatever it is, it is surely something that we do not understand."

"Well, I say God." Says the officer. "If you don't know the answer, it's God."

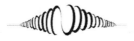

10:33 am
Jacob Javits Convention Center

An escort leads Maximilian to a small conference room. Sitting around the table are Joseph, Police Commissioner Wilson, and the woman that he was not looking forward to seeing. At all.

"Dr. Oroko," says Secretary of State Fender, standing up and extending her hand. "It's good to see you again."

Maximilian's entire body reacts with a tingling wave of disgust and anger, which he manages to hide with award-winning stoic indifference. He shakes her hand.

"It is good to see you too, Madam Secretary," he says, managing his emotions.

"I don't believe you," says Fender.

"Well, I guess we will both have to do our best to believe," says Maximilian.

"I'm glad you're here, Max," says Joseph trying to break the tension.

"I would not miss it, old friend," says Maximilian, looking down at a stack of what looks like ledgers sitting on the table in front of Joseph.

"I wanted you to see these," says Joseph, sliding the ledgers over towards Maximilian. "They were found yesterday."

"Shipping manifests, eh? That is pretty elaborate for a hoax," says Maximilian as he opens the first book. The logo at the top of the page catches his eye immediately. It's detailed and ornate, featuring a large elephant in front of a castle. The initials "R.A.C." are integrated within.

"What does that mean?" asks Fender, "R.A.C.?"

"Royal African Company," says Maximilian. "The largest slave trading company in the world during the 18th century. There were known to export over 20,000 Africans to the Americas and the Caribbean per year. Which ship is this?"

"The Fredensborg." Says Joseph.

The Secretary of State steps in immediately to say, "Our research tells us that it was—"

"A slave ship that sank in the late 1760s," says Maximilian. "What are the other ships called?"

"The Leusden and the Henrietta Marie," says Joseph.

Maximilian looks up. "The Leusden and Henrietta Marie? You have got to be kidding me."

"I kid you not."

"You know these ships, Dr. Oroko?" asks Fender.

"They are very well known, yes," says Maximilian. "Slave ships that sank at sea. The Leusden was probably the worst of them all. The cargo hold—"

"Was nailed shut," says Joseph. "And it was."

Maximilian flips through the books, in quiet amazement at how detailed and authentic they look.

"If I knew any better," says Joseph, "I'd say that those books were real. And I like to think that I know better."

"Well, these are just books," says Fender. "How about meeting the people? Do you think you can talk to them?"

Maximilian looks up at her. "Let us find out."

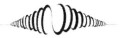

10:58am

Onorede is watching everyone eat. There is plenty of food, mainly rice, chicken, and vegetables. They seem content. They have become accustomed to their new environment. That makes him uncomfortable.

Among a sea of cots, Onorede is located in the back corner. He likes the idea of having a wide field of vision so that he can see everything. But even from this vantage point, with all the people milling around, it is difficult to see absolutely everything.

Volunteers set up stations along the back wall where the refugees can get food and water, additional clothing, toiletries, medical supplies, etc. The room is loud and alive.

"*Ah, Onorede!*" says Fakih in their native Krou, approaching Onorede with two plates of food in his hands. "*Let us eat!*"

"*You have been gone for a long time,*" says Onorede, taking a plate of food. No cup full of slop not suitable for an animal to eat, like their previous ghosts provided.

"*What do they call this?*" asks Onorede.

"'chee-chin,' *or* 'chih-kahn,' *something like that. It is bird meat, with boiled grains and beans. It is very good. I must tell you what I saw!*" says Fakih with the enthusiasm of a nine-year-old. "*One of the sentry's showed me his picture stone. It was amazing, a shiny black stone, about the size of your hand, with moving pictures on the front! He touched it, and the pictures changed to other pictures! He showed me pictures of the large boats and the moving of our people to this place. And there were other pictures! It shows things that I have never seen before! Did you know that they have structures that can fly—flying! In the air, like a bird!*"

"*Do not let yourself get wrapped up in their magic and trickery,*" says Onorede. "*Structures cannot fly. They are showing you things to fool with your mind.*"

"*Maybe,*" says Fakih, "*But it sure is fascinating!*"

"*If I did not know you any better, I would say that you were enjoying your captivity,*" Onorede sneers.

"*I would not say that,*" says Fakih defensively. "*You said yourself that these people are harmless. We are not prisoners here.*"

"*We are not prisoners, yet we cannot leave. And even if we could leave, where will we go? We are in a strange place with strange people. That was the risk that we took by agreeing to this mission. We always knew there was a chance that we could not get back home. We did this voluntarily, you and I. And Oluchi, may his spirit rest in peace. Masinu as well."*

"What do you think happened to Masinu and his group?"

"I am assuming they had a similar fate. I can only guess the outcome."

Fakih sits his plate to the side. *"So, what do we do?"*

Onorede shakes his head. *"I do not know. I think these people have lost faith in me."*

"Foolishness!" says Fakih. *"We tried. And we will try again soon."*

Three men approach Fakih and Onorede. One of them, with a beaming expression on his face, steps forward and speaks to Fakih in his native language. He speaks quickly and excitedly, pointing to the direction he came from.

Fakih looks at the man curiously, as if he didn't quite understand what he said. Fakih speaks to the man. The man answers, continuing to point.

"He says there's a man that can speak to us," translates Fakih.

"Great, another stooge," says Onorede, rolling his eyes.

"No," says Fakih, *"he says this man speaks directly to us."*

"So it's another stooge with a magic plank."

Fakih turns to the man and speaks in his language. He uses his hands to illustrate the use of a 'magic plank.' The man shakes his head vehemently, then motions with his hands over his mouth. He points again in the direction he came from.

"He speaks to everyone in their language, without a plank."

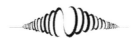

10:42am

When Maximilian first steps into the convention center hall, a large pit grows and sits so heavily in his stomach that it stops him in his tracks.

"You okay, Max?" asks Joseph.

His throat is so tense it's like his heart has leaped up inside of it. "It is more overwhelming in person,"

Joseph puts his hand on Maximilian's shoulder. "I was about to walk out the first time."

"That explains the crying," grins Maximilian.

Joseph sucks his teeth. "Fuck you, Max. Let's go. You're holding us up."

The two step into the hall, followed by Commissioner Wilson, Secretary Fender and four officers in military gear. A few of the Africans stop what they are doing when this group enters the room.

Maximilian spots a young African man standing a few feet away, staring at back at him. He makes a quick study of this man's features—the spacing of his eyes, the fullness and shape of his nose and lips, his ear shape. Maximilian steps up to the young man, and in Yoruba says *"My name is Maximilian, can you understand me?"*

The young man smiles, and says *"Yes, I can."*

As Maximilian speaks to him, others watch, then approached the two. He sees a woman with features indicative of someone of the Ibo tribe. *"Can you understand me,"* Maximilian asks in native Ibo. The woman cries immediately and hugs Maximilian like a long-lost child.

Joseph watches and smiles wider than he has since before this event occurred. *I knew it*, he thinks to himself. Joseph activates the video recorder app and watches through his NAVI as he captures the situation.

"Good call, Professor Healey," admits Secretary Fender. "Mr. Oroko is a brilliant man; he always has been. He's also an enormous pain-in-the-ass."

"Always has been, Madam Secretary," Joseph nods. "He means well. He's the most driven, passionate person I know. I think he puts a little too much of himself into his work."

"Mrs. Oroko?"

"He's single. Max has never been much of a dater."

Secretary Fender nods. "That explains it. He needs to get laid."

"*Where are we?*" shouts a man in Mande, "*Please tell me what is going on?*"

Maximilian begins by saying exactly what he was asked to say: "*I am a representative of the government of the United States of America. You are safe. We will provide you with food and shelter and whatever you need to make this transition as smooth as possible. Can you please tell me your name, where you come from, and how you ended up on the ship?*"

"*My name is Afar,*" the man says, "*I am a warrior of the Soninke people. I was captured in battle by Marabout warriors and traded to a group of dead-skinned people, who took us onto a massive river and put us on...a very large structure on a raft. We were stacked and crammed like meat on a shelf for smoking. And after what seemed like half a day, new people removed us from our prison and brought us here. Why were we brought here? What is this place?*"

Maximilian listens carefully. Soninke and Marabout. A battle. He knows of an Islamic holy war between the two tribes, but that was over 400 years ago.

A young woman standing next to Maximilian grabs his arm, with tears welling up in her eyes.

"*Can you help me?*" she asks in a language that sounds to Maximilian like Kwa, spoken by the Akan. "*They took me as I gathered water for my village! I just want to go home!*"

"*I will help you the best I can,*" answers Maximilian in the best Kwa he can muster up. "*These people are here to help you. We are looking for answers like you.*"

As Maximilian turns to speak to the next person, Onorede bursts through the crowd that has surrounded him. Fakih steps up next to him.

Joseph steps up to Maximilian and whispers to him, "That's him! That's the one from the other day!" He says this while looking at Onorede, who is starring Joseph down. Joseph sees this and fades back.

Maximilian looks at Onorede, but cannot place his ethnicity. He tries Mande, *"Hello, my name is Maximilian. Can you understand me?"*

Onorede says nothing; he just stares at him stoically.

Maximilian tries again, this time in Yoruba. *"Can you understand me now?"*

Onorede smirks. *"Another stooge."*

Maximilian is startled by Onorede's words. He hears a language that he has not heard since he was very young, and even still, he heard it from someone that was the last known person to speak it. Maximilian did his college dissertation on the language, mostly to show off and impress his professors. But to hear it being spoken by a relatively young man, in the 21st century…maybe he is mistaken.

"Can you understand me?" Maximilian asks in Krou.

Onorede's smile vanishes. He looks at Fakih, who is looking back at him in astonishment.

"You understand me, do you not?" asks Maximilian. *"You speak Krou. How do you speak Krou?"*

Onorede looks insulted. *"How do you speak Krou?! You are not Krou!"*

"I am not," says Maximilian. *"I am from Nigeria. I am a descendant of the Hausa and Fulani from the northern region."*

"How can this be?" asks Fakih.

"This is a trick!" says Onorede. *"More trickery from this stooge! How is he able to speak to all of us this way? He must be using some type of magic allowing him to read our thoughts and our language and give it back to us. It is a lie!"*

86

Onorede spits at Maximilian, hitting his shirt. This rouses the crowd of Africans, and in turn rouses the officers who begin to move in. Maximilian holds up his hands "Wait!" he says.

Joseph continues filming, although he has the hand holding the camera extended, his eyes slightly squinting, awaiting what he believed could be an inevitable attack.

Maximilian steps closer to Onorede, who at this point is confused by this man's calm. "*I can speak your language, and the languages of the others, because I studied them. You are currently in a gathering center, typically used for celebrations and meetings. We are very curious about how you got here. The more we know, the better we can help you. Can you help us understand*?"

Onorede again looks to Fakih, who just shrugs. He looks back at this man that calls himself 'Maxmilia,' as he hears it. Like it or not, this man could be his only hope.

CHARLES A. CONYERS, JR.

8

Difuu-Ɔsandaa[6] 1741
Kuruwukuo, Midday
(August, Wednesday, 1:43 pm)
North West Africa

Onorede leads a group of 35 warriors, crouched and stalking slowly towards the crest of a hill, at the opening of an expansive line of trees 2000 feet away. When going into battle, Krou warriors are dressed in a dark goatskin loincloth, and their bodies are painted with scale-like bands of white ashen war paint on their arms, legs, chest, back, and face. Their shields, made of thatched bark woven in copper within an iron frame, are held up over their backs in their left hands. In their right, long iron javelin spears with serrated blades at the tip, held at the ready. From behind, their procession appears like an armored snake slithering slowly towards its prey.

He stops, as do the others behind him, crouching down awaiting instruction. He looks at the man to his right, his second in command.

"There they are, Masinu," he whispers, pointing at the trees. "Oluchi was right."

Masinu gestures to the warriors behind them. That's the ready signal.

"I count 58," Onorede whispers.

Masinu shakes his head. "I had 62."

"Well, one of us is right. Let us find out ."

With a smile, Masinu raises his right hand, spear gripped firmly and let out a deep-throated yelp.

---

[6] The Krou follow the Akan calendar.

The warriors bolt from their position, charging in unison. Within seconds, the Krou warriors spread out in formation, seven rows of five. Each row, one after another, with a mighty running start, throw their javelin spears toward the trees.

Many of the Gola warriors are not fast enough. Like iron missiles, the Krou weapons slam into their targets, bursting into trees, chests, legs and skulls. The surviving Gola charge in spite of the attack. The Krou javelin throwers brandish knives from their belts to continue their assault.

Of the 62 Gola warriors, only ten survive, and are taken as prisoners. The Krou have only lost one. Onorede orders the surviving Gola warriors to dig graves for their fallen brethren. A marker is left so that a Krou artisan can erect a statue of this battle to honor the fallen.

The graves are completed by dusk. The war paint is all but gone from their bodies, as the sweat of a difficult battle melts it away and cools them in the warm and hefty breeze. The Krou warriors march back to their village, laughing and singing songs of their triumph. Their Gola prisoners, draped in blood-red cloth and adorned with an array of red and golden beads, are bound by the wrists with leather rope, flanked by their captors. Tailing the procession and not partaking in the celebration are Onorede and Masinu.

"This is the third attempt to attack our village in this cycle," says Masinu. "There is something happening around us."

"Agreed," says Onorede.

"You have an audience with the Elders, what do they say?"

Onorede looks ahead as he speaks. "The elders do not appear to be disturbed. It is almost as if they have been expecting this."

"It bothers you, does it not?" asks Masinu. "It is more than the frequency of the attacks. We are not at war with the Gola, yet they have attacked our people, and they tried to attack our village."

Onorede only nods and listens.

"Does this have anything to do with the pale face ghosts? Many people in the village hear very scary things."

"I've heard the stories. The soulless, dead-skinned creatures that snatch men, women, and children in the night."

"Not just at night. They say the ghosts walk with our people, and they use spells to trick us into snatching our brothers and sisters for the ghosts. Walking with the devil to betray your own!"

Onorede laughs. "You sound like the children with their creature stories."

"Ah, but these are not children's stories. This is reality."

"I hear things as well. But if the elders have no fear, neither should we."

Masinu gives Onorede the side eye.

"I can feel that look," smirks Onorede.

"I cannot believe that you're giving me the Elder line," scoffs Masinu.

"Masinu," groans Onorede, "You are very inquisitive, and that is an admirable trait. Not in this case."

This stops Masinu in his tracks. "Why not?"

Onorede turns to Masinu, and takes a deep sigh. "My friend. My brother. I mean no offense to you. You are a great warrior and leader of men."

"Then why keep me in the dark?"

"Because the little I know is not worth you knowing at this time. When I am ready to share it with you, I will. Understand Masinu, the only thing that matters is protecting this village."

Masinu shakes his head, "Of course protecting the village matters, that's exactly the idea!"

"Not only from the outside but inside as well. I've already said too much."

"There was a time when you used to share these things with me."

"Times are changing. Also, my friend, your mouth runs like the Prah."

"You know that's nonsense," Masinu scowls, shaking his head.

Onorede laughs, slapping Masinu's back. "I promise you, Masinu, you will know when the time is right."

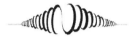

Fomene, Morning
(Friday, 10:10am)
Village of Okenna

"Master Madaki, excuse me. I was told to inform you that a group of Dainke traders is approaching the village."

Onorede is kneeling in front of a tomato plant when he receives the news from the young girl wearing a dress wrap with a complex mosaic design distinct to the Krou. He wipes the dirt from his hands as he stands upright.

"Thank you, Ama," smiles Onorede, "I will greet them at our meeting place momentarily."

Onorede is the son of a member of the Elder Council, and one of its two youngest members (next to Fakih). He is also the leader of the village of Okenna's warriors, as well as husband and father of three. He likes to unwind by tending to the small garden behind the large clay-brick and thatch-roofed home he and his wife built. It's a more elaborate dwelling than most, with multiple sections for rooms and an attached, two-level cylindrical structure to store, dry and smoke foods. There are a few things the Krou are known for; engineering, architecture, agriculture and warfare.

Onorede steps into the family dwelling to change into a boubou. As he steps out, he finds Fakih waiting for him, also wearing a boubou.

"Do you think they will have anything good this time?" Fakih asks.

"They usually do," answers Onorede as he steps onto the clay-brick path leading to the center of Okenna. "Their spices and fabrics are always impressive."

Fakih follows Onorede down the path. "But they do not produce any of those things."

"Does that matter?"

"I like trading with artisans, builders, farmers-- they know what they are dealing with. Traders only know what they have to trade, and sometimes they do not even know what they have."

Onorede smiles, shaking his head. "Such a pessimist, Fakih."

"A realist, Onorede-- realist."

When they reach the village meeting place, they are greeted by six members of the Dainke tribe; three men are dressed in gold and blue Kente robes. The other three, a woman and two men, wearing only kente skirts, have laid out and arranged items to be traded from the large baskets, wraps, and bundles they carried. The Krou have a friendly and prosperous relationship with the Dainke, and Onorede has been looking forward to their return. The leader of the group is Dembe, who speaks to Onorede and Fakih in Mende.

"He asks if we have any prisoners we could sell to them," translates Fakih.

"What perfect timing," answers Onorede.

As expected, the Dainke are more than pleased to take the 10 Gola prisoners. Onorede summons Ama to have the prisoners be prepared for transport and brought for the Dainke right away. Onorede is sure the prisoners are presented well; they were well fed, allowed to bathe and were given clean garments. Onorede has heard stories of other tribes that starved or beat their prisoners. This makes no sense to him. Brutality and maltreatment always seemed to breed dissension and proved to be too dangerous. Under those conditions, sooner or later, the tables could turn; no one wants to be killed by their prisoners.

In return, the Dainke do not disappoint. In addition to the spices and some fabrics, another object catches Onorede's eye. Dembe smiles at Onorede and speaks to Fakih.

"He says you have good instincts," says Fakih. "Really, Onorede-- you need to brush up on your Mende."

"Do not act like you don't enjoy these visits," smirks Onorede.

Dembe holds up what looks to Onorede like a carved wooden handle holding a steel rod. He offers an explanation to Fakih to translate.

"He says it's a weapon called a 'ri-fel,'" translates Fakih. "It is capable of shooting a small ball of steel that can pierce the skin over 400 feet away."

"Ask him to demonstrate it," requests Onorede. "I want to see it work."

Dembe barks out something to one of their shirtless companions, who runs over to a Mopane tree about 300 feet away. The shirtless Dainke man smears a large white ash circle target on the trunk of the tree.

As Dembe prepares the weapon, he describes the steps as Fakih translates.

"He is measuring out a powder to pour into...the muss-el, the long metal tube. Now he takes that piece of cloth...and he uses that to help that metal ball move down into the muss-el. That bigger ball is to pound the metal ball into place."

"This seems like a lot of work for one metal ball," Onorede says watching Dembe remove the ramrod from the side of the rifle to shove the metal ball down into the muzzle. After he replaces the steel rod, Dembe holds up the rifle.

"Finally," says Onorede.

"He's not finished," says Fakih.

"You are joking."

"Now he is filling more of the powder into that...the pan. He says 'not too much powder'. He says pull back the hammah, I believe he is saying."

As Dembe cocks the hammer, he holds the rifle in firing position, with the butt firmly against his shoulder, aiming it at the white circle on the tree. Onorede watches the other Dainke cover their ears and grimacing. Dembe turns to Fakih and speaks.

"He says it makes a very loud sound," he translates.

Pulling the trigger jerks Dembe as a deep and ear-splitting crack lets off a puff of smoke. A burst of bark and splinters spray from the white circle target. Birds scatter from the trees. Fakih practically jumps out of his skin.

Onorede's eyebrows raise involuntarily. "Impressive," he says, nodding.

Fakih rubs his ears. "You can go deaf as you defeat your enemies."

"Please," Onorede smirks, "I've heard the last screams of desperate, dying men in my ears. A sharp pop is nothing."

"How was that lion's heart you had for breakfast," jokes Fakih.

Onorede shakes his head and smirks as Dembe hands him the rifle.

"Where does this come from," Onorede asks.

Fakih addresses Dembe about the rifle. When Dembe answers, Fakih looks surprised.

"He said he got this from the white people," Fakih replies.

Onorede is perplexed. "What are 'the white people?' Does he mean the pale faces?"

Fakih rolls out a description to Dembe, gesturing with his hands over his skin. Dembe answers, nodding. Onorede sees concern growing in Fakih's face.

"He says he trades with the Gola, and they got this from the pale faces."

Onorede is surprised to hear this. "They got these weapons from the Gola? I haven't seen them use these weapons in battle."

Dembe continues talking.

"The Gola have a lot of these weapons, and they don't typically trade with them," translates Fakih, "He says the Gola are hoarding them. They traded this rifle because they needed food."

"How lucky for us," says Onorede examining the weapon. "We would be foolish not to take it."

Onorede looks up from the weapon to spot Ama escorting a few Krou warriors as they guide the prisoners to be traded. A small group of Krou villagers has gathered as well, wondering where that loud sound came from.

"I apologize for the sound, everyone," Onorede calls out.

He shifts his attention back to Fakih, who is speaking to Dembe and is seemingly surprised by what he is being told. When Dembe finishes and turns to his people to make arrangements to secure the prisoners, Fakih steps to Onorede.

"Dembe has quite a story to tell," he begins. "He asked if we have encountered the pale faces. I told him we had not, but have been hearing about sightings. He says that these white, pale faces are abducting people from tribes all over. He says...they are taking men, women and children to be eaten."

"Eaten?" says Onorede, taken aback. "He told you the pale faces eat women and children? Are you sure you heard that correctly?"

"That is what he is saying," says Fakih. "He said they were taking our people to be eaten. That is what he said he heard."

When the Dainke pack away their remaining items and secure their Gola prisoners, Dembe offers a parting gesture by raising his hand, then extending for Onorede and then Fakih to claps arms and shake. Onorede and

Fakih look on as Ama guides the Dainke to the opening gate of the Krou village.

"I know you don't believe them," says Fakih, "But I have heard these stories as well."

Onorede gives Fakih a strange look. "You have never told me anything about this."

"To be honest, I did not take these stories seriously. It can't be a coincidence that we have been under constant attack over the last few cycles."

Onorede smiles. "So you think we are being attacked so that we can be taken and eaten by pale ghosts in the night? You sound like Masinu, afraid of what is not seen and is spoken of only in stories. I, for one, am not afraid of children's nightmares, and you should not be either."

"I'm not afraid," says Fakih. "Contemplative, but not afraid."

Whenever Onorede speaks to the elder council, he feels far less than his 26 years. He may be a man who has been given tremendous responsibility, but to this group of seven elders, including his father Elder Jahi Madaki, he is still very young and inexperienced. Onorede's personal pride aside, he is very concerned about the safety and wellbeing of the Krou. The fear of more attempted invasions and the talk of the pale-faced ghosts and their abductions are growing day by day. He feels that sitting around and waiting is not an option. They need to act more preemptively to keep the threat from overtaking Okenna. He feels it necessary to strengthen their alliances with neighboring tribes and build up their defensive forces.

"Nonsense," says Elder Matata. "We've had a surge in attacks lately, yes. The Krou have faced greater challenges than this. As far as these pale faces are concerned, they pose no threat to us."

"With all due respect, Elder Matata," says Onorede, "I think that this is far from being nonsense. I know that we have faced attacks in the past, even with similar frequency. I believe that the threat of the pale faces is real and should be taken very seriously. They are bold and use very dangerous weapons that shoot projectiles from hundreds of yards away. They are not to be underestimated."

"Have you seen these pale faces? " asks Elder Zola.

Onorede knows where this is going, and he is not pleased. "No," he admits reluctantly, "I have not."

"Yet you want us to alter our entire way of life to accommodate an invisible threat?"

"Invisible to us at the moment," Onorede insists, "but it is only a matter of time before this becomes our problem. Surely you cannot be blind to this!"

"Onorede!" exclaimed Jahi. "You will only speak with respect to the council!"

"Forgive me, Father. Forgive me, Elders. I cannot allow this to rest another day with no action. I request permission to form and lead a party to investigate this impending threat."

"Permission denied," says Elder Zola. "We cannot have you roaming the countryside for days or weeks while our village is unguarded."

"Manisu will go in my place," Onorede offers. "I will continue to press this point for as long as it takes to convince you."

"Jahi," says Elder Ade, who has sat quietly and observed this exchange from the beginning, "I suggest that you have a talk with your son, to make clear to him that he is a long way from dictating decisions about anything involving matters of this village."

"Yes, he does, Ade. He and I will have a long talk this evening," says Jahi.

Elder Ade, the oldest of the Krou village elders, has been watching Onorede closely over the years. He does not appreciate the insubordination, but he recognizes his urgency. "You may form a party of no more than seven to investigate these so-called claims of invaders with pale faces," he says. "You have one week to present evidence to us of this threat. If you make a convincing argument, only then will we make decisions regarding the future of this tribe."

Onorede bows respectfully. "Thank you, Elder Ade."

"Do not thank me yet, young Madaki," warns Elder Ade. "Whether you are right or wrong, we will have much to consider."

At the end of the meeting, Jahi asks his son to walk with him. Dusk is setting in, prompting the lighting of torches along the paths in Okenna, giving everything a warm, golden hue.

"You are petulant and impatient, Onorede," Jahi begins. "I love you, son, but you must learn that there are some moments that require no comment from you. You do not address the Elder Council as if they are commoners."

"I am sorry, Father. You know I mean no disrespect, but they are deaf and blind to our problems. If we continue to ignore this threat, there will be no Elder Council, there will be no village, there will be no Krou! I know you can see what is going on!"

Jahi sighs deeply. "Your disrespectful tone betrays your good intentions."

"Why does the council have to be so thin-skinned about this?"

"It is not about thin skin, son," explains Jahi. "They are cautious. Okenna has a long and proud history going back twelve generations. Conflict and adversity from the outside are nothing new."

"I know of our history, Father," insists Onorede, "This threat is new. I've never heard stories of Krou, or Gola, or Yoruba, or Igbo being taken and eaten by pale-faced men. That is what we hear now."

"Eaten?" Jahi stares at his son curiously. "That's a new one, son," he says laughing.

Onorede is so frustrated he wants to scream, but that won't get him anywhere faster.

"This village is well-protected," assures Jahi. "We worked very hard to maintain and secure Okenna from outside threats. You helped build some of those safeguards yourself, you know." Jahi puts his hand on Onorede's shoulder. "You got them to agree to your suggestion, that is good first step. Don't spoil that."

"But you are on the council, Father-- why can't you talk to them?"

"You assume that I have not," Jahi answers. "Even my influence has its limitations. You requested this expedition, and it was approved. Assemble your team, and let us see what happens."

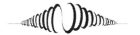

Kurubena, Afternoon
(Tuesday, 12:22 pm)

Masinu, accompanied by six Okenna warriors, are two days into their scouting mission before they are ambushed. He and Onorede had discussed at length the path they thought would be best to explore. Since the Dainke spoke of a relationship between the Gola and the 'ghosts,' they felt their party should travel north to the Prah River, and follow it south where the river ends and right before the mountains divide. From there, they could make their way back home. The entire trip would take about a week to complete.

"Be mindful. Use your eyes. Stay out of sight at all times," Onorede reminds his old friend. He has known Masinu since they were both old enough write their names in the Krou script that was taught to all in the tribe, but was not mandatory; since Masinu's grandfather was also on the Elder Council, it is demanded of him.

The Krou warriors had walked eight miles of flat land, bleached by the sun in glowing orange and light green, until they reached a cliff from which they had a view of the country in front of them. There was a lush forest awaiting them at the bottom, that stretched out for miles, with the Prah River snaking through the inside.

At the crest of the cliff, Masinu finds the mouth of a small path. The path leads to a series of steps that were carved into the blood orange rock face. The steps lead to a small plateau. It is here that the smell of burning flesh hits Masinu's nostrils.

"Is that meat?" asks one of the Krou warriors, turning his nose.

"That smell is unlike any meat I know of," says Masinu. He spots a small column of gray smoke rising from the trees.

They continue their descent down another series of steps, followed by a sloped path before they finally reach the bottom and the entry point for what looks to be an unforgivably dangerous, living and breathing jungle. The smell is thicker.

"Keep your eyes open, men," says warns Masinu.

The group moves in a line, slowly. The sound of their leather sandaled feet stepping through a jungle floor thick with twigs, rocks, leaves and other forms of plant life, overwhelms the background sounds of animal life and wind-blown trees.

Masinu is tense. The burning smell is really strong now, and the air is slightly smoky. They are close. There is a small clearing up ahead. He stops, as do the other Krou warriors. After a moment of thought, he gives a hand gesture, which signals the others to fan out around the clearing, and move in slowly.

The first thing that Masinu sees when he breaches the clearing is the pile of at least eight bodies lying in a pyre. The bodies, exposed in between plumes of pouring smoke, are charred severely as the fire rages and pops underneath.

While the others hold their noses, Masinu does not. He is too scared to do much of anything; he had never in his 26 years seen anything like this. Just as he is about to announce an immediate retreat from the area, he and the other Krou find themselves surrounded. He watches his men drop their weapons, holding up their hands and moving in towards the center of the clearing. Behind them, warriors from the Dainke tribe. When Masinu sees this, he is relieved.

"*It is okay,*" he says in Mende, "*We are Krou.*"

Dembe steps forward.

"*What has happened here?*" Masinu asks. "*Why are these bodies being burned? Did you see who was responsible?*"

Dembe smiles. "*That does not concern you,*" he says. "*I think you have more important things to worry about right now. We spotted you coming down the mountain. Why are you here?*"

"*We were seeking assistance from the Dainke,*" says Masinu, "*We thought you could join forces to help us defeat a common enemy.*"

"*A common enemy,*" Dembe asks.

"*We were hoping you could help us shed some light on the invasion of the pale-faced peoples coming into our land.*"

Dembe shakes his head. "*We cannot help you. But you are going to help us.*" He shouts a command to the other Dainke. They hold their weapons up, ready to attack.

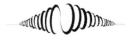

Monobena, Morning
(Tuesday, 8:17 am)
Village of Okenna

Four attempts have been made to attack Okenna.

Onorede and his men are tired. They have never been in multiple battles with the frequency that they've experienced recently. Masinu and the others are presumed dead or captured. When the first week came and went, Onorede became more and more restless. He was furious at himself, but more so of the Elder Council. Their complacency is so puzzling to him that immediately after the fourth battle, he approaches them, and throws down his blood-soaked spear in protest.

"We have been fighting and fighting, and for what? None of you have given me an adequate answer. Unless you tell me what you know, I will fight no longer!"

Onorede braces himself to receive his lashes for what he thinks will surely be considered a mutinous act. No amount of lashing would equate to the weariness of the constant loop of battles.

Elder Ade stands up and looks Onorede dead in the eyes.

"This day has been long coming, since before you were born," he begins. "The pale men have been moving into our lands for nearly 100 years. It was only a matter of time before we would have to deal with them. They are building alliances with other tribes, bringing in their weapons, and their tools, and their liquid potions. They are building a new world, and need us. They trade for land, and for people."

"How do you know all of this?" asks Onorede.

"Because they have already approached us," answers Elder Jahi. "We turned down their requests. This was many years ago, before you were born. We had managed to keep them at a distance. Now, however, it seems that they are more powerful and more influential than we had previously anticipated."

Onorede is blindsided. "You are telling me that you have known this all along? You called me out, made me look and feel like a fool for merely speaking of this danger, and you knew this the whole time!"

"Our countrymen are weak," says Elder Ade. "They are easily swayed by jewels and weapons. That is why we have been under constant attack. They have allowed their senses to be corrupted by the pale men. They will stop at nothing to fulfill the wishes of their new masters."

"No," demands Onorede, "We can stop them!"

Elder Ade looks at Elder Jahi. "Indeed," he says, nodding.

"No! No! Absolutely not!"

Ifé is furious when Onorede tells her of his mission. He didn't expect his wife to take it well, but due to the Elder Council's betrayal by way of avoidance, he has no choice. He will bring five men with him, and walk to the Prah River, where the pale-faced ghosts are known to stalk. Then he and his men will allow themselves to get captured. Once inside, they can find out what the ghosts have been doing with their people. He may even be able to find Masinu and the others.

"You are mad," Ifé barks. "You are speaking madness to me! What about your sons? What about me— well, you obviously don't care about me...! What about your home? This village! We have been under constant attack, and you are just going to leave?"

"This village will always be safe from attack," says Onorede. "Okenna is well-protected. We have the finest, strongest warriors in the kingdom. We have hidden traps circling the parameter of the village if our enemies get too close. Everyone will be well-protected."

Ifé shakes her head in protest. "With you gone, there is no guarantee that we will be safe."

"If I don't do this," insists Onorede, "there will be no village for us to protect. There will be no Krou. Those pale faces will spread through our land like a plague and kill us all. You're seeing it happen now! These tribes that attack us are being pushed out of their villages because of the ghosts. They are building alliances with the ghosts and betraying their own countrymen!"

"And you think allowing yourself to be caught is the only way to do this? This is insane—YOU are insane!"

With that, she storms away from him, moving into their sleeping quarters. Onorede gathers his supplies next to the entrance of their home before joining her. He looks at his wife, lying on the bed, back facing him. As his eyes follow the contours of her body, he feels regret and anger. He regrets having to leave this beautiful woman behind, and angry that circumstances have led him to this decision.

Onorede lies down next to her and puts his hand on her hip.

"You know that I do not want to do this, Ifé," he says.

"Then you should not," she says softly.

"I have to," he says.

"You just made this decision without me. You didn't even give me a chance to have a say in this."

Onorede kisses her gently on the back of her neck. She moves her head back, allowing him to kiss the side of her neck as well.

"This is bigger than you and me, love," he says. "These pale faces are seductive and crafty. They would have to be, to have the ability to corrupt our people so easily."

"They are not corrupting our people," insists Ife. "If our people go to them, then it is our people who are already corrupted."

"I make no excuses for the weakness of some," says Onorede. "But they do not represent the many who are being taken. They have no voice or say in their situation.

"Is there anything that I can do to change your mind?" she asks.

He pulls her closer. "I'm sorry," he says gently in her ear.

She turns over to face him, cradling his head in her hands and arms. "I need to feel you inside of me. Now."

9

Nkyiafi, Midday
(Friday, 3:02pm)
Prah River

"I do not know how you managed to talk me into this, Onorede," says Fakih, craning his neck back and forth as they move down the path through the forest that runs parallel to the river. "This entire thing is spooky to me."

"I just don't want to get into trouble," says Oluchi. "I am already in bad favor with the Elders."

"If I had known I was inviting children on this mission, I would have come alone," says Onorede.

"Well, you are a noble, mighty warrior. I am a mere translator," says Fakih. "Oluchi is supposed to be the brave one!"

"I am a brave one," says Oluchi. "I just don't want to jeopardize my spot on the council."

"You have many suns and moons to go before you have to worry about that," says Onorede. "They say you always have to be on the edge of your life before you are given a chance to lead. Ridiculous! Age and wisdom are not necessarily married."

"Onorede!" Oluchi whispers. They freeze.

"Someone's here?" whispers Onorede.

"All around us," Oluchi says. "We walked right into it."

They watch as several warriors pop out from all around, surrounding them, pointing their wooden spears at the five.

"The Gola," says Onorede. "Do not panic. This was part of the plan."

"They'll kill us for sure," says Oluchi.

"They would have killed us already," says Onorede, as he drops his weapon and holds up his hands. Fakih, Oluchi, and the three other Krou warriors do the same.

"I hope that wisdom of yours works out," says Fakih.

In a wood-thatched hut in the middle of the Gola village, four other prisoners wait along with Onorede, Oluchi, Fakih, and the other three. They are given plenty of food and water.

"Say what you will about the Gola," says Fakih, "But they make great food."

"How can you eat or try to be funny at a time like this?" whines Oluchi.

"This is Fakih's way," says Onorede. "Humor through adversity. I find it comforting."

Gola guards enter the hut and say something to the group of ten.

"He wants us to come with him," says Fakih.

They stand up and file out of the hut. They are forced to line up, while other guards flank around them. That is when Onorede sees a pale-faced man for the first time in his life. His skin is light pink, with red blotches. His gold and brown hair is stringy and tussled.

"Is that a hat?" Fakih asks. "Why does the pale man wear dead grass on his head?"

"I would like to know the tribe that walks with him," says Onorede, referring to the five dark-skinned men that appeared to be with the pale man.

"They even dress like the pale man," says Fakih

A Gola ambassador speaks to the pale man. One of his dark-skinned escorts translates for the pale man as he steps to the line of prisoners. He stalks up and down the line, scrutinizing each of them.

"This is it, isn't it?" asks Oluchi?

"Be calm," says Onorede. "This is what we are here for. Remember our mission."

The Gola ambassador speaks to the pale man.

"He is talking about us," says Fakih. "He says that we are very stro-"

Fakih is unable to complete his thought before a Gola guard steps to him, barking at him. Fakih knows that the guard has told him to be quiet.

The pale man says something to his translator, who relays it to the Gola ambassador. After a few words to the guards, they immediately move in on the prisoners, forcing the ten prisoners to move in line towards the mouth of the village.

When they stop, Onorede sees the wide open expanse beyond the village. At that moment, his hands are bound with rope, along with the other prisoners. Around their necks, choker harnesses made of two thick branches tied together with twine, giving a snug fit around the neck. Large wooden planks with forked ends rest on their shoulders, closed with a small steel spear through the teeth of the fork. Every two prisoners share a plank. They are heavy enough so that the prisoners could do nothing more than walk.

"What is this?" shouts Oluchi.

"Shut up, Oluchi!" says Onorede.

"I can't breathe!" he says.

"Then stop talking!" says Onorede, who is having a little trouble breathing himself. *So this is it,* he thought.

As the train of prisoners is led off, Onorede can only think of his wife and son. What if this happens to them? He knows that he cannot allow it. That's what this mission is all about. He would rather die than let his family end up like this. He will fight to make sure that it does not happen, if he doesn't die first.

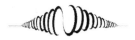

Kwakwasi, Early Morning
(Saturday, 6:42am)

Three large pale-faced men with three big row boats wait at the shore for the procession of prisoners. In the distance, on the ocean, a large cargo clipper ship.

One of the prisoners stops and moves back, either unaware of or ignoring the fact that he is sharing a harness with another prisoner. When he falls, his partner falls with him. The three pale men run towards the group.

"This is not good," said Oluchi.

The pale man next to him yells something at Oluchi. Fakih, having been listening very closely to the language, discerns that the man is saying something that sounds like "sha-dup" or "shah-TUP." He assumes that this means "stop talking."

Onorede does not fight back when one of the pale men grabs his arm and pulls him towards one of the row boats. The water is cold as they stomp through it. One of the men holds the boat steady as the other guides Onorede inside. As Onorede steps in, he is forced down to sit on the floor of the boat. Two of the other prisoners are put into his boat before it is pushed off. Two of the pale men ride with them.

He watches as Fakih and Oluchi are forced into another boat. He is surprised by how calm Fakih has been, but also by how frightened Oluchi is. Oluchi is one of his finest warriors and always seemed to be brave in the face of the greatest danger. It's a lot easier to be brave when you have an army on your side.

When Onorede is on board of the ship, his rope bindings are removed and replaced with steel cuffs for his wrists and his ankles. He sees a large hole being opened by more pale men on the deck. For the first time in this mission, Onorede is scared.

A wave of putrid and grotesque smells rushes out from the darkness below, pushed out by a burst of hot, humid air. The smell is so severe it makes Onorede cough and gag. When one of the pale men tries to move him down the stairs, his legs stiffen. He now regrets this entire mission. He wants nothing more than to be back in his bed with his wife. He wants to run and play with his sons. He wants to get yelled at by his father, for being so stupid as to think that this was a good idea. Another pale man grabs his arm and forces him down the stairs.

It is dark, save for a few slivers of light that make it inside. Onorede is glad that he cannot see what he is hearing; the cries and moans of grown men. He cannot be sure, but it sounds like there are hundreds down there. The floor is moist, a little slimy and sticky under his feet. The air is not only sour and rancid but thick and oppressive. As Onorede's breathing gets heavier, the smell grows more intense. So much so that he vomits. The men hold him forward, to avoid getting splattered. They push Onorede down an aisle with two-tiered shelves on either side, each shelf with about three feet of space separating them from top to bottom. Shelves made for holding men; as many as the pale-faced ghosts could cram in.

They force Onorede onto the top shelf. His shackles are chained to the edge of the shelf, inhibiting much of his movement. He is practically frozen. Next to him, three of the other prisoners he was with at the Gola camp. He does not see Fakih or Oluchi. After the commotion of stacking the remaining prisoners, the pale ghosts disappear. It is dark. It is loud with misery and despair. The man next to Onorede speaks to him in Mande, continuously asking if they are going to be eaten. He keeps saying that he does not want to be eaten. He listens to the man repeat this, over and over again.

"*Be quiet!*" Onorede demands in Mande, but the man keeps repeating. It only gets worse when the ship begins to move.

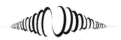

Onorede has held his bladder and bowels for over 4 hours, and can no longer do so. His muscles cannot fight the urgency that his body's functions are begging and pleading to release. The shelf surface below him is made up of planks with gaps in between. He tries to position himself over the gaps to aim as much as he can through them. He does not know where his waste would go underneath, but at that point, he does not care. Finally, his body gives in. He loosens his muscles and releases everything, including tears. He is mortified and humiliated, reduced to nothing more than an infant.

The sounds of agony around him are constant. He knows that the other poor souls are not warriors like he and his comrades. He can imagine that they are much worse off than he is, who had put himself into this situation of his free will. This situation is much more ghoulish than he ever imagined.

The pale-faced ghosts come through every several hours. One group brings buckets of ocean water, dousing the Africans, then using mops to wipe over and around them. This is meant to clean them of their waste but ends up pushing it around more than it cleans anything. Another group comes through with buckets of what looks like mush and slop. Onorede sees the others holding out their hands in cup shapes to take the slop, which they eat. When the men bring it to him, he does not offer his hands. Instead, one of them men grabs a handful and tries to force it into Onorede's mouth. This does nothing but make him choke and gag. He has to pretend to eat it so that they leave him alone.

Never in his life has he seen such treatment of men. Even the most savage of tribes have some humanity. This is beyond anything Onorede has ever experienced, or had ever thought was possible. The regret of his decision grows deeper. He closes his eyes and tries to put himself back in his bed with his wife. He tries to drown out the noises of his fellow captors. He tries to forget the dipping and rocking movement of the vessel. He tries to replace the smells with memories of the oils and flowers Ifé loved so much. No matter how hard he tries, he is still on this shelf, on this ship, in the bowels of demons and beasts.

Monokwasi, Night
(Sunday, 2:18 am)
Atlantic Ocean

Onorede feels he is ready to escape. Every moment with the pale ghosts brings him closer to figuring out how to get free and make his move. He watches them as they release the chains connecting him to the shelf. He looks around the ship as they are forced to march around the deck to exercise their muscles. He knows their schedules and movements almost as well as they do. It is only a matter of time before the opportunity presents itself. That moment comes with the death of the prisoner to his left on the shelf.

Some of these pale ghosts do not appear to be very bright. Onorede is lucky that the ghost with the keys is one of the dumbest ones. The dumb ghost unlocks the chains, first of the Mande man on his right that Onorede comes to know as Kante. Next, the ghost unlocks Onorede and then discovers the dead man.

Onorede is patient. He waits for the dumb ghost to call his companion over. He waits for his companion to unlock the chains of the dead man. He waits for the dumb man with the keys to take one more step back towards him as they lower the dead body to the ground. Onorede falls on top of him, maneuvering his body to wrap his bound hands around his neck. Kante leaps over and falls on top of the other man.

Pulling harder than the harness of a wild mare, Onorede yanks the ghost's head back, squeezing his neck like citrus fruit. Then comes the snap. The man stops moving, his body collapses. He looks up to see that Kante has killed the other.

"*Quickly*," whispers Onorede in Mande.

Onorede searches the body of the dead ghost and finds the large ring of keys. After a few attempts, he finds the proper key to unlock Kante's shackles. Kante then unlocks Onorede's.

"*I must find my friends*," says Onorede.

Kante follows as they step over the three bodies. They go down the line, through the aisles, searching each man.

"Fakih!" Onorede whispers, "Oluchi!"

He feels a hand grab his wrist.

"Fakih?" He unlocks the chains and helps him up. Fakih is in a daze, almost as if he is sleepwalking.

"Fakih, it's me," says Onorede. "I need you to be awake for me now." He slaps his face. "Fakih!"

Fakih blinks and shakes his head. Through the slivers of moonlight and spots of lantern light cutting through the darkness, Onorede can see the despair and anger in Fakih's eyes.

"We must find Oluchi," says Onorede, "I have not seen him, have you?"

"He was sick," says Fakih. "They threw him over the edge and into the water."

Onorede grits his teeth hard.

"What kind of creatures are these?" asks Fakih.

"The kind we are going to send back to the underworld, my friend," says Onorede. "You and I have work. Let us get to it."

Things are quiet on the deck of the ship as Onorede and Fakih make their way up the stairs. The moon shines bright and full in the sky, giving muted white highlights where the dim orange glow of the lanterns did not reach. Both make it up the stairs at the same moment that one of the ship's crewmen spots them. Just as he lets out a scream of alarm, Fakih jumps him and takes him to the ground.

The sounds of footsteps come from everywhere on the deck, as the pale ghosts emerge and the freed Africans charge up the stairs. The sailors watch in horror as the furious wave of Black rage charges at them. Some sailors manage to grab rifles and are even able to squeeze off a few shots before they are overtaken. The Africans scream and wail and punch and kick and grab and strangle. The crew is outnumbered, and even with their weapons are no match for the force against them. Then suddenly, out of nowhere, the sky sparks, and flashes with a great white light.

Everyone on the deck freezes. It's as if a star popped up out of nothingness, right along side of the ship. There is a snapping sound, like a match being struck in one's ear, then a pin of sharp, bright light that swirls and grows into an oval-shaped disc as large as the ship itself. No one can tell if it is moving towards them, or they are moving towards it.

Onorede does not know whether or not this is some trick or illusion created by the ghosts. He looks at the crewmen and the Africans both and sees the same exact expression. He wants to guide everyone back down into the bowels of the ship, but before he can say anything, the light makes a deep, steady, rhythmic pulsing sound. It then expands out towards them. There is nothing but blinding white.

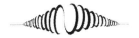

August 8th, 2041
11:02 am
Lower Bay, New York

The sun is shining. It is a warm, clear, beautiful day.

Onorede, Fakih, the Africans and the crewmen are still frozen on the deck of the ship. The light is gone. In the distance, land.

Fakih is bewildered. "Onorede?" he asks, "what just happened?"

Onorede steps slowly towards the deck rail, squinting his eyes, seeing the land and the strange looking structures on it. He turns around and is startled to see that there are two other similar-looking ships right next to theirs.

"Is this…is this…are we in the afterlife?" asks Fakih.

"I…I do not know," says Onorede. This is the second time that he is overwhelmed with fear.

"Where did those other vessels come from?" asks Fakih. "They were not here before."

"Do we know where 'here' is?" asks Onorede.

Some of the Africans panic. Fakih calls out in whatever language he can hear and understand for people to be calm, but it is no use. Onorede and Fakih can only watch as chaos breaks out around them. They make their way through the madness to the other side of the deck to see the other two ships.

"We all could not have come to the afterlife like this," says Onorede.

"How do we know?" asks Fakih. "Have you ever been dead before?"

Onorede's attention is drawn to one of the other ships. "This is my first time," he says. "Look at that," he says, pointing at the other ship, "More ghosts."

"What is he pointing at us?" asks Fakih.

A crewman on the other ship is pointing a rifle right at them. A puff of smoke, a bang, and the wood on the railing in front of them splinters.

"Get down!" yells Onorede, grabbing Fakih and pulling him down.

"It's one of their weapons, stay down!"

"What about the others?" asks Fakih.

Just as Onorede is about to answer, there is a strange sound coming from the distance; a low-pitched, rumbling sound. And it's getting closer.

"What now?" asks Fakih.

Kante runs to Onorede, dropping to the ground next to him. "*They are coming! They are coming!*" he says in Mande.

"Who is coming?" asks Fakih.

Onorede, keeping low, moves towards the back of the ship, and spots a smaller vessel approaching. Fakih comes up behind him.

"What is that?" he asks.

"Why do you keep asking me these things—I do not know!"

CHARLES A. CONYERS, JR.

11

August 11th, 2041
6:49 pm
Manhattan, New York

Kiki steps down the corridor as fast as she can, considering that she is holding a 15 lb. piece of equipment. She is 4 minutes late to the recap meeting of the days' events. She hates being late. She is especially looking forward to hearing what Dr. Oroko has to say about the situation. She has heard that he made a great deal of progress in speaking with the refugees.

The device she is carrying, which looks more like an oversized salt and pepper shaker, is of her own design and creation; she calls it an "electromagnetic analytical conduit," or EAC for short. It's similar to an air purifier, in that the hardware inside extracts particles from the air. Instead of dirt and dust, it pulls in and examines protons, electrons, and neutrons for analysis. Perfect for taking samples from the ships, to see if they match samples taken from the locations of the series of electromagnetic storms that occurred a week earlier. She had planned to install two of these devices on each ship when she realized that she was going to be late. The one she is carrying was to be the last to be installed. For now, the Henrietta Marie would have to settle with one.

As Kiki enters the conference room, Dr. Oroko is standing and addressing the room. He looks at her and smiles. She smiles back and mouths "Sorry," and finds a seat.

The room is not as packed as she thought it would be. She sees Police Commissioner Wilson, both Mayor Jú and Governor Steele, professors Joseph Healey, Brad Spencer, and Secretary of State Fender.

For the next 7 minutes, Kiki is caught up-to-date on what Maximilian has found out through speaking with the Africans. Through a connection made from his NAVI to the large monitor hanging on the wall, Maximilian goes through several maps of Africa, highlighting the locations of the tribes and languages he encountered throughout his conversations.

Kiki is simply fascinated, not only by Dr. Oroko's depth of knowledge but by the specifics of the findings. The most interesting fact is that these men and women have such rich and detailed stories of the how and why they ended up on those ships. There's also the fact that the details in those stories are more consistent with the past than the present. All of these variables put together could, in Kiki's mind, really only equal one thing.

"So, Dr. Oroko," begins Secretary of State Fender, interrupting his presentation, "You are telling me that your 'professional opinion' is that these people have traveled through time."

"You asked me to find out where these people came from," says Maximilian. "That is what I have tried to do here. None of these people sound as if they are from this era. Each one of these people that I spoke to was living a life consistent to tribes from over 300-400 years ago. This man, for example," he says, tapping his NAVI and bringing up a video clip of himself speaking to Onorede.

"This man," Maximilian continues, "and the man standing next to him, are members of the Krou people. The Krou haven't existed for over 180 years. They were completely wiped out, yet there were these two men."

"If they were wiped out," says Secretary Fender, "How were you able to speak to them? How could you know the language of people that do not exist?"

"It was my dissertation in graduate school. I met a 94-year-old African man from a neighboring tribe, who learned the language from an ancestor of a surviving member of the Krou when he was a child. That was over

20 years ago. As of now, I am likely the only person on Earth that speaks Krou. Until now."

With a few more NAVI taps, he shows more videos of himself interacting with the refugees as they crowd around him. "It's not just the Krou— each of these people has a rich history. Each of them describes their journey through the Middle Passage. And each one of them describes a 'storm of light.'"

A pit socks Kiki right in the stomach, and ripples out in tingly waves throughout her body.

Fender turns up her nose. "What do you mean by 'a storm of light'?"

"They said it was like an oval of light," Maximilian says, holding his hands together to form a shape. "Like an egg or a lemon shape. They said it grew like a swirl—- a few of them made a swirling motion with their fingers. They describe a snapping sound right before it appeared, and a sound like a heartbeat as it grew. It grew quickly, overtaking them, and in an instant, they appeared here. From what they described, it all happened within a matter of seconds."

"So they *are* connected," says Kiki.

"Connected to what?" asks Fender.

"These storms that I've been tracking—these so-called electrical storms that have been occurring since last week! There have been four, including the one that accompanied these ships. And these storms have left the same electromagnetic signature each time!"

"We all know how smart you are, Kiki—dumb it down for the rest of us, please?" asks Fender.

Kiki smirks. "I think these storms have something to do with these ships arriving here. In fact, I don't think they're storms at all. I think they're worm holes."

"Worm holes, now," sighs Secretary Fender. "All right then, it sounds like the two of you are suggesting that I go the President of the United States and tell him that these ships and the people on them traveled through time."

"These people are not from this time," says Maximilian. "I am convinced of that. I do not know how they got here, or why they are here. Miss Bishop's explanation is the closest thing that I have heard to a reasonable explanation. I do not know what she knows about the science, but I do know that there is no other sensible or logical reason why these people are here."

Fender looks to Brad and Joseph. "And you believe this as well?"

"I'm not saying that," says Brad. "To me, time travel exists in stories and nowhere else. That's just what I believe."

"And what do the crews of the ships have to say," asks Maximilian. "They believe they are over 300 years in the past, do they not?"

"That's what they say," says Brad. "But who the hell knows—they could lying, or brainwashed or—"

"Oh, give me a break," Kiki groans, rolling her eyes. "You're telling me that someone brainwashed over 1000 people for a 'stunt'? Can you explain how they got past NORAD's defense system? Were they brainwashed, too? How did those ships get here without anyone spotting them?"

"I don't know—you're the scientist!" says Brad.

"That's right, I am the 'scientist,'" says Kiki using air quotes, "And as a 'scientist' when I see two phenomena that are connected to each other, I draw whatever conclusions are possible from the data that's available. If anyone in this room has any other theories that can be supported by the Scientific Method, I would love to hear them."

"Yes, Miss Bishop- we all want to adhere to the Scientific Method," says Secretary Fender. "I think you have some compelling evidence. Dr. Oroko's analysis is also interesting. But I'm telling you right now, I am not going to say 'time travel' to the President of the United States. I just don't see it, and at this point it sounds too crazy to risk presenting that."

Kiki throws her hands up in the air out of frustration. "Madam Secretary, the reason why we're all here is crazy. It's insanity!"

Fender shakes her head. "I'm sorry. I need more. We've had a very successful day, we've discovered a great deal. We need to know more."

"So, let's pick this up tomorrow morning," says Governor Steele, "We've all had a long day, and I agree-we accomplished a lot today, thanks to Dr. Oroko and the rest of you. We should reconvene tomorrow when we're all a bit more clear-headed."

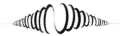

9:04pm
Furious Studios, New York City

"...I have to tell you, ladies and gentlemen, that when I woke up this morning, I felt...great! I did, I mean it—I felt this overwhelming sense of calm. Peace! And do you know why? Because I believe in God! I believe in God—I believe in God! You know, there used to be a time when I was embarrassed to say that. You know, all of us are. The snobs, the intellectuals—they make you afraid to believe. They'd tell you that it wasn't okay. Or it was okay, but just don't talk about it. Keep it to yourself. Never, ever talk about religion out in public. Well, I'm not afraid anymore, because I know that God is real. I know it, and you know it too. So let's not pretend anymore. Let's not act like it's this private, personal thing that we can't and should not express out in the open. That's who we are! We are a God-loving nation. Why fear that? Why not embrace that?"

Gerry Baines is on fire tonight. His ratings have gone through the roof over the last two nights, which is spectacular considering that The Gerry Baines Exchange was known to have a very specific core audience and hadn't previously had much universal appeal. But ever since the Event, and his overly-interpreted so-called prediction of the event, more and more people are tuning in to see what this guy is all about.

As usual, at the beginning of his show, he stands in front of the large monitor, which displays shots of the Africans inside the convention center.

"My grandmother was, well…she was not an educated woman. Educated in the sense that she didn't have a fancy degree from some elitist university. She was a hard-working woman, who had to drop out of school to support her family. You know what she used to say to me? She used to say 'Gerry, you ain't <u>nothin'</u> without God. None of us ain't <u>nothin'</u>…without the Lord by your side. And you can pretend She's not there, you can pretend She don't exist, if you dare. At the end of things, we'll all have to face Her.'"

Gerry has to stop for a moment to catch himself; his emotions get him so carried away, and he hates it…but it makes for great television. "'…Either way,' she said, 'you need to believe.' That's what she said to me. And you know what? She was so right…she was more right than I ever knew. You only need to look around today to see that. Look at everything that has happened in the last three days. We are all in pain. You can feel it, I can feel it. And right now…you know what's happening right now? There are scientists, and specialists, and professors, and intellectuals, and people like this that are out there trying to figure out what is going on. You know what? They don't know. They <u>don't</u> know! You know why they don't know? Because there are things in the world that science just cannot solve. Now wait, I know a lot of you are going to say 'well, Gerry, I mean—what about cars, and medicine? What about computers?' Well, sure. Of course, we need science, and we need medicine, and we need math to figure out how all of those things work. That's a given. But can a scientist explain a miracle? Can a scientist explain prayer?" He steps to the camera, for effect, looks into it, and shakes his head 'no,' with a shit-eating grin.

"Where is science to explain this," he says, pointing to the monitor showing the African refugees. "Sure, you can explain how this screen, this monitor was made— what electrodes and other nonsense are inside to make it work. But you can't explain what's showing right now, can you? You can't explain how over 1000 people showed up on our shores the way they did. You know why you can't explain it? Because science didn't bring them here. God did! And just like God brought them here, God will take them away. And you won't be able to explain that either. Oh, you'll try, you'll always try! But with you it's all talk, isn't it? It's all talk because you don't want anyone to know that <u>you</u> <u>don't</u> <u>know</u>!" Gerry chuckles.

"It's amazing how the intellectuals, the elitists can never admit when they don't know! The 'intelligencia,' the 'know-it-alls'! When it comes to God, you don't know anything! Just accept it! But you know what? Don't believe me. You don't have to believe me—I'm just some schmuck on TV. All you have to do is wait. Wait and see. You'll be proven wrong."

9:12pm
Slmbr[7] Inn Hotel, New York City

Maximilian shuts off the television.
"My God, what a lunatic," he says.
"What?" a voice comes from the bathroom.

---

[7] Pronounced "slumber."

"This Gerry Baines, he is a lunatic," repeats Maximilian, loud enough to be heard through the bathroom door.

He's is glad to be back in his hotel room. This seemed like the longest day he has had in ages.

The toilet flushes. Joseph emerges from the bathroom and collapses face-first onto the bed.

"How are you feeling?" asks Maximilian, smiling.

"Good!" says Joseph, with his face buried in the bed. He picks up his head, and says, "Maybe I had a bit too much rum…"

"Do you think?" asks Maximilian sarcastically.

Joseph turns over on his back. "Oh man! Man, I'm glad Kiki's not here to see this."

Maximilian smiles. "Well, I doubt that you would be drinking this much with her around."

"Yeah. And I wouldn't want to have to compete with Brad either."

"No competition there, my friend," says Maximilian. "She is far from interested in him. I thought you said that she had a live-in boyfriend."

"Yeah. But still…"

"But still," Maximilian says, holding up his glass then taking a sip of rum.

"I'm so glad you're here, Max," says Joseph. "You were amazing out there today with those people."

"It is quite remarkable," says Maximilian. "I have no idea what is going on, but those people do not belong here. I do not think I can explain it any further than that."

"Time travel," says Joseph.

"You do not believe that."

"No, I don't. But you do. You and Kiki both do."

"Do I?" asks Maximilian. "I do not know. I do not know if I do. I only know that what those people described to me is not the world that we live in today. I keep thinking of Onorede. Everything he described was consistent with life in the early to mid-1700s. The detail with which they described their lives, their abduction, the Middle Passage itself. To say that these people were brainwashed is insane. These people would have had to either be raised from birth to believe these stories in their own context, or these things happened to them."

"So it's time travel, China, or God," says Joseph.

"It's hard to believe that in the year 2041 these are our only options. There are Lucy Fender and her people selling China, and Gerry Baines selling God. The sad thing is that most people are uneducated enough to believe in either one of those things. Or both."

"China and God working together?" Joseph laughs. "People are crazy. The seeing misleading the blind, the blind leading the blind…where does that leave us?"

"Fucked," says Maximilian, downing the rest of the rum in his glass.

9:42pm

Security Office, Jacob Javits Center, New York City

Jacob Morgan is very confused. He knows he is in trouble. That's the risk he took for slaving beyond Emancipation in the first place. This is not the kind of trouble he was expecting. He knows he is a long way from home. But how far off is very troubling.

He is told that he is in New York City, in the year 2041. That alone makes absolutely no sense. That would mean that he has traveled over 300 years through time. And as far as he knows, there is no such thing as time travel.

Everything around him is unfamiliar. He is in a room equipped with a black box on the wall that these strange people call a "television," with actors in plays that are called "shows" and "movies" and "news." He sees amazing things that are at first frightening, but it is explained that everything is an illusion; fake. The clothes and the shoes, or what they called "sneakers" that he and the crew are given are unlike anything he has ever seen before. Even the food is odd, held in strange boxes and paper wrapping. And the way these people speak… it's English, and he can understand what they are saying for the most part. There are certain words, certain phrases that these people use that are alien to him and the others. No part of this seems real.

It has been three days. Every time he wakes up, he is expecting to be back in his bed in Yorktown, or back on the ship at sea. Instead, he finds himself back in this strange room in this strange place; back in New York City, the year 2041.

People have asked him many questions over the last few days, including a university professor named Brad Spencer. Spencer seemed to know an awful lot about what Jacob was doing, where he was coming from, and where he was going. It is from this professor that Jacob is told that the institution of slavery had been abolished for nearly 200 years and that the Negro race, who were now referred to as African Americans, had integrated into the society. They were doctors, lawyers, actors, professional athletes, business owners, mayors, and even two Presidents of the United States.

Jacob almost falls out of his chair in astonishment and disbelief in the face of these facts. "Niggers have been Presidents of <u>these</u> United States?! Niggers can't lead, they can't even think for themselves! How far has this nation fallen when niggers can be President?" he asks in earnest. Brad, going along with what he feels is a brainwashed crazy person, tries to explain that everything Jacob believed about Black people was a lie- propaganda sold to people of "his time" to support a system of free labor. Even as Brad showed him video footage, Jacob was convinced that this was also an illusion, just like the television shows and movies that he was shown. It was then that Jacob began to think that maybe that bright light that he saw that night on the ship was God, and that he was now in heaven, or the afterlife. Or was it hell?

On the morning of this, his third day, he was visited by a man that introduced himself as his lawyer. He called himself David Schaumburg, which sounded a lot like a Jewish name to him, but he did not want to offend anyone in this place for fear that he would get into more trouble—especially if he were to make his way into heaven.

This lawyer, this David Schaumburg, explained to Jacob that he could be charged with the illegal trafficking of African refugees for use as slave labor, a charge that could get him up to 40 years in prison. However, due to the unusual circumstances, no charges have yet been filed until it can be determined exactly what has happened. Since Jacob, the crew of his ship, and the crews from the other ships were seemingly baffled and confused by where and how they arrived in New York City, there has been a request made to administer lie detector tests on everyone to determine truth from lies. A judge could rule as early as tomorrow, August 12th, whether or not this would be permitted, and if it is they would be given the test immediately. Jacob is horrified by the notion of a machine that could determine truth from lies.

There is also the matter of the detective that grabbed him by the throat upon their arrival to this strange, backward world. The lawyer informed him that if wanted to file charges against the man, that he was well within his rights to do so. However, the lawyer advised against it. He felt that it would deliver a bad message ahead of an already sticky situation. Schaumburg reminded Jacob that slavery of any kind is frowned upon, particularly the enslavement of African Americans, which carries a tremendous weight of animus and shame among Blacks and Whites alike. *Dirty, tricky Jew*, he thought, *I always knew they weren't to be trusted!*

On the night of his third day, Jacob Morgan finds it difficult to sleep at first. The thoughts eat at him like a starving swarm of locusts in a lush field of crops. The only thing that can comfort him is his prayers to God that something, anything, can save him from this place, this world, these people. As his eyelids get heavy, and his head grows lighter, he begrudgingly comes to terms with the fact that no matter what happens tomorrow, it is God's will. It doesn't matter if he doesn't know why these things are happening to him or the others. As his mother had always told him: when you don't know, God knows.

12

August 12th, 2041
6:17 am
Manhattan, New York

The light from the auto-illuminated daylight simulator alarm clock on the nightstand has been increasing over the last 15 minutes, to wake Gerry Baines slowly from his sleep. The only way he feels he can get the perfect night's sleep is in a dark, windowless room at night, and a slowly-lit room in the morning. He always wakes refreshed and ready to fight the good fight for another day.

From the bed, he heads to the bathroom to begin his morning ritual; "piss, shit, shower and shave," as he likes to call it. As he works his way down the list, he can smell the coffee from his autotimer coffeemaker in the kitchen. By the time he leaves the bathroom and enters his wardrobe closet to change, he can smell the bacon, poached eggs, and toast cooking in his 'Brekkyman' automatic breakfast maker.

Gerry enters the kitchen to find the plate in his breakfast device has ejected with his meal, piping hot and ready to eat. Little things and modern conveniences, that's what he likes. He takes a bite of his food and activates his NAVI. The beeping tells him that he has voice mail messages. Fifty-three of them. *That seems high*, he thinks. Just as he is about to check the messages, the NAVI rings. The name "Tom" appears on the screen, meaning his producer Tom Busing.

"Good morning, Tom," says Gerry. "This is earlier than usual—"

"Jesus Christ, Gerry—where the hell have you been?" Tom yells into the phone. "I've been trying to reach you since four this morning!"

"It's called sleeping, Tom, you should try it sometime," says Gerry, sipping his coffee.

"They're gone, Gerry!"

"Who's gone?"

"Who the hell do you think? The Africans! They're gone! Vanished without a trace! There were guards—they blanked out, and no one remembers a thing! Jesus Christ, Gerry are you seeing this?"

"TV on," Gerry says out loud. The monitor on his wall switches on, and every channel he swipes to has variants on the same headline: The Africans have vanished!

"Do you hear me, Gerry?!"

Gerry's mouth is agape as he continues to swipe through the channels.

"The network wants you here as soon as possible! They're already talking about it everywhere—they're saying you predicted it!"

Just as Tom says that, Gerry sees video of himself on PNN, their ratings rival, with the words "Lucky guess?" in the banner below his image.

"I'll be right there," says Gerry. "No, wait! Send a crew over here first. I know how I want to begin tonight's show."

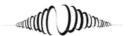

10:23 am
West Chester, PA

The first thing that Maximilian does when he enters his apartment, after dropping his bags at the front door, is slump down into his favorite chair. He is beat, defeated, and emotionally drained.

He was jerked out of his sleep at 4:41 am to the dual sounds of his NAVI ringing and banging on the door of his hotel room. It was Joseph in both cases, to tell him that 23 minutes earlier, the Africans had vanished. As groggy and half-drunk as he was, and as confusing as it had sounded, Maximilian just assumed that maybe the Africans had been moved and the powers that be just failed to inform them. But when Maximilian and Joseph arrived at the convention center, it was clear that they had not been moved. They did, in fact, vanish.

All of the cots, clothing, blankets, uneaten food, everything had been left where it was. The guards each told the same story. Everything was there one moment, and in the blink of an eye, they found themselves on the ground, completely disoriented. And when they got up, they found the Africans gone. The sailors and crews were also gone. The three ships, gone.

Maximilian's breathing was heavy, his stomach was pitted. Still locked in the rum-induced stupor from a few hours before, this all seemed like some kind of weird dream. The arrival of the Africans was mysterious enough, but their disappearance in the presence of dozens of people...this was, as Joseph put it, "some fucked up shit here."

The first of the security footage they watched was from the dock. When the timecode reached 4:18:29.03, there was a blip of whiteness, a white flash. At 4:18:29.05, the ships were gone. Not a ripple in the water, nothing to indicate where they had gone. The only things left were the guards, many of whom were so startled that they either fell to the ground or jumped as if they had seen a ghost.

Security footage from inside the convention center revealed the same thing. The Africans were seen as plain as day. Then, at 4:18:29.03, there was a flash, and at 4:18:29.05, they were gone. All of them were gone as if they just evaporated into the air. "It's like they were raptured," Maximilian overheard an officer saying to another.

Secretary Fender was nowhere to be found. Some said she was heading back to DC. Mayor Jú and Governor Steele were gone as well. It seemed as if no one wanted to be around to have to answer for this disappearance.

"I wonder who disappeared faster," Maximilian sneered, "Fender or the Africans."

In the rush and heat of the moment, Maximilian caught a glimpse of Kiki holding one of her machines and yelling at one of the guards at the dock. No one had any answers, especially the people brought in to find them.

The most uncomfortable and disconcerting thing of all was when Maximilian and Joseph were approached by two men in dark suits wearing mirrored, chrome-like visors. Each of the men pulls them aside individually. Maximilian could feel his teeth involuntarily grinding; he knew what was coming.

"You are advised not to speak to anyone about what you've seen here today," the man said.

"Excuse me? What exactly have I seen here today?"

"Don't be a smart-ass, Doctor," the man said. "You saw the security footage."

"So what? In a few hours everyone in the world will see it."

"No, they won't," the man said. "One more time, Dr. Oroko…you are not to mention or discuss that footage to anyone."

"You have got to be kidding me," Maximilian groaned in disgust. "Why would people not be able to see it? What is going? Are you trying to cover this up? Are you going to blame China for this? Where is Fender? Why is she not here?"

"That's not your concern, Dr. Oroko," says the man. "You've been warned."

"Excuse me? Are you threatning me." asks Maximilian.

"It's not a threat. It's advice. For you own safety."

Just like that, Maximilian Oroko's involvement with the Event was at an end. The two men asked NYPD officers to escort Maximilian and Joseph back to where they belonged.

It was 13 minutes after 7 am when they finally left. There was a mob outside of the convention center. There were hundreds of people outside ready to tear the building down. He looked out from the tinted car windows at the screaming throngs of people, who gave up on any meaningful chants. Mass hysteria. Police in riot gear walked next to the cars, shields in hand, to make sure they got out safely. Bottles, full cans of soda, and lithium-ion batteries are thrown, most deflected by the police shields. Maximilian feared for his life, even after he got back to the hotel to grab his things, and even after he got back into the car that would drive him the 103 miles back home; he was horrified.

Now he sits in his chair, staring off into space, reflecting on it all. In the calm of his apartment and the comfort of the big burgundy armchair, he is bombarded with a flock of frustrating questions that were left behind in New York City.

The whirlwind of thoughts continue as his eyelids get heavier. He had only been asleep for a couple of hours, and even then it was a restless sleep. Now that he is finally at home, in his chair, alone with his thoughts, he is relaxed enough to let his body's natural desire for rest take over. He closes his eyes.

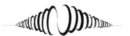

7:09 pm

Maximilian opens his eyes. He looks at the time on his NAVl; he's been asleep for nine hours. He lifts himself from his chair and prepares to spend the rest of the night trying to relax and forget the nonsense. He cannot stop thinking about how, once again, he was screwed by *that asshole* Fender. Even as he showers, where he is usually the most relaxed, he is tense. As he towels himself off, he thinks about how he expects to watch the news and see someone from the Lopez Administration beating the drum harder about a pre-emptive war with China.

He finds some four-day-old Indian food in the fridge; chicken korma and rice. Good enough. He pops that in the microwave, then pours a generous amount of rum with a dash of cola; the ultimate bachelor's dinner.

As the microwave beeps, his NAVI rings. He doesn't recognize the number, but from the first word he knows the voice.

"Hey Dr. Oroko, it's Kiki."

"Miss Bishop," says Maximilian, smiling, "How are you?"

"Oh, I've been better," she says with a sigh. "How are you doing?"

"The same," he says, taking his drink and sitting down in his chair.

"I guess you're home by now, huh?" she asks.

"Yes. I got home this morning."

"I'm sorry I didn't get to see you before you left. It's been such a shit-storm today.'"

"Yes, I saw you briefly, actually," says Maximilian. "You were yelling at someone."

"Ha! You'll have to be more specific, I've been yelling at people all day—the bastards! Did you get your threat," asks Kiki.

"I did," Maximilian smirks. "Apparently, we are risking our lives right now by talking about it."

"Fuck them," she growls. "So, what do you think happened?"

"I was going to ask you the same thing."

"I think you and I may very well be the only sane people involved in this thing. Can I send some stuff to you?"

Maximilian links his NAVI to the monitor hanging on his wall. He finds the icon with Kiki's picture and taps it.

"I'm ready," says Maximilian.

Maximilian's screen comes to life with a graphical representation of what looks like an elaborate planetary map with a beautiful geometric array of arcs and lines in different thicknesses and colors.

"Okay, you see that?" asks Kiki.

"It looks like a star map," says Maximilian.

"Kind of, yes. First of all I should explain that when I got to the dock this morning to recover my equipment, I discovered something very interesting. I had an array of instruments set up on the dock and on the ships. Some were connected wirelessly, but others were hard-wired because the electromagnetic fields tend to interfere with wireless communication. What I found this morning with the wired devices...the wires were melted. Not cut, not pulled, but melted."

"What does that mean?"

"It means that we have a wormhole. A super-powerful electrical energy force able to open, hold, and close the wormhole. Each action requires a burst or a surge of energy. And the heat from that energy is what melted the wires."

"So, how did this happen?" asks Maximilian.

"That's the mystery of our age. It's not just this one, by the way—it's more than one. That's how they were able to get the Africans out of the convention center; it was probably several smaller wormholes to get them out. But that wouldn't explain the security footage—oops, can't talk about that."

Maximilian laughs. "Okay, if they go into these wormholes, where do they go? How do they get from one time to another?"

"Well, that's the tricky part," says Kiki.

"I was afraid you'd say that..."

Kiki giggles. "Typically we perceive time as only linear, in 2 or 3 dimensions. See, the Earth is always in motion. It rotates on its own axis, and around the Sun, and the Universe itself is constantly expanding. So if we were to go back, say, five years, the Earth wouldn't be in the same place. You would end up floating in outer space, or maybe on some other planet or something. So, in order for time travel to work, you have to travel fourth-dimensionally."

"I have a feeling that this is the point in the conversation where you lose me," says Maximilian.

"I'll try to use small words, Maximilian," Kiki chuckles. "Look at the map I sent you."

He watches the map on his monitor begin to animate.

"That blue dot is the Earth, right? See, it's moving along with everything else—the moon, other planets, the sun, etc."

The animation stops. Two red markers appear on different parts of the screen; the first near the center left, the other in the middle towards the bottom of the screen.

"Now, let's say that the first marker represents today. And the second marker represents some random date in the past, let's say June 12th, 1994. Now, even though the Earth was originally in the location of the second marker, we could not travel back there from our current location without ending up in space; the Earth is here now, and no longer there, right?"

"Right," says Maximilian, taking another sip of rum.

"So, what we have to do is travel in the space between the two points. But we can't do that in 2 or 3 dimensions. The fourth dimension is the space you cannot see.

"For example," Kiki continues, "if you raise your hand, and move it back and forth in front of your face, you can see a blur or a streak as it moves from the left to the right, and back again. That blur is the fourth dimension—it's the space between space. So the wormhole acts as a bridge from one point to the other, allowing us to revisit the space once occupied by the Earth, and therefore travel through time."

"That sounds very complicated. I say as I take another sip of rum."

Kiki busts up laughing. "Max Oroko, you are a funny, funny man!"

"Does that surprise you, that I have a sense of humor?"

"I have to say, it does! It does surprise me! You are a very intimidating man, you know."

Maximilian laughs. "Impossible!"

"Oh, come on! My God, you're like the leading man in your field! You have this enormous reputation proceeding you, and...you know, you never know what to expect from someone so brilliant, you know?"

"I could say the same thing about you, Miss Bishop," says Maximilian.

"Well, when you deal with as much kooky shit as I do, you have to have a sense of humor. Keeps you sane. Hey, honey!"

Maximilian feels a swelling in his chest, followed by fluttering butterflies. "Excuse me?"

"Oh no, my boyfriend just walked in—sorry."

"Oh," says Max. "I thought for a moment that we had been elevated to a nickname basis."

Kiki laughs.

"I should let you go now," says Maximilian. "You should not keep your man waiting."

"He sees me enough, but yes, you're right. It was great talking to you."

"It was great for me too, Kiki—thank you for sharing your insight."

"It's my pleasure. Have a good night."

"You, too," Maximilian smiles.

He disconnects the call on his NAVI and leans back in his chair. He continues to sip from his glass of rum, looking at the animated star map on the monitor.

CHARLES A. CONYERS, JR.

13

8:13 pm
The White House, Washington DC

All television programming is interrupted. Local and national news anchors announce that President Lopez will be addressing the nations from the Oval Office.

As he sits at his desk and waits for the red light on top of the camera, President Lopez swallows deeply. He worked with his speechwriter and cabinet members for hours. Everyone had their own idea of what he should say. The problem is that everything they suggested was bullshit.

He looks up at Secretary of State Fender, who stands on the other side of the room, near the door. He knows what she wants to hear. Or, more to the point, he knows what "her people" want to hear. They want him out. And once again, the Vice President is nowhere to be found. At this point, he is isolated. He wants nothing more than for all of this to go away. But now, the red light comes on, and the teleprompter starts to roll.

"My fellow Americans," he starts. "We have had very mysterious, curious, and baffling few days. It all began three days ago, when we came in contact with three ships that somehow appeared on our shores, filled with the images and horrors of our past, represented by nearly 1000 African refugees. We rescued them. We fed them and gave them medical care. We housed them the best way we could. And early this morning, they disappeared without a trace.

"You're going to hear a lot of theories and a lot of proclamations. Everything ranging from a Chinese government conspiracy plot to an act of God. The truth of the matter is that at this time no one, I repeat, no one knows what has happened. No one knows why they appeared, and no one knows why they disappeared. We will eventually figure all of this out, but the most important thing for all of us is to stick together and unite to continue to move our great nation forward."

As he says these unscripted things, he sees Secretary Fender roll her eyes and swearing under her breath. He doesn't care.

"I know all of you are angry and confused. Now is not the time to divide this country. There is never a time to divide this country. We are a nation of stronger stuff than that. I cannot stress enough how important it is for all of you to stay strong and be resolved. Together, we will all continue to make this the greatest nation in the world. God bless you, and God bless the United States of America."

Secretary Fender storms out of the room, and marches down the hall. "Fuck!" she says under her breath, right before her a call alert appears on her NAVI. Without even looking at the number, she knows exactly who it is. She ducks into an empty office to take the call.

"Yes," she says.

"What the hell is going on, Lucy?" says the voice on the other end, with an eerie calm.

"This is what you get for putting an independent mind in the Oval Office. I told you people from the beginning—"

"You told us that you could handle it," said the voice. "You said that you could control him."

"This is different. Who the hell knew this African slave shit would happen? You want to push the needle while trying to make it work with this supernatural refugee crisis, and it just won't work!"

There is a long pause. She continues, "To tell you the truth, I don't think it will work with Matthew at all. You picked the wrong guy, so don't pin that on me."

There is another long pause before the voice speaks again. "Supernatural, eh?"

Fender sits down in a chair, rubbing her forehead. "It's obviously not the Chinese, and I'm an atheist." She sighs deeply. "There's a theory that these are time travel events. Temporal wormholes that brought these ships here and sent them back, perhaps. The evidence is more consistent with that than anything else."

"Do you believe in time travel, now?" the voice asks.

"I can't believe what I saw. I can't believe any of it. Honestly, I would like to forget it."

"We know this is unexpected," says the voice. "We did not plan for this. That does not alter our direction. You must find replacement."

Fender's eye widen before she bursts into laughter. "Just like that!"

"Yes, just like that," answers the voice.

"And who the hell do you think you're going to replace him with?" she asks…

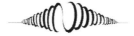

9:00 pm
Furious Studios, New York City

The Gerry Baines Exchange opens on Baines himself, standing at his kitchen counter.

"Hello, America. Welcome to my home. My kitchen, to be exact. You may be thinking to yourself, 'why is he opening his show from his kitchen? Am I watching the Food Channel?' Not exactly. I'm opening the show from here because, well…this is where it happened. It was here, in my kitchen, that I believe that I was touched… touched by the Divine.

"Now, when I spoke about this a few days back, when I spoke of God's message to us, about God sending us a sign, many people thought I was crazy. They said

'Oh, that nutty Gerry Baines—what a kook!' You know what? I started to believe them. I started to believe all of those people that thought I had, as they said, finally gone insane. I almost let the nay-sayers convince me of that—they're very powerful that way, very persuasive. But then it happened. God brought those poor, poor people here. People from our past, like phantom ships in the light of day."

Gerry pauses for a moment, allowing the emotions to overwhelm him.

"I'm sorry, I just...when I think of those images from that first day, it just breaks my heart. Those people were brought here—not by some crazy scientific theory, not by a geopolitical ploy to seek revenge against us...but by <u>God</u>. Do you know why God brought them here? She brought them here, to us, because She loves America. She loves this country, and She loves all of us. She sees that we are a people divided by anger and hatred for each other, for the worst possible reasons imaginable. She wants to show us that we, in all of our stupidity, really need one another.

"It's the whiny white folks that continue to wallow in the same ignorance that drove their ancestors to commit atrocity and terrorism in their own land. It's the complacent Blacks that wait around, unmotivated, to be rewarded for things their ancestors endured—horrors that they will never know in their lifetimes. We look at those ships and the people that have arrived here, and then we look at ourselves. How far we have come! None of us is where we were 200 years ago. Where are we now?

"While we fight with each other, Mexicans are moving in right under our noses, rebuilding our decimated neighborhoods and cities, building little Mexicos all over the country. You know who else? You know who else- the Chinese and the Arabs are also coming to this country, taking our jobs! Not the blue collar jobs that no one wants. The white collar jobs—running our companies and corporations! All this is happening while Blacks and whites fight over 400-year-old issues. Is that what you want? God doesn't want that! And She told me so…right in this kitchen.

"Everybody laughed at me when I told them God would test us. Everyone mocked me when I told them that God brought these Africans here, and that She would take them away, and that no one—not even all the scientists and college professors in the world—would be able to explain it. Look at what happened today. Where are your explanations? Where are your scientific methods, your rules that govern the Universe, all that malarkey—where is it all now? Oh yeah, God took it!

"We'll be right back after this."

A quick-cutting montage of footage of the Africans arrival, followed by the Africans in the convention center and ending with the shots of the empty convention center. In a large, thick font, the words "GOD'S WILL" move onto the center of the screen, before it fades to black.

9:32 am
West Village, New York City

Kiki has been staring at the computer screen for over forty minutes, waiting for something—anything—to magically appear. Numbers. Formulas and equations. Variables and strings. Metaphysics, quantum physics, quantum mechanics…it's enough to make someone's head explode.

Kiki rubs her eyes, incidentally catching a whiff of the latex smell left on her fingers. She looks over at her boyfriend Michael, passed out in the bed. It had been a while since they last had sex, and they made up for it, with a vengeance. It was a good thing for both of them, especially her; good sex always cleared her head.

Right now, all the good sex in the world couldn't clear up what's in front of her. She has so much intriguing data—all of the readings from her equipment returned some amazing results. She was able to take the data and form a computer visualization of what could not be seen. What she was able to see was a horizontal vortex. The mouth of this vortex opens up, creating a circular portal, that funnels back and stretches snake-like for several feet, like a tornado on its side. When it closes, it's mouth-first, leaving its snake tail trail until it shrinks and disappears.

The data is there. But without physical evidence, it's practically useless. And even if there was physical evidence, there's still the question of how is it possible to produce the kind of energy required to create these results? It's impossible in this era, that is. The technology required to make a wormhole is several centuries away if that. All the theories in the world won't convince anyone living today of the possibilities of future generations. These days people are willing to believe that their God or gods is or are responsible. Science has always had a hard time competing with deities.

Kiki is tired of staring at the monitor. She reaches for the joint in the ashtray on the desk that she and Michael started earlier. She lights up and takes a nice, long drag. She holds her hit as she hears echoes of her father's voice saying to her what he always used to say; "Honey, you think too much." She lets out a stream of smoke, followed by long, wet raspberry with her tongue. *I think too much—bullshit*, she thought. *No such thing! People don't think enough—that's the real problem!*

Unfortunately, her brain is insisting on rest. Which is fine- she's tired of trying to make other people understand something that she knows is real. She can't sleep, though. So that means television. She remembers that she recorded a streaming news special about the Henrietta Marie, one of the ships that had appeared with African passengers. A crew of divers and researchers got together with mini submarines equipped with video cameras, and set out to prove that the ship is still submerged underwater, and therefore proving that it is impossible for it to have been involved in the event.

Kiki fast forwards through all of the overly dramatic spectacle and build up, and gets right to the nitty-gritty. The footage delivers what the show promised. The mini-subs, equipped with lights and cameras, pan across the ship's submerged wreckage. The ship is crusted with coral and teeming with marine life. This is all pretty typical, as underwater exploration footage goes.

Then comes a moment that produces a deep, surging flourish of tension, anxiety, and shock. She taps her NAVI and rewinds the video to a specific spot in one of the panning shots of the deck of the ship.

She is convinced for a moment that she is just over-tired and stoned. She rewinds and plays the panning shot again, and this time she pauses the video. At first, she refuses to acknowledge what she sees and wants to just go to bed immediately. But she can't. There it is, as plain as day. Right there, on the deck of the ship, crusted and weathered with the rest of it, an object that looks like an oversized salt and pepper shaker. An instrument of her own design and creation; her electromagnetic reading conduit, or ERC for short.

9:57 pm
Central Park, New York City

For the group to survive, Thabiti has to do things that he would never do under normal circumstances. He steals clothing and blankets from street vendors. He steals fruit prominently on display in stands outside of grocery stores. He steals baskets of bread from people eating outdoors. At this point, it doesn't matter. Ever since they escaped from the large building with the others, they have been in hiding. They had no other way to get food, other than stealing it.

He brings everything he can get back to the others, back to the hiding place that he found underneath a bridge in what seemed to them like a small forest. He waits for any people in the area to pass before he approaches the bridge. He has to climb over the edge and jump down to get to the others. Three others; a young boy named Mbwana, and two women named Abi and Gabra. They are startled at first but relax when they see that it's only Thabiti. He steps to the group and hands them the food. They tear into it.

As Thabiti watches them eat, he thinks of home. His life was full and rich before any of this insanity. He was a metal smith- the best in his village. He and his family lived in peace, until a renegade tribe raged through, taking his wife and his son. They took him in bondage and handed him over to a tribe of what looked like pale, sick-looking people that appeared as if the color in their skin had been drained by some mighty serpent or some other blood-sucker.

There is a noise. They all freeze. Thabiti steps out from under the bridge slowly and cranes his neck back and forth. He sees nothing. He turns and consoles the others. He could communicate clearly with Abi, but Gabra and Mbwana speak a tongue he has never heard before.

He doesn't know why they followed him. He has always been good in rough situations; his wife always told him that he had a calming presence that was good to be around. But this situation is different. He is typically able to cope well because there was always something familiar to fall back on for comfort. There is nothing familiar to him here. All the noises, the smells, the people, nothing here seems normal or comfortable. On top of all of that, he knows that he cannot keep doing this for much longer. He will eventually get caught stealing, and the others will most definitely get caught. Then what? He fears the pale-faces would take him, and suck his blood, and possibly the others; they could, he believes, become ghosts themselves. He does not want that.

He steps out from under the bridge and looks up into the sky. He can only see a few stars—the sky is so difficult to see here. There is too much light around them. He could usually find his way with the stars. They are the only familiar things in this alien world. He has no idea how he is going to get home, or if he will ever get home. The one thing that he knows for sure: he will never see his wife and son again.

August 13th, 2041
5:55 am
West Chester, PA

Maximilian wakes up with his head throbbing, his throat raw, and his stomach sour. It is a monumental challenge to drag himself out of bed. Every muscle he attempts to move induces a sensation of wanting to collapse or vomit his guts out. The shower will bring him all the relief he will need. A shower, and two headache capsules, and as much water as his stomach will allow him to ingest.

As the hot water hits his body, he lets his mind wander. Suddenly, it hits him. He had a very weird dream last night. The details are a bit sketchy, but from what he can piece together, he remembers waking up and seeing someone standing in his room. It was dark, but he could make out an outline from the glow of the wall monitor.

He remembers saying "Hey!", and it sounds like the man said something about a dream. That was it. The only thing he remembers distinctly is a snapping sound, like someone striking a match.

It was so unlike the dreams that he had been having lately. In the last few days, he had been having dreams of being back home in Africa. Or, at least, it seemed like he was back in Africa, but it wasn't Nigeria; Ghana, maybe. He was married to a beautiful woman, and they lived in a beautiful village. It was like the past, but it wasn't…it was like a futuristic past. A neo-present perhaps?

He shakes his head slowly. "Such weird dreams," he says.

PART II
EMANCIPATION

CHARLES A. CONYERS, JR.

14

Sha'Ban 10, 1463
(August 8th, 2041)
4:44 am

Masomakali Kébé opens his eyes slowly. He lies still in his bed for a few moments; he wants to remember everything with as much detail as possible. He moves very deliberately as he turns himself over on his back. He allows his eyes to adjust to the darkness. The moonlight fills the room, lightly accenting everything it touches; the bed, the nightstand, the desk, the chairs. Once he can see as much as he can see, he pulls himself out of bed. He opens the sliding doors that lead to the balcony.

It's a beautiful night. A warm breeze lifts the sweet smell of the flower patch on the ground below him. The moon illuminates everything that does not have a light attached to it. There is enough light to see the entire village stretched out before him. He can just make out the stone walkways, making paths through a formation of cottages that look similar to his. He can hear the subtle chorus of distant birds singing along with the babbling brook just behind his house. In the distance, against a star-filled sky, the painterly view of trees and mountain tops.

He feels warm hands touch his waist, and arms wrap around him. She kisses him on the back of his neck. Masomakali smiles and closes his eyes, taking in the soothing calm that only his wife can bring him.

"More dreams, Mas?" asks Nyah.

"More dreams," says Masomakali.

"What was it this time?" she asks.

"This was the strangest one yet. It was as if I was myself, but I was not. I was another person, in a different place. The same time as now, but…it was a completely different world. We were slaves."

"Slaves?" Nyah smirks.

"It was our history. Our people were enslaved and brought to another country, and were forced to build a society where we had no power or control."

Nyah giggles sleepily. "You have the strangest dreams," she says lovingly. "So you were a slave?"

"It wasn't just me. It was millions of us, over hundreds of years. An entire history of struggle and strife."

"If we were the slaves, who were our masters?"

"The Caucasians," he says.

"Oh brother," she says with a laugh. "You should write speculative fiction, Love."

"You know what was strangest of all," he says, "It felt so real. It was like a real, lived-in life. I felt like I had lived that life for as long as I have lived this one. It's as if I know everything there is to know about that world and its history."

Nyah smiles, hugging him closer. "Well, Mister History," she says, moving her hands down to his penis, "Why don't you come back to bed, and make some history with me."

Masomakali likes that kind of history. He turns to face her, and they kiss while moving back to the bed.

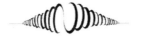

The next morning Masomakali and Nyah have a peaceful breakfast outside on their patio table, as they usually do every morning, except for days when it's raining. Nyah likes to pick fruit and berries from a few of the trees and bushes in their yard to mix with nuts and a sweet bread that she makes on the weekends. Masomakali usually sits at the table, reading the news from his HANDI[8]. This is the morning ritual before both of them go off to work.

The two walk to the hydro-electric trolley stop, located five minutes away from their home. They usually walk together, hand-in-hand, chatting away about what neighbor is doing what and saying what about whom. On a typical day, there are four other people waiting with them. They usually exchange pleasantries, even though they don't know them. It's usually a man in business attire who always seems to be twittering away on his HANDI. There's a young woman that looks as if she works at a music shop or a trendy clothing store. And there are the two young men that Nyah suspects are also a couple; "They are almost as cute a couple as we are," she usually says.

If they're not paying attention, the trolley usually sneaks up on them. It very quietly rides on a cushion of air over a magnetic track. Masomakali and Nyah usually find a seat in the middle of the trolley's second of three cars, on the left side facing forward. There's usually a slight nudge before it starts moving. After that, it's almost always a smooth ride.

There is a vast, beautiful countryside to look at from the window as the trolley whisks them towards the city. Masomakali and Nyah enjoy their morning ride together; it's the last time they see each other until they each get home after work. Every day of their 20 years together has seemed like a first date. Masomakali has always been engaged in everything Nyah says, just as Nyah always listens intently to Masomakali with the emotional energy of a grade school crush. It's not that they don't have arguments or disagreements; they tend to be resolved fairly quickly. Their love is strong and enduring, and passionate and stable. In the quiet moments of their trip, as the trolley passes over the bridge that stands over the

---

[8] "HANDI" is the nickname given to a handheld portable tablet computer.

river that leads into the city, Masomakali holds Nyah's hand, and her head rests on his shoulder. He feels completely and totally at peace.

The trolley pulls up to the first stop in the city, right in front of the University; this is Masomakali stop. Nyah kisses him full on the lips, her hand planted on his chest as he gets up from his seat and steps off. He waves goodbye, and blows her a kiss like he usually does. Sometimes he feels silly, like people are sick of watching him and his wife be so loving with each other. Who cares. You only live once. As the trolley speeds off, Masomakali enters the campus.

Due to the warm climate, most of the classrooms are built outdoors, with canopies available in case of rain. It is early yet, and except for a few other teachers, the campus is relatively empty.

Masomakali grabs a cup of coffee from the cafeteria before heading to his classroom. He usually has 20 minutes to himself before his first class starts. He teaches three different classes, each dealing with history in various stages: The History of Africa, Africans and World History, and Pre-African Civilizations. His classes are rich and deep with a lot of reading, but students always love his lectures for his masterful storytelling. Masomakali not only loves history and knows it well, but he is always able to pepper his lectures with stories and insights that always keep his students engaged. He has been teaching full time for 11 years and loves every minute of it.

As Masomakali looks over his lesson plan for the day, as he usually does, he suddenly hears a voice that he usually does not hear; at least, not as often as he used to.

"Good morning, Professor Kébé," the voice says.

Masomakali looks up. A sharply dressed woman steps into his classroom, with a smile that he could never forget.

"Well, I will be damned!" says Masomakali, smiling widely. "Johana Matsuke!" Masomakali stands up and gives his old friend a hug. "My goodness, how long has it been?"

"Almost three years," says Johana. "And I accept the blame for that. I'm sorry, old friend."

Masomakali flags his hand. "Nonsense," he says. "It's what happens when we get old. We get busy. Time has a way of slipping by us when we are busy."

"This is true, this is true," says Johana.

"What brings you here so early and unexpectedly?"

"I need your help," begins Johana. "We found something out at one of our dig sites. Something that I can't explain."

"One of your dig sites? Still mining dead dinosaurs for the Europeans, eh?"

Johana grins. She remembers the last time she had this conversation with Masomakali, and would very much like to avoid listening to yet another lecture about the "Petroleum Problem."

"Mock if you will," says Johana, "but petroleum is one of the most versatile substances in the world. It's the wave of the future."

"Says you. Every time they try to revive petroleum, it fails. People don't want a dirty, toxic energy source. But far be it from me to tell you your business. You said you found something?"

"Yes, we did. I need you to come take a look at it."

"Okay, well, I can check my schedule to see when I'm available…"

"I need you to come out a bit sooner than that. Like today. Like right now."

Masomakali looks at Johana as if she has three heads. "Johana, I have a job—I have classes to teach. I can't just pick up and leave—"

"I cleared it with your dean. Or rather, the government cleared it with your dean."

The *government*?

"What's going on, Johana? What did you find?"

"I can't explain it. It's something you're going to have to see. We've known each other a long time, and

I'm asking you to trust me. Know that I wouldn't be doing any of this if it were not important. I promise to have you back home to Nyah in time for dinner."

Masomakali has never been on a military jet before. He knows they are very fast. In fact, the only other planes that were as fast were way out of his price range, reserved for the super rich and famous. When Johana said that he would have Masomakali home by dinner, she wasn't kidding!

They are on board the plane a little over five minutes before it takes off. Masomakali watches the wings turn vertically, and feels the plane levitate from the ground. As soon as they are several hundred feet in the air, the wings return to their horizontal position and shoot the plane forward.

"I'm very impressed, Jo," says Masomakali. "Nyah won't believe that I was actually on a hover jet!"

"How is Nyah doing these days," asks Johana. "She's still teaching, right?"

"No. She left teaching, and starting painting again," says Masomakali. "She does a few paintings a month for this advertising firm. It's good money, though not as much as teaching."

"That's great! See, I always had a feeling that she should be doing more art stuff—that's great!"

"Yeah, it's great. She's very happy. Which makes me happy, of course."

"Are you happy?" asks Johana.

"Absolutely," says Masomakali. "Not just because of Nyah, although she's a big part of it. I'm right where I want to be, doing exactly what I want to be doing. We're making money, we have a great cottage in a great village. It's an amazing time."

"Kids?"

"We're getting there," says Masomakali. "It will come soon, I'm sure. As much as we make love, I'm surprised it hasn't happened already!"

"Thanks for rubbing it in," says Johana.

"Well, what's going on with you?" asks Mas. "What happened with you and Gladis?"

"Oh, that ended a long time ago," says Johana. "Turned out that I was an absolute cunt. Who knew?"

Masomakali laughs. "Well, 'absolute,' at the very least."

"Ha-ha. These days I'm just focused on work. I have a lot going on right now, so…"

"Not getting any younger, are we?"

"I feel young," says Johana. "That's all that matters, right? Hey, at least I'm doing what I want to be doing. I'm not slaving away at some thankless job for unappreciative people."

Masomakali smiles introspectively, nodding his head a bit.

"It's true," insists Johana.

"No, it's just…I was just thinking about something Nyah said to me this morning. I've been…eh, never mind."

"Oh come on, don't leave me up in the air like that…! You've been what?"

"I've been having these dreams lately. Last night was the most vivid of them. It was about Africa. Our people had gone astray, our land and our people were raped and pillaged. A great many of us were enslaved for hundreds of years. Millions of us were brought to other countries to work as free labor. It was this entire history where we had been enslaved by Caucasians from Europe—the British, the Dutch, the Spanish…"

"You've been having dreams that we've been enslaved by Caucasians?" Johana asks, laughing. "Wow! If this teaching thing doesn't work out, you have a future in speculative fiction, my friend!"

Masomakali smiles. "Nyah said the same thing," he says.

"I mean really," continues Johana, "the very idea of Caucasians enslaving anyone is laughable, to say the least! They can't even govern themselves properly! I mean look at them—the Germans, the Britons, the Spaniards, all of Eastern Europe…they've done nothing but fight their way into poverty. Their generations have wasted blood and treasure to wage wars that they not only can't afford, but they cannot win! And for what? Their 'white supremacy' mythology! That's the most laughable thing of all- but who am I telling, this is your specialty! I guess that's why it's even funnier, coming from you!"

"It's very strange, that's all," smiles Masomakali.

"Think about it—where would they be without us? All of their energy, resources, education, industry, everything comes from us. There are many reasons why Africa is the center of the civilized world. We have the greatest minds, the greatest military, the greatest technology in the world! The Caucasians aren't even close, but meanwhile…they lie to themselves about how superior they are."

"Is that why they're such an easy sell with petroleum?"

"It's cheap, ultimately. Cheap and powerful, and we can sell a lot of it. Yes, it's toxic, too. But maybe in your dream world they make it work for them!"

"Well, they are just dreams," says Masomakali. "Odd dreams, but dreams nonetheless. I wonder what they mean, though? Our dreams are supposed to be visual representations of our subconscious. So it must mean something, don't you think? Other than the obvious literal interpretation, that is."

"It means that your subconscious has a wild sense of humor, that's what it means!" says Johana, laughing.

In less than 40 minutes, the plane reaches the desert-based landing pad, which sits next to a large dune. It slows to a hover, the wings rotate vertically, and the plane lowers slowly until it rests with a slight nudge.

Masomakali follows Johana out of the plane and onto the pad, towards a path that leads to a set of ascending stairs against the dune. The two armed military men standing at the stairs step aside as the two make their way up. Johana reaches the top of the platform first, then looks down at Masomakali as he makes his way up.

"This is it," says Johana as Masomakali gets to the top. He looks down into the large dig site in front of them and freezes. He swallows deeply as he feels that his heart is about to jump up his throat. There are two wooden cutter ships, each partially submerged in the sand. One is on its side, and the other nose down, with only half of its back end exposed and leaning up against the first. Dozens of workers mill around the ships with digging machines and other equipment, as armed military men stand guard.

"What in the name of Allah is this?" asks Masomakali.

"I told you, you had to see it to believe it," says Johana. "Come on."

The two take the next set of stairs down to the dig site. Masomakali is mesmerized by the scene in front of him.

"We had staked out this site to dig," begins Johana, "Then there was an electrical storm about a week ago. A day or two after that, the military shows up, telling us that their scientists picked up some strange readings. Something about electronic magnets or something."

"Electromagnetic," says Masomakali, still in a daze as they get closer to the ships.

"Yeah, that's it. Anyway, they did some scans of the area, then started digging."

They reach the first ship, which is tilted on its side. Masomakali reaches out and touches it. He looks up a back end of the second ship, which hovers over them like a fallen tree.

"What do you think?" asks Johana.

"British, maybe Spanish. How the hell did they get out here? These ships might be about 300 years old, and there was no water here 300 years ago. They would have had to have been buried here, in the sand, for thousands of years."

Masomakali looks at Johana suspiciously.

"This is a joke, right? This is a joke."

"Are you kidding me?" asks Johana. "Do you think that I have the kind of time and resources to drag you all the way out here for a joke?"

"This is not possible," says Mas. "None of this is possible."

"But here we are," says Johana, pointing at the ships. "Come here, there's something else."

Johana brings Masomakali to a series of tables off to the side of the ships. Sitting on top of and around the tables are various artifacts taken from the ship; barrels, cups, cutlery, shackles and chains...

"Shackles and chains?" Masomakali steps to the heap, picking up one of the shackles. "These are used for slaves."

Johana nods. "Look at this over here," she says, pointing to an object that looks like an oversized salt and pepper shaker.

"We found this on the ship, along with the other things," says Johana as he picks it up from the table. Masomakali takes it from him, turning it in his hands and examining it.

"What is it?" asks Masomakali.

"I was hoping you would know," says Johana. "We found three of them so far. The scientists took the other two. I kept this one for you to see."

Masomakali holds it up. It's weighty for its size, about 15 lbs. He looks at the sides, through a blue-tinted window in the front. He sees some of the mechanics inside, which seem somewhat familiar, but a bit off. He can't explain how.

"I am at a loss, Jo," says Masomakali looking up at the ships, then looking at his friend. "Two ships that were built for slaving during a time when there was no slaving at all. And this thing. No one knows that this thing is?"

"Not a clue," says Johana. "A few of the scientists speculate that they could be sensors of some kind. They were attached to the decks of the ships, but they're not a part of them. Whatever they are, they were put there by someone."

Masomakali cannot wrap his head around what he saw. None of it was logical, and the only other explanations he could come up with were the stuff of movies and fantasy books; and that only infuriated him. He considers himself a reasonable and logical man, who also has an open mind. To him, the things that he saw today require a mind far too open. It is a lot to consider. So much so, that it's giving him a bit of a headache.

Johana finally steps into the plane and finds Masomakali sitting where they sat on the way to the site. When she joins him, Johana can tell that Masomakali's mind is swimming.

"It's confusing, isn't it?" asks Johana as she sits down.

"Confusing is one thing. This is impossible," says Masomakali. "The only reasonable explanation I can think of is that beings from outer space put them there. I'm not willing to believe that. Not right now, anyway."

"Aliens, huh?" smirks Johana. "Little green men?"

"Think about it. Aside from the fact that those ships should not exist for the function which they were intended, how could those ships end up buried deep in the sand?"

Johana shugs.

"They would have had to have been…beamed into the sand. Teleported, or something like that. Their molecules broken down, then reassembled under the sand. That could also explain those electrical storms you mentioned. Maybe they weren't storms at all."

"That is way too far out for me," says Johana. "I had a bit of an easier time believing that they were sitting there for thousands of years, gradually being covered by sand."

"Okay, let's go with that," says Masomakali. "How could that be? The only way is to..." he pauses.

"What?" asks Johana.

"Or they come from some place else," answers Masomakali.

"What place is that?"

"Some place like ours," says Masomakali. "Are you familiar with the world/time theory?"

"Never heard of it," says Johana.

"The theory says that there are infinite numbers of realities, or dimensions, that run parallel to our own. These realities, for the most part, are almost identical, with some slight variations. Maybe in another world/time, you are an Asian business person or a Caucasian farmer."

"Please let it not be the farmer," says Johana.

"Or, maybe in another reality you are a slave of the Caucasians."

"Like your dream," says Johana. "Are you saying that you can see other realities, or world/times or whatever?"

"Not necessarily like my dream, but...maybe. After today, I'm open to that possibility."

"Are you saying that those ships are from another dimension?"

"I'm saying that it would not surprise me," says Masomakali. "It might make sense. Otherwise, what are we looking at? To bring those ships back thousands of years earlier, set them on the surface, then allowed them to be covered over time. The only problem with that is would they be this well preserved if they were buried thousands of years ago? These ships look like they're at least 15 to 20 years old."

"So they traveled through world/time?"

"Time and space."

"For what purpose?"

"To be hidden perhaps," say Masomakali. "I don't know why, but why else would you bury something, unless you want to get rid of it?"

"All I know is that my dig site will be shut down until they can get these things cleared out of there. Unbelievable. Of all places, this had to happen at my site. We could be delayed for another week or two while they figure all of this out..."

As Johana continues to complain, Masomakali's headache gets a little more intense. This is followed by a bit of nausea and slight dizziness.

"Jo," he says weakly.

"Hey, are you alright?" asks Johana. "You look horrible—what's wrong?"

"I just need to close my eyes for a moment," says Masomakali. "I don't know. I think it could be motion sickness."

"It can happen on these planes sometimes," says Johana. "Even the best pilots can get sick. Go ahead, close your eyes. I need to make a few calls. I'll wake you when we get back."

While Masomakali has his eyes closed, he focuses on the sound of the plane. The engine's sonic breath creates a lulling hum, like a deep dial tone. As he slips out of consciousness, he feels as if his body is sinking through the plane's seat. It is an odd sensation that normally would have frightened him. But he feels as if it is okay, like this is supposed to happen; as unusual as this is.

CHARLES A. CONYERS, JR.

15

August 26th, 2041
5:43 pm

The first thing that Maximilian is aware of before he wakes up is the droning of an engine. His eyes open, and he sits up startled. The train. He is sitting on the train. He is sitting on the train, coming home from work. It all comes back to him. The last thing he remembers is a headache and a feeling of nausea before he left the school. He barely remembers getting on the bus that took him to his commuter train. In fact, the only reason he knows that is because it's his usual routine. Now the headache is gone, and his stomach feels fine.

He reminds himself that he needs to call his doctor about these odd sensations. It's been about a week now since he got back from New York City, back from the middle of the Event. He's been interviewed by media outlets from all over the world, recounting his experience with the "African Refugees." Every day since then, he has had these odd bouts of dizziness, nausea, and headaches, to the point where he lies down, blacks out, then wakes up to find himself someplace else. It's as if he's continued with his day uninterrupted, like sleepwalking, without the sleeping. And every single night, he has had the dreams. He dreams of what he now calls "the other place," and what he thinks of as his "other life." It's getting to the point where is familiar with faces. It seems as if, with a bit more time, he'll even know names.

There is something happening to Maximilian; something that he cannot control, and is so alien to him that it's freaking him out. He is more afraid to tell anyone about it, even a doctor. The last thing he wants is for anyone to think he is some lunatic or crazy person. After the infamous "Philadelphia Incident," he did not want to add fuel to a dying fire.

The incident in question wasn't his fault, after all. Not entirely, anyway. Uncovering a slave graveyard buried underneath a patch of land in the middle of downtown Philadelphia was a major find. A few of the gravestones were well-preserved, and all of the bodies were intact. It made Maximilian sick to think that there was so little regard for Blacks at that time in American history, so much so that they didn't even bother to move the bodies. They just simply built over them, gravestones and all. He felt that the site should be deemed hallowed ground and that whatever monstrosity of a hotel they had planned on building could be relocated.

He had plans for that site, and for those forgotten souls paved over and desecrated for the sake of so-called progress. How else was he to react when he discovered that work crews had clumsily dug up the bodies and the gravestones, transferring them into crates and even damaging some of them in the process. No respect for their deaths, and no respect for their afterlife. Yes, he lost control of his senses. Yes, he chained himself to one of the construction vehicles in protest, when no one else took his side. Everyone was easily bought, but not him. It was a shame and a disgrace.

They all thought he was crazy—hell, some still do! He never really understood what could be so crazy about respecting the dead, especially when it came to the enslaved people that practically built this country. If that made him crazy, he believed, then lock him up and throw away the key. So be it.

As for these narcoleptic-type episodes, he figures that it may just be some post-traumatic stress, but even that sounds a bit far-fetched. This has been a stressful time, and everything—the odd feelings, the stress—all of these things will pass. For now, he just has to get through the next few weeks and hope things will return to normal as quickly as possible.

6:31 pm
West Chester, PA

Walking into his apartment, Maximilian has two things on his mind that he wants to relax with: rum, and EWF.

Maximilian discovered the group Earth, Wind, and Fire in college. His girlfriend at the time was a big fan and had every single one of their albums. His favorite was their 1982 album "I Am," which begins with one of his all-time favorite songs: "In The Stone." He wirelessly connects his NAVI to his speaker system and puts the album on. It's the horns at the beginning of the song, the trumpeting, the battle-cry that says "We are here, and we are going to rock the HELL out of you!" He dances into the kitchen, grabs the bottle of rum and pours a short glass.

As he steps back into the living room, he hears a loud snapping sound, He looks to be about Maximilian's age, with a lighter complexion and short curly hair. There is something about him that looks familiar, but Maximilian is too horrified to compute why.

As the vortex disappears, the man speaks. "Do you remember me?" he asks.

Maximilian says nothing, still in shock.

"Do you remember me?" the man repeats.

Maximilian shakes his head wildly. "No! No—what the hell is going on? Who are you?"

"It doesn't matter," says the man. "I need your help." The man pulls a small electronic device from one of the

pockets of his suit. The man taps on the screen, and a
holographic display projects in front of him. He motions
with his free hand over the image, which changes as he
moves.

"I'm looking for four people," he says, "Two
women, a man, and a boy. Africans that escaped from the
others." He continues to manipulate the hologram. "They
were at the convention center and split from the group
during an attempted escape by the others. You saw them
this afternoon. I need to know where they are."

Maximilian is horrified and confused. Aside from the
fact that a strange man just jumped out of some light
portal in his living room, and is now using some weird
holographic projector, he is talking about something that
Maximilian does not understand.

"What Africans?" he asks. "Do you have something
to do with the Africans coming here?"

"Where are they?" asks the man, "The four?"

"I do not know what four you are talking about!"
says Max.

"You were contacted this morning by the police,
asking you to help interpret for some Africans they
picked up in a park," says the man.

"What are you talking about? I have been at work all
day. I have no idea what you are talking about!"

The man manipulates the hologram on his device.

"What day is it?" he asks.

"What?"

"The date, is it the 27th?"

"It's...it's the 26th..."

"You're right," he says. "It doesn't happen for
another 14 hours." He looks up at Maximilian. "We need
to go to New York."

"What?"

The man makes a few motions over the hologram
before it disappears. The snapping sound announces a
pinpoint of light that opens up into a vortex of white light
that appears on the other side of the room. The man looks

down at Maximilian, who has been on the floor the entire time.

"This will feel a little strange at first," he says, "But it will only be a few seconds."

He grabs Maximilian's arm and pulls him off the floor. Before he has time to marvel at the strength that this man possesses, Maximilian is pulled into the vortex, which closes behind them as both disappear inside.

August 27th, 2041

2:14 pm
Downtown Manhattan, New York

On a sleepy side street, a small pinpoint of light expands into a vortex of white light, spitting out the man in the black flight suit, followed by Maximilian. He is in a state of shock and panic. A few seconds before, he was in his living room. Now, after being pulled through a circle of light that felt as if he jumped through a shower of ice water that made his body feel like a "sleeping" limb, he found himself on a New York City street. He looks at the man in the flight suit, who is consulting his holographic device.

"Who the fuck are you?" demands Max.

"You should be getting a call any moment now. You need to tell them that you will be right there—and you're bringing an assistant professor to observe." The man pockets his device and presses a button on the belt of his flight suit. The suit flickers as if it were itself a holographic image, and then a full dress suit appears in its place.

Maximilian yelps then turns to run away. The man grabs Maximilian and stops him in his tracks.

"Get your goddamn hands off of me!" Maximilian yells.

"Maximilian, get yourself together!" the man yells back. "This is not helping! We need to do this, and we need to do this together. Otherwise, this world/time will be in jeopardy!"

Maximilian calms down, staring at this strange man.

"How do you know my name?" Maximilian asks.

"There are a lot of things that I know," the man says.

"You are a time traveler," says Maximilian.

"Yes, I am," the man says.

"It was you. You brought those ships here. The slave ships—they were from the past," says Maximilian. "How are you doing this? Why did you do this?"

"That was an accident," the man says, "They were not meant for this world/time. There were some miscalculations made, to say least. It took me three years, eight months, four days and almost six hours to figure out where they were. It took another two months, two days and 33 minutes for me to discover that four of the passengers were left here. On top of that, it took about two weeks, five days and 17 minutes to calculate whether or not I should be contacting you at all. We shouldn't even be interacting right now, let alone bringing you here in one of the portals. But I had no choice. Mathematically, there's no other way to get those four back."

"Who are you?" asks Maximilian.

"It's not necessary for you to know that," the man says. "I'm sorry that I have to be so vague, but you have to understand how risky this is. You really cannot know any more about me."

At that moment, Maximilian's NAVI rings. He looks at the number but does not recognize it.

"It's them," says the man. "It's the police telling you about the Africans."

Maximilian answers. "Hello?"

"Dr. Oroko, this is Commissioner Wilson, how are you today?"

Maximilian looks up at the time traveler.

"Hello, Commissioner. I'm fine, thank you. How are you?"

"Well, I've got a bit of a situation here," he says. "We received a few calls about a homeless man stealing food in Central Park. We sent a few officers out, and they found a group of four people; a man, two women, and a young boy. The thing is that they don't speak any English, and may speak some African language. No one has alerted the media yet, but I think they could part of the group of Africans that disappeared a couple of weeks ago. I'd like to know if you could come in and talk to them, so we can find out what's going on."

The time traveler nods at Maximilian.

"I will be right there," he says.

"Great," says the Commissioner. "When do you think you could get back to the city?"

"Actually," says Maximilian, "I'm already in town."

"Oh, well, that's great," says the Commissioner. "Well, they're at the 13th Precinct right now."

"I should be there shortly," says Maximilian. "I have one of my assistant professors with me, if that is okay."

"That should be fine, Doctor. Thank you very much. I'll let them know you're coming."

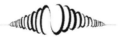

2:24 pm

Maximilian's time traveling friend does not say much of anything in the taxi on the way to the precinct. He notices that the man is spending a lot of time playing around with his portable hologram computer, keeping it lowered and in his lap so that it does not draw attention.

Maximilian takes this opportunity to get out his NAVI to send a text message to the first person that he thinks of since this man entered his life. He calls up Kiki's name, and quickly enters the following: "CAN'T TALK—HAVE ANSWERS—MEET ME AT 13th PRECINCT ASAP."

As the taxi pulls up to the precinct, Maximilian feels a pit in his stomach. Walking in is the first stress test they needs to pass. Maximilian is convinced that his time traveler friend will set off the metal detectors with his special devices, which would then have to be inspected, and his cover would be blown. To his surprise, they pass through with no alarm.

An officer escorts the two to an interrogation room, where they wait for the Africans to be brought in. Maximilian is getting more tense and nervous. So much so that he is startled when the time traveler speaks to him.

"What?"

"We will need to be alone with them when they are brought in," the man says.

"We will see what happens," says Maximilian. "I cannot promise anything."

"Please try," the man says.

"So, how do you think you will get them out of here?" he asks.

"I'll take care of it," says the man. "You don't have to do anything, as far as that's concerned."

Maximilian grits his teeth. "You know something, I cannot take any more of your cryptic, evasive words."

"I'm sorry, Maximilian. You've been a great help to me. I know you didn't have to do any of this."

"Are you kidding me? You did not give me any choice! You grabbed me and jerked me from my living room through some wormhole thing—you gave me no choice whatsoever!"

"That's true," the man nods. "Again, I'm very sorry Maximilian. I wouldn't be doing any of this if it weren't for the greater good."

"What greater good? Whose greater good? Why is any of this happening in the first place?"

The door to the interrogation room opens. The four Africans walk into the room. Maximilian's heart rate jumps. The boy and the women look frightened, but the man looks angry. Maximilian studies the features on the man's face and determines that he should probably try Yoruba.

"My name is Maximilian. I am here to help you. Can you understand me?"

Thabiti looks at Maximilian cautiously. Ever since the group was picked up by the police, he has been on high alert. He feels guilty that he let the others down. He did as well as he could, but it was not good enough. After finally getting captured, he has been stung with a wave of anger and resentment that he cannot shake—that he does not want to shake. Even though he is facing a man—the first man since he's been taken from his home, since they showed up in this strange world—that speaks his language, he does not want to trust him.

"Can you understand me?" repeats Maximilian, sensing that Thabiti does.

"Who are you?" demands Thabiti.

Maximilian smiles, then looks up at the officer.

"Could you leave us alone for a few moments please?" he asks. The officer nods and leaves the room.

When the door closes, the time traveler pulls out his holographic computer.

"We want to help you. You have nothing to fear from us," says Maximilian.

"I fear nothing!" barks Thabiti. *"I want to know who you are, and why you walk with the pale-faces!"*

"I am here to take you home," says the time traveler, in perfect Yoruba. Maximilian looks at him stunned.

He taps a few buttons on his device, producing a holographic display. The women and the boy gasp. After

175

making some motions over the hologram, the lights flicker slightly. A few more motions, there is the sound of a match-snap, followed by the pinpoint of light, then the appearance of the vortex.

The women and the boy scream and cower in the corner. Thaibiti backs up slightly, trying to keep a brave face to mask his fear. As the time traveler steps forward to try to calm the Africans, Maximilian reaches into his pocket and pulls out his NAVI. He activates the video camera, hits record, and casually sets it up on the table.

"*Please, stay calm,*" the time traveler says to the two women in Mande. "*This is nothing but a door of light to take you back to your home. It's okay. I will show you.*"

The time traveler enters the vortex. It closes. After a few seconds, another opens up, and the time traveler emerges. This feat does nothing but frightens them more. When the vortex reopens, Gabra jumps for the door and tries to open it. It is locked.

"*Please be calm,*" says the time traveler, trying to speak over their screams of panic. "*You do not have to be scared. You can go home now. Do you understand me? You can go home. You do not have to stay in this strange place with these strange people!*"

The screaming stops. Maximilian wonders why no one has barged in yet to see what is going on in here.

"*You can go home,*" the time traveler says to Thabiti in Yoruba. "*You can go home now.*" The time traveler turns to the boy, Mbwana, and says in Bantu, "*You don't have to be afraid. I am here to make sure you get home. You don't have to stay here. You can be free again, away from this strange place.*"

Mbwana looks at the vortex, then looks at the time traveler and smiles slightly.

"*What is your name?*" Mbwana asks.

The time traveler smiles back. He peers over to Maximilian, who is in absolute awe of what's going on in front of him.

"*My name is Davis,*" he says to the boy. "*Let's go home.*"

As Mbwana steps forward, Thabiti and the women try to keep him back, but he pushes his way through, and steps to the time traveler.

"*It's okay,*" he says. "*I promise you.*"

Mbwana smiles. He turns to the vortex and jumps in. The women shouts for him. He is gone.

"*It's okay,*" says the time traveler in Mande. "*The boy is just fine! And you can go home, too!*"

"*I don't want to go to the afterlife!*" cries Gabra. "*I don't want to die!*"

"*You are not dead,*" says Maximilian says to the women. "*You are as alive as I am. I know this seems strange. I know you are frightened. But I believe him. This is a way for you to get home. I have walked into the door of light, and it works. It works.*"

Abi looks Maximilian directly in the eyes. She believes him. She looks at Gabra, who is still unsure about what she should do. Abi steps to the vortex. Before she enters, she says something that Maximilian is not familiar with, that has no real direct translation, but is a phrase that is used by someone who throws caution to the wind. Loosely translated: "*Fuck it.*"

When Abi disappears, Gabra clenches her fists and grits her teeth. She steps to Thabiti and says something to him. Thabiti turns to Maximilian.

"*She wants you to go with her,*" says Maximilian. Thabiti looks at Davis, who nods at him.

"*What is on the other side of this light?*" he asks suspiciously.

"*It's home,*" says Davis. "*It's trees, mountains, rivers, lush green lands…it's where you belong.*"

Thabiti sighs deeply. If this is truly the end of his life, he wants to get it over with. He is too tired to argue or fight it anymore. As he steps towards the vortex, Gabra grabs his hand. He looks down at her, trembling like a cold, wet kitten. She too is tired and weary. He squeezes her hand and walks with her to the vortex. He looks inside at the white and light blue swirls of light. It is silent. The air is still around it, although it seems like he should be feeling some breeze. He takes a deep breath, and takes a big step inside, with Gabra trailing right behind him. They disappear into the light. Davis motions over his device, which closes the vortex.

"We did it," Davis says with a sigh. "You've been a great help to me, Maximilian Oroko. Thank you!"

As he reaches out to shake his hand, Davis' device starts beeping.

"Shit!" he barks.

A few motions over his device and another vortex opens up.

"I have to go," says Davis. "I can't take you with me."

"Whoa, wait a minute," says Maximilian. "You are not going to leave me here! Take me back home! How am I going to explain this to these people?"

"I'm sorry, I know this is…well, it's fucked up, but…"

"You are not leaving me here like this!"

"This was a big enough risk for me. I cannot stay here a second longer. I can no longer have any further contact with you, or this world/time."

As Davis steps into the vortex, Maximilian reaches out to grab his shoulder. He misses, and loses balance, causing him to fall into the vortex as well. Both vanish inside the light as it closes.

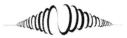

2:43 pm

When Kiki arrives at the 13th Precinct, she is told that Maximilian and a colleague had arrived 15 minutes prior. As she is escorted back to the interrogation room, the lights, monitors, even NAVI displays flicker and blink momentarily, which elicits curious glances and reactions from everyone in the building.

"The fuck?" says the officer, but immediately covers his mouth looking at Kiki. "Sorry, ma'am."

"No fucking sweat," says Kiki with a smirk.

The officer opens the door to the interrogation room to find it empty.

"Where'd they go? Did they leave?" he asks the officer posted at a desk near to the door.

"What are you talkin' about, no one left..." he says as he stands up and peers into the empty room. "What the...?" Both officers sprint away.

Kiki walks into the room. Something feels very strange to her, but she cannot put her finger on it. She looks down at the table and sees a NAVI propped up on its side, with the red camera light on. She picks it up and stops the recording. After the clip processes and saves, she plays it back. She watches Maximilian set the NAVI down, and sees everything up to and including her walking in the door, and picking up the NAVI.

CHARLES A. CONYERS, JR.

16

Sha'ban 16, 1463

(August 16th, 2041)

3:41 am

Knock-knock-knock-knock:
"Mas? Masomakali!"
Bang-bang-bang!
"Masomakali Kébé! Will you answer me, please?"
"Yes…!" says Masomakali. "Yeah, I'm coming, I'll be right there…"
Masomakali Kébé finds himself hunched in the corner of a small bathroom. At first, he can't figure out why the bathroom is so small. He thinks about where a bathroom this small could exist. He is not in a trendy club because there is no music. The only sound is the constant sonic drone of hydrogen-powered jet engines, which is currently being drowned out by rapid and heavy knocking from the other side of the bathroom's door.
"Mas, are you okay?", says Johana.
"Yeah, I'm okay." Masomakali takes a deep breath. His nausea is gone. His headache is gone. He feels strength coming back into his legs as he stands up.
"I'm all right," he says. "I'll be right out."
Hearing Johana's voice brings it all back to him. The government scientists discovered another electromagnetic storm. He is currently on a jet because Johana asked him to join her team as a translator. He would be translating from Ojigwe to their native Bantu. He had to dig up a few of his old language books and notes to upload onto his HANDI. He hasn't had to speak any of the Algonquian languages in several years, since university. That's when he remembers…they're going to The Great Turtle Island[9].

Or, as it is known to its countrymen, Anowarakowah. It was what the Europeans called "The New World," until they lost it; they lost it before they even had it. The Haudenosaunee-European War raged for 15 years, exhausting the efforts of the Dutch, French, and British forces. The Haudenosaunee Confederacy reached far down from the northern plains to the southern shores and stretched back nearly to the middle of the continent. They are smart, govern well, and have good relations regionally as well as internationally. Rubbed the wrong way, however, they are known to be volatile and aggressive, and if pushed will strike with great fury and brutality.

The top representatives of the "H.C.", as the British newspapers call them, would be meeting and escorting them to the site of the disturbance. Then they would have a nice dinner. That's one of the things that Masomakali remembers about the last time he visited the Turtle Island; the food is spectacular. Fresh. Tasty. Delicious. The prospect of having great food picks up Masomakali's spirits. He is hungry, which must be why he was feeling so light headed. He looks in the mirror to make last minute adjustments and opens the door.

Johana is doing some work on her HANDI when Masomakali sits down in the seat across from her. Johana looks at him and smiles.

"I can't believe you're air sick," laughs Johana. "I don't mean to be so insensitive—how do you feel?"

"Fine," says Masomakali. "I feel fine. I don't know what happened—I just felt dizzy and light-headed, and the next thing I knew...I was sitting on the bathroom floor."

"How much did you have to drink?" asks Johana.

---

[9] "The Great Turtle Island," otherwise known as North America, was named according to the legend of the Woman Who Fell From the Sky. The story says that she fell into the water and was rescued by a large turtle that collected dirt from the ocean floor on its back to provide the woman with land to live on. As the turtle grew, the land grew into a continent.

"I had three glasses of wine, but it wasn't that. This has happened a few times lately, though not as severe. This time it was like I was dreaming. But the dreams seemed so real…"

"You were dreaming in there?" asks Johana. "I could never fall asleep in bathrooms. Yes, I know they're all auto-cleaned, and it's thorough, and they did all those tests, and it cleans better than a human can. It still sickens me to even sit on the bowl. Do you know how many people use public toilets? They had to invent this technology because people are disgusting."

"Oh, how I enjoy your anti-bathroom lectures," says Masomakali smiling.

"It's not anti-bathroom, more than it is anti-inconsiderate and dirty people. So, anyway, you say you were dreaming in the bathroom. Not the Caucasian thing again."

"Yes," says Masomakali, rolling his eyes, "It's 'the Caucasian thing' again. But it's not about them—that's just a small part of it. That's just part of this world these dreams take place in. That is the crazy thing. It's as if I am a part of this second life. I don't know how else to say it…but it feels like I'm living this other life in another world. It's like I have a window into another dimension."

"Another dimension?" Johana laughs. "Whoa, Captain Kébé, let's land the starship!"

"I'm serious!" Masomakali insists. "It feels real, but it's different. It's been happening almost every day now, usually when I'm tired. You know, when my guard is down. That's when I start to slip. I get dizzy, I close my eyes, and then I'm someone else."

"Is this more of that space and time stuff you were talking about?" asks Johana.

"Not space and time, world/time. And I don't know."

"Are you sure you don't have multiple personality syndrome?" asks Johana.

"No, I do not have multiple personality syndrome." says Masomakali, frustrated that he's unable to properly articulate this sensation. "This man, he's…a teacher. And he has friends, and he commutes to work on something that looks like a train. It is a train, but not like ours. Everything is like that—it's similar, but a little different."

"That sounds like another dimension," Johana says sarcastically. "Speaking of Caucasians, do you think we're going to see any niggers[10]?"

Masomakali flinches, a little taken aback by Johana using such an impolite word.

"I don't know," says Masomakali, "But do us a favor, and don't say that word out loud."

"I'm not stupid, Mas—of course, I won't say that out loud. If there are 'niggers' around, I'll hold my tongue."

"Very funny," says Masomakali.

'Nigger,' of course, as in the name the British use when referencing the ancestors of the original colonists of in the Haudenosaunee Confederacy, formally know as "the New World." After the war, the Haudenosaunee set aside small regions of land allowing the remaining and surviving settlers places to build homes and schools and churches, and their own shops. That did not last long, as renegade Iroquois bandits took to burning down and destroying almost anything the whites built, making it difficult for them to evolve as a culture or people while constantly having to defend themselves and their families and their possessions. Their lack of education due to decades of inaccessibility took its toll with the passing of each generation to the point where only a relative few of them are intellectually or emotionally capable of building success in an Haudenosaunee society.

Ever since then, the name stuck. And even though it is not likely to be said out loud in public, most use it in private.

---

[10] In the early 20th century, a British journalist, upon visiting one of the many white slums in the Haudenosaunee Confederacy, wrote an article for the British newspaper The Daily Telegraph, which he called "Anowarwakawa's Niggers", describing the "H.C. whites" as "...the poor, lazy, uneducated, unskilled, undesirable masses."

7:54 am
The Island of Montauk, Anowarakowah
(New York City, USA)

The Island of Montauk is a long sliver of land with tall buildings mixed with lush greenery. It's considered one of the most technologically modern and culturally progressive cities of Anowarakowah, and the world itself. Masomakali peers at the island through the window of the plane as it circles around to make a landing on the airstrip at the southern tip.

Johana and Masomakali follow the team as they disembark from the plane. Standing at the base of the stairway, four students from the University of Montauk, two male and two female, dressed in the hippest of modern Montauk fashion; clothing inspired by a blend of European styling with a Mohawk aesthetic. They are very stoic and serious-looking.

Johana gets a look at the two women and quietly asks Masomakali, "Would it be rude of me to ask to see them naked?"

"You have to show them yours first," says Masomakali.

"That's not fair," says Johana.

"Life rarely is," Masomakali smirks.

When they reach the bottom of the stairs, one of the male students steps forward. He smiles a little, and bows slightly.

"Welcome to Montauk Island," he says in perfect Bantu.

Masomakali and Johana also bow slightly.

"*Thank you*," says Masomakali in perfect Algonquian. "*I am Masomakali Kébé, and this is Johana Matsuke.*"

"*Yes*," says the representative, switching to Algonquian. "*I am called Abooksigun, and known as Book. This is Chogan, and this is Yamka and Tiva. We are here to escort you to the site. The others are waiting for us there.*"

"They're here to escort us to the airport," he translates for Johana.

"All of them?" asks Johana.

"*Excuse me*," asks Book. "*Do you speak many languages?*"

"*Not many*," says Masomakali. "*Zulu, Swahili and Algonquian, of course…some Mandé, a little bit of French, and English, actually.*"

Book's eyes light up. "*You can speak English?!*" he asks ecstatically. Masomakali had a feeling that his English speaking would come in handy, particularly with the Haudenosaunee youth. The society deemed English a "gutter language", or the language of the poor.

"We both do," says Masomakali in English. "Johana has had a bit more practice than I have had recently."

"It's true," says Johana.

"That's great!" says Book in English. "Well, this should be an interesting ride!"

8:18 am

Masomakali never liked the smell that emitted from the hydro-electric engines used in Anowarwakowah to power their vehicles. Although many would argue with that, the hydro-electric engines did not emit an odor at all.

In fact, their emission levels were lower than most, particularly Europeans and their use of the black oil.

"I don't smell anything," Johana says to Masomakali quietly.

"It's an acidic smell," says Masomakali. "Like something being pickled."

"You lost me there," says Johana.

Johana is a little disappointed that they are not taking a more scenic route to the pier where they were to meet their party. Instead, they took the major road that circles the entire island. The left side of the road is lined with thick, lush trees. Between their branches and trunks one can make out buildings and homes, including many variations of the traditional "Longhouse" style. On their right is the ocean, with beaches and small villages scattered along the coastline.

"It would take us a lot longer to cut through," says Book. "We should not keep Professor Zacharie waiting. Maybe we can see more of the island after dinner."

"That would be great," says Johana.

Masomakali was looking forward to meeting the professor. Oren Zacharie was one of the leading scientific scholars in the League of Nations, and allegedly quite a history buff, with a nearly encyclopedic knowledge of the Haudenosaunee.

"How long have you worked with Professor Zacharie?" Johana asks Yamka, who is sitting behind her and Masomakali.

"I don't work with him," she says, "I'm one of his students. The four of us are."

"How old are you," smiles Johana.

"Twenty," Yamka smiles back.

Book takes a right turn, and guides the vehicle down a steep hill, then onto a street that takes them through a poor neighborhood. The structures are dull and not well-kept. Trash has collected in pockets all along the streets. Whatever vehicles are around are either run-down, or hollowed out and converted into housing or garbage receptacle.

"Where are we?" asks Johana. "Is this a white neighborhood?"

"One of only a few slums on the Island," says Yamka. "There's one here, one on the North Western edge, and another on the other side of the Island."

Book slows the vehicle to a stop, as the traffic light ahead of them changes. Masomakali looks out the window, at the crossing in the street. In front of their vehicle, he watches a Caucasian family of five and a half crossing in front of them.

The woman is scrawny, with a protruding pregnant belly, shuffling herself across the road; tired, faded, with bitterness and frustration etched in her eyes. She says something to the three kids following behind her. Masomakali does not understand what she says, but whatever it is the anger in her face does not indicate that it is a good thing. Trailing behind the woman and the kids is the father. He looks as worn out, if not more so, than the woman. As he crosses and looks up at the vehicle, he and Masomakali make eye contact. The gaze is broken as Book honks the horn.

"These niggers are so slow," he says. Johana immediately turns to Masomakali with a broad smile on her face.

"Is that what you call them?" asks Johana? "I thought calling them 'niggers' was a bad thing."

"Well, we're not supposed to," says Yamka. "In public, anyway."

"We're supposed to be nice to them, and show them equal respect," says Book. "There's a national campaign to help their community, but…look at them. They're lazy, dumb, and all they do is drink liquor, take drugs, and have kids that are dumber than they are. Besides, it's not our word, it's theirs. Nigger is a European word. It's a part of their language. It's one of the few things that Europeans have contributed that's worthwhile."

"Well, that, and shoes," says Yamaka. "Italians make the best shoes!"

"Their food's not bad either," says Johana.

"Okay, so there's food and shoes," says Book. "I think we can draw the line there."

8:55 am

"We are about 1200 feet from the location," announces Professor Oren Zacharie in Algonquian from the cabin of the boat.

The professor is not what Masomakali was expecting. Zacharie, with his rugged, almost bushy appearance looks more like a fisherman, or a musician than an esteemed scholar. Not that it should matter because it doesn't. It's just a little strange, and amusing to Masomakali that he would make such a blind assumption.

Johana's team members have been tooling away with their instruments since they first set foot on the boat. Meanwhile, Johana has been flirting with Yamaka, who along with her colleagues, changed into clothing more suitable for employ on the professor's boat. Johana finds the cut-off shorts, moccasins, and cotton tunic blouse Yamka is wearing to be quite sexy.

"I've got something," one of the team members says, tweaking the controls on the instrument.

Johana excuses himself from Yamaka and steps over to see for herself.

"What is it?" she asks.

"It's faint. It's very faint. But it's a residue of some energy mass. Whatever it was, it was big and extremely powerful."

"This storm happened almost two weeks ago, and it's still leaving a residue. What could produce something that strong?" asks Johana.

"What did you find?" asks Masomakali.

"It appears to be the same signature that we found at our site," says Johana. "It's weaker, but it's the same thing. And it still registers after nearly two weeks. Can we get a visual?"

The team member flips open a separate viewer and taps a few keys. On the screen, a ghosted mass shaped like a tornado on its side, which funnels out into a stream that snakes out for several yards.

"There it is," says Johana. "It's weak, but this is it."

"*We are at the center point of the location,*" announces Zacharie. "*You should be able to detect the signature.*"

"*They do,*" Masomakali answers back. "*It's the same as ours at home.*"

Zacharie says something to Chogan that Masomakali doesn't not quite catch, but when he sees Chogan enter the cabin and Zacharia approach them, he assumes he asked to take control of the boat.

Zacharie looks at the screen. "*It looks like a lemon or a walnut,*" he says.

Johana looks up. "Did he just say walnut?"

"He said it looks like a walnut, yes," Masomakali answers.

"Can you ask him if he knows what could have caused this," Johana asks Masomakali.

Masomakali translates to Zacharie. He shrugs, and answers by gesturing at the screen and the sky.

"He says that there were witnesses that said they saw what looked like a pin of light at first, then a blinding flash, before it disappeared. It happened almost instantaneously."

As Zacharie continues, Masomakali feels a slight headache coming on.

"He said one of the witnesses said that it did not seem natural. Like it was…it was like someone switching on a light, or…no, it was like someone making a light? I guess he is saying that it was artificial."

"That's impossible," says the team member. "It would take the energy of countless suns to produce a burst of energy like this artificially."

"Well, how else can you explain this phenomenon," asks Johana. "How do you explain wooden ships in the middle of the desert? Ships that are maybe centuries old, buried for thousands, if not millions of years in the sand?"

"Well, I cannot explain that either," says the team member. "I'm not discounting that these things didn't happen. I can say that if these events are human-made, or artificial in some other way, I am not at all sure how."

"Mas, could you ask the professor...Mas?"

Johana notices that Masomakali is swaying back and forth slightly with his eyes closed.

"Hey Mas, are you okay?" asks Johana.

"I'm fine," Masomakali slurs as his knees give. The last thing that he sees is Johana rushing to him with her arms open.

17

June 13th, 1730
Night
The *Little George*, Atlantic Ocean

A flash of white light is instantly extinguished as Maximilian falls forward onto the planked wooden deck. It is dark and raining hard. All around him, there is screaming, and yelling. Bodies fall. Feet pound and stomp next to him. He scrambles to move away from what seems like the floor of a massive riot.

When he is clear from the immediate cluster of violence, he rises to his knees. He is on a ship. There is a frenzy of people around him. There are men, Black men, barely dressed. He sees some of them wrestling and struggling with other men, white men, who are dressed in tattered and weathered clothing. All of this looks familiar. These people look like the visitors from the convention center. But how? The last thing he remembers is standing in the interrogation room of the police station. He reached for the time traveler as he entered that door of light. And now, he is on a ship.

Through the screams and yelling, he hears a voice shouting out: "Hey! Hey! Get up!"

Maximilian looks around, trying to find the direction of the voice.

"Get up!" the voice says again.

He still cannot see who is speaking, but somehow he knows the voice is speaking to him.

"Get up now! You have to follow the stream!"

Maximilian stands up. *Follow the stream?* he thinks. *What stream?* He looks left and right and then stops. He sees something hovering in mid-air, but he is not sure. It

looks like a long, transparent earthworm-like tube
suspended horizontally in the air, and stretching down
along the deck towards the back of the ship. Is this the
stream?

"Yes, that stream! Follow it now! <u>Now</u>!"

He stops thinking and starts following the stream
down the deck. As he follows the stream, it gets thinner;
it's slowly disappearing. Maximilian sprints after it,
around a corner. Before he can react, he slams into a
vortex waiting at the end.

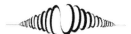

At first, it's a blinding shield of light. Ringlets of
darkness are gradually introduced creating the appearance
of a tunnel. Through the rings, the darkness shifts,
revealing glimpses of what appear to be stars and
planets—and not just Earth. The speed and the colors
increase. The sounds are garbled and mixed, as if
someone is surfing radio station channels, between
pockets of silence.

Maximilian feels as if he is suspended. It looks to
him as if he is falling, but his body does not feel that way
at all. He feels his limbs moving slowly as if he is
swimming in a vat of pudding. The visuals pick up speed,
blinking rapidly through lightness and darkness, earth and
stars, moving and spinning out of control like a yo-yo in
zero gravity. He is too stunned to scream.

February 1st, 2387
1:32 pm
Old South Beach, Florida

Maximilian stumbles into the shin-deep water. The land underneath his feet is hard, like asphalt. The sun is shining, blasting a stinging heat. He turns to face the vortex, but it has disappeared. Instead, he sees homes on his right and hotels on the left, and beyond the hotels is a body of water so massive that it could only be the ocean.

The water has overwhelmed the land and the structures. The buildings look as if they have been abandoned for several decades. The waterlines on the faces are high, over 8 feet. This is low tide. At high tide, he'd be treading water right now.

These sights are enough to temporarily distract him from what he should be doing: following that stream. He whips his head back and forth, searching for signs of it.

"Shit," he says. "Shit! Where in the hell do I look?"

He spots a rippling effect in the air in front of the large former beachfront hotel 400 yards in front of him. He stomps through the water towards it.

He wades through the gaping hole that used to be a picture window of one of the most luxurious hotels in the country, now reduced to a flooded, weather-beaten relic akin to a ceramic castle one would find in a fish tank.

Maximilian can see the stream clearly now. It snakes inside and curves upward through the ceiling. He navigates through a cluster of junk and garbage and whatever the tide managed to bring into the building. He runs up a set of stairs that hug the wall and curve upwards to the second-floor balcony overlooking the lobby. The moldy, dank, putrid stench of rotting chemically-treated, centuries-old furniture, wood, and vinyl were all destroyed in the late summer of 2115 by Hurricane Silus.

These are the results of an event that Maximilian would not see in his lifetime.

The stream curves up and penetrates the ceiling up to the third floor. He continues up the second set of stairs, his shoes squishing out more and more of the water they had accumulated.

The third floor is more deprived of the intense sunlight than the others, but he can still see the stream rippling in the air like heat off of hot asphalt. It's getting smaller and extends straight down the hall, and out a window at the end. When Maximilian gets to the window, he looks down. Twelve feet below the window, the vortex is shrinking.

He climbs out the window and positions himself to make the jump. Suddenly, a screeching sound erupts above him. He looks up and sees a man, lowering down in front of him, suspended by what looks like two small scale jet plane engines strapped to his back. At first, Maximilian thinks that his brain has broken because he swears that he hears this guy speaking to him Mandarin. Since he doesn't speak it, Maximilian only could give a blank stare. He looks down to the flag emblem on the man's uniform. He is confused by the four flags merged into one design. The stars and stripes are unmistakable, but are arranged differently, confined to a pie shape with three other flags. The blue field in the back end with only three stars showing. The others have colors and symbols that represent flags of China, Iran, and Russia. The man himself looks Asian, but with brown skin.

Maximilian watches the man remove a small device from his belt and hold it to his mouth. When he speaks into it, the device says: "This is a restricted area. Step down from the window immediately."

Instead, Maximilian jumps out the window as the jetpack man reaches out for him. He can't tell if the man can see the vortex, and by the time he hits it, he doesn't care.

The sound is deafening-- large, robust swooshing sounds, like two sets of helicopter blades chopping in his ears. Maximilian spirals through ringlets of darkness and hoops of light. The darkness is accented by views of space and planets. The red sands of Mars and the icy mountains of Saturn mix seamlessly with the grassy plains and massive oceans of Earth.

It's moving faster, and the views are blurring. He is nauseous, and wants to turn away or close his eyes. But he cannot. He will not. He understands that this must be one of those wormholes that he's heard Kiki talk about. That was his final thought before hitting the wall of light.

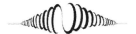

Maximilian lands knees first, then flat on his chest, with his hands breaking the rest of his fall, preventing him from a face plant. It's too dark to see anything, but he can smell, feel and hear the moisture. He also hears the hum of machinery. The sounds of dripping water are all around him, both close up and far away. The metal grating on the floor below him suggests that he is on some sort of structure.

As his eyes adjust he sees spots of light. He gets to his feet, holds out his hands and slowly moves towards an inviting array tiny of blue lights, which form a path that point to a doorway. He steps slowly, feeling around for any obstructions that may be hidden by the darkness. He takes several steps before he feels something butt up against his waist. He drops his hands immediately onto the railing he has walked into. It's wet, and very slimy.

"Disgusting," he says out loud.

He picks up the pace, using the railing as his guide. As he gets closer to the blue running lights, his heart beats faster. He has no idea where the stream is, or where to even begin looking. All he wants right now is some light. He has a mini flashlight on his keychain, but his keys are in his apartment. His NAVI is at the police precinct; it would have more than likely been reduced to an expensive flashlight because he doubts he would be able to get a signal from wherever he is.

When he reaches the blue lights, he breaks into a sprint. Almost immediately, he triggers a motion sensor, which activates the floodlights installed over the elevator door. He covers his eyes and stops in his tracks, so hard he lurches forward and has to regain his balance to keep from stumbling over. He looks away from the lights, rubbing and blinking his eyes to recover from their intensity.

When his eyes clear, he looks up and sees a lit section of big, gray skyscraper. He rubs his eyes again and looks. The building is still there. Hollowed out, moist, dank, moldy. On his left and his right, the light reveal that he is on a steel walking bridge suspended in between two flood-damaged skyscrapers. If he believes what his brain is processing, this walkway is running down the middle of what used to be a city street. This is a city that was flooded centuries ago. Three hundred feet in front of him is the open elevator door, connected to a steel wall that looks impossibly large, and cuts right through the two buildings.

Maximilian steps inside the elevator; a large glass cylinder that looks a lot larger inside than it does from the outside. The glass walls show the interior of the grayed and blackened tube and pipes and other bits of machinery inside.

He turns toward the door, spots a panel screen, and touches it, bringing up a line written in six different languages; Chinese, Spanish, Russian, Hindi, Japanese, and at the bottom, English: "Please choose your language." Maximilian clicks English. A graphic image of a building profile divided into colored sections. Next to the building graphic, the following words:

Welcome to Kamon Tower
Please select your destination

If he is reading the building map correctly, there appear to be 620 floors, and he is currently on the 30th. Maximilian touches the blue quadrant on the graphic; the 400 block. He picks a random floor; 444. The elevator door closes with a hiss, and it gently, quickly lifts upwards. He rubs his hands together with a deep sigh. At this point, he doesn't know what to do. He lost track of the stream and has no idea where to look.

The elevator counter climbs very quickly; the numbers jump in 10s almost every 5 seconds. The glass wall is still showing the innards of plumbing and mechanical boxes. The touch screen displays an advertisement for some device. An attractive woman holds it in her well-manicured hand. She taps a few buttons and a holographic image projects over it. She motions her hands over an icon and photos appear. She motions again, and it's an address book. He remembers the device that the time traveler was holding. It was nothing more than a consumer product, but unlike any that Maximilian had ever seen before.

The advertisement fades out, and the following appears:

January 18th, 2648
1:09 pm
Temperature in NUEVA NEW YORK: 92 degrees

The elevator makes a whistling sound, like a flute playing ascending scales, then the elevator floods with sunlight. Maximilian turns to the glass wall. As he takes in the view, his jaw drops lower and lower.

There are so many things to look at: a pedestrian promenade, shops, and restaurants, a massive park, all littered with thousands of people, all seemingly floating among a forest of the biggest skyscrapers he has ever seen. They are bigger than mere skyscrapers…they are like atmosphere-scrapers. Every time he turns his head, he sees something new. There are walking bridges that float around and through buildings. There are speckles of digital screens and holographic advertisements selling everything from singers to soap. Organized clusters of flying vehicles move in grid-like patterns at many different altitudes. There are people all over the place; a group of girls stepping out of a shop laughing, a little boy playing tag with a toy android, a couple at an outdoor restaurant ordering dinner from a holographic menu. All of these sights go on for miles and miles in all directions.

"They have built a new city on top of the old one," Maximilian muses to himself. The world is nearing the 28th century, and they've found a way to survive. All of that talk about global warming or climate change, whatever you want to call it…it was real. The New York he knows, the New York he was in just over 20 minutes ago, was long gone. He looks out over the landscape of glass towers, spires, domes, pyramids and other structures he had never dreamed of seeing. It's a city in the sky.

Maximilian notices a group of people walking into a domed structure that looks as large as a small office building, shaped like a saucer and resting on a cylindrical platform. As he watches people entering this building, he realizes that the elevator's speed as slowed a bit. According to the screen, he is on floor 263 and climbing about one floor every second. He looks back at the saucer just in time to see the tracking lights around it come to life cycling around the rim. There are people standing at its windows, looking out.

By the time Maximilian's elevator is above it, the saucer slowly lifts off the platform. After a few moments, it picks up speed and rapidly lifts into the air. He looks up at the saucer, seeing the array of black cylinders undulating and vibrating underneath. He has to use his sleeve to wipe the string of drool that has dribbled from his mouth while his jaw was agape.

18

September 1st, 2041
2:14 pm
Brooklyn, New York

It's been five days since Joseph has heard from Maximilian. He has called and left messages, but there's been no reply. He called the school, but they haven't seen or heard from him either. The police went to his house but found that he was not there, and no one seems to have been there in days.

Joseph is concerned about Maximilian after the way they were shepherded out of the convention center. He thought his friend might go off the deep end again and do something foolish. Joseph thinks that maybe Maximilian has been "silenced." He is not sure if that could be possible, but after everything that has happened, it wouldn't surprise him.

His NAVI's incoming call tone breaks this train of bad thoughts. The number is one that he doesn't recognize; it's an international voice call as well. Curious.

"Hello?"

"Professor Joseph Healey?" says the voice on the other end.

"Yes, who's calling?"

"Professor Healey, my name is Youssef Hakeem. I am the curator of the Secret Archives here at the Vatican in Rome."

Joseph looks at the number on the NAVI. "I'm sorry, did you say that you're calling from the Vatican?"

"Yes, I am the curator of the Secret Archives at the Vatican here in Rome."

"And...I'm sorry, your name is..."

"Yes, my name. It's Youssef Hakeem. Yes, I have a Muslim name. And yes, I work for the Vatican."

Boy, Joseph thinks, *I guess business is bad enough for them to broaden their horizons.* The Catholic Church has become more progressive going into the mid 21st Century. First, they relaxed their policies on homosexual priests, and then they allowed women into the priesthood. That inclusiveness appears to be extended to other religions as well.

"The reason I'm calling Professor Healey is that I am wondering if you happen to know how I can get in touch with Dr. Maximilian Oroko? I have made several attempts to contact him, but have had no luck."

"Dr. Oroko has gone missing, Mr. Hakeem," Joseph says somberly. "It's a real mystery. I've been to the police as well."

"I'm sorry to hear that, Professor Healey. I hope that he's okay."

"So do I, Mr. Hakeem."

"Well, Professor, you were the next name on my list of contacts. Maybe this is something that you want to see."

"See what, exactly?" asks Joseph, his curiosity continuing to pique. "You said you were a curator of the archives?" asks Joseph.

"We have many, many works that have not been seen by anyone outside of these walls for hundreds and in some cases thousands of years. I don't want to say too much on the phone, but...my work here over the years has revealed some very interesting things, as you can imagine. I believe I may have something here that could pertain to the 8/8 and 8/12 events."

Joseph freezes as Youssef's words marinate.

"I..." he starts. "I'm sorry again, are you saying that you found something connected to the appearance of the African refugees?"

"A few things, yes," says Youssef.

"I mean...can...can you send it?"

"I cannot, Professor. I am not authorized to release anything. I had to get a special request from the Pontiff himself to allow you and Dr. Oroko to see this. That's why I'm calling. I'd like to invite you to Vatican City to see what I've found."

September 3rd, 2041
11:11 am
Vatican City, Italy

Youssef Hakeem was a young man when he first took the job out of college as a student of theology and history to work in the Archivum Secretum Apostolicum Vaticanum, otherwise known as The Vatican Secret[11] Archive. Since Youssef was a child, he had always been fascinated by Vatican City, mostly for aesthetic reasons. The architecture, the grandeur of it all was very impressive to him, which caused a bit of concern for his conservative Muslim parents. They were a bit confused, to say the least and would have rather had their son take an interest in their own faith. But they love their son and wanted to support his interests. *Terrific*, his father would say to his mother behind closed doors, *it's bad enough to deal with these anti-Muslim whites- they would never accept him.*

Learning about the Vatican Archive only intrigued Youssef more; the idea of having access to history on that scale became an obsession for him. By his Sophomore year of high school, he was studying abroad in Rome. His thirst for knowledge and love of history helped to propel him throughout his academic career. By his Junior year in college, he was not only fluent in Farsi and English (he grew up with both), but also Latin and Italian, with a little bit of French and

---

[11] "Secret" meaning "personal", as defined in the 17th Century parlance.

German. He also took to studying the art of handling and even restoring ancient manuscripts. He did not have much of a social life since all of his time was devoted to studying. He was a nerd, and proud of it.

His greatest undertaking came in the late 1990s when he proposed to digitize the entire contents of The Vatican's archives and library. It was a massive undertaking, for there are millions upon millions of pages of documents and manuscripts, in addition to illustrations and paintings that were to be committed to digital storage. Although everything would eventually be digitized and available to scholars and researchers in ways that have never been before, there were some pieces that would not be available for viewing. In fact, there were very few people in the history of the Catholic Church that has ever laid eyes on some of the contents of the archive.

It was only he, and members of his small team, that were allowed to see what many others had not. His team was required to not only sign non-disclosure agreements, but also take a sworn pledge to never, ever expose to anyone the contents of specific pieces. In a little over fifteen year's time, the entire contents of the archive had been thoroughly digitized; millions of pages of information, and Youssef has laid eyes on every last one of them. He is the only living man that has. He never spoke about any of it to anyone. Until now.

When Youssef saw the slave ships on television and heard the descriptions of the Africans as translated by Dr. Maximilian Oroko, it sent a chill up and down his spine that shook him to his core. What Dr. Oroko described, the white light and the "storm" that the Africans spoke of, struck him with a feeling of déjà vu. He had seen these things before.

There are certain things in Youssef's research, in the eleven years since he completed the digitization process, which had etched an impression in his mind. He kept pages upon pages of notes that he committed to a brown leather-bound journal; his private catalog and reference guide to the most interesting bits in the archive. Upon seeing the events involving the African Refugees in America, he remembers discovering several pieces that he believed were connected. It was this event, in fact, that gave him the clarity of context. The things that he had seen in those pieces finally made sense.

Since Professor Healey was the leader of the team dealing with the Africans, he was the next-best choice. Youssef was a little disappointed about not being able to share his findings with Dr. Oroko himself. From the media clips, he seemed to be such a sincere, intelligent and thoughtful man—someone who would have appreciated these pieces. Instead, he gets to share his findings with the guy who was crying like a baby on his knees in front of the entire world. He doesn't know why he finds that clip so funny; it has over 30 million views, and he feels he's contributed to at least half of them.

Youssef meets Joseph at the security desk in the main hall of the Vatican Library. As he approaches Joseph, he keeps thinking about that damn clip; Joseph blubbering through a stream of tears. But as soon as he looks the man in the eyes and shakes his hand, that clip isn't so funny anymore.

"It's good to meet you, Professor Healey," Youssef says.

"Nice to meet you face-to-face," smiles Joseph. "I'm excited to be here." Youssef does not look the way Joseph pictured him. He looks stockier and older than he pictured, and the mellow, cheerful cherub-like demeanor was also unexpected.

"I'm excited to show you what we've got," Youssef says as he leads Joseph through the main hall to a doorway on the other side.

"I'm still a bit surprised to be here. I can't imagine what you could have to show me," Joseph says.

"Well," says Youssef, "prepare to be more surprised..."

As Youssef escorts Joseph to one of the study rooms, Joseph finds himself generally, and quietly underwhelmed. He was expecting something a bit more ornate. Instead, it looks a lot like the study section at his high school library. It's not garish or overdone. It's all very practical and lived-in.

"There are a lot of rumors and legends about this place," says Joseph.

"I'm sure," smirks Youssef. "If you have any questions, ask away. I can't promise I'll answer everything, though."

"I did a little bit of research," says Joseph, "but I'd like to hear it from you. What exactly is stored here?"

"We have historical documents, records, artifacts, illustrations, sketches, paintings, and manuscripts dating back to the late 8th and 9th Centuries—we have a couple of pieces going back to the 2nd and 3rd. Over 50 miles of storage houses the entire collection. Correspondence between Pope Pius IX and Abraham Lincoln, The Doctrine of the Immaculate Conception…"

"The Ark of the Covenant?" asks Joseph.

"Sorry," Youssef giggles. "No Holy Grail either. No hidden pornography stash. None of that stuff."

"No space aliens," adds Joseph.

Youssef doesn't say anything, just smiles and continues walking. "Like I said before, I'm excited to show you what we've got."

They enter one of the study rooms, where Youssef has set up a terminal with everything they need. Joseph sits down and feels an incredible wave of anxiousness. The lump in his throat feels as if his heart is drowning and trying to come up for air through his mouth.

Youssef sits down next to Joseph and touches an icon on the screen, calling up the first image.

"Here we go," Youssef says. "I found this painting years ago, locked away in a crate with a few others. You're the first person outside of myself and the team to lay eyes on this painting in over three hundred years. This is 18th century, painted by a well-known artist of the era named Giovanni Battista Tiepolo. He painted many religious scenes, most known for his 'Death of Hyacinth.'"

"It looks like a religious painting," says Joseph. He allows his eyes to move freely over the image to take it all in. It's a painting of a slave port, with several docked ships. In the foreground, there are chained Africans being led by leather leashes by Caucasian slavers. They are all looking at something in the background. There are smiles on some of the Africans faces, and there are looks of fear on the Caucasians. In the sky, there is a bright white and light blue burst of light, and a massive Nubian army emerging. There appear to be thousands of African warriors, some on foot, some mounted on horses, and others on armor-bearing elephants and rhinos, charging towards the shore. Over their heads, hovering in the sky, there are three flying saucers.

"Are you shitting me?" says Joseph, immediately covering his mouth. "Excuse my language, I'm sorry."

"Not a problem," says Youssef. "I said the same thing when I heard about Dr. Oroko's translations."

James gestures over the screen to enlarge the image of the white light, the army, and the flying saucers. "This is over three hundred years old?" asks Joseph in disbelief. "I can't believe this is real."

"This isn't the only one," says Youssef, clicking on another icon. "This, believe it or not, is a Rembrandt."

This painting is very similar to the first. An image of a slave port, with dozens of cargo ships in the scene. On the shore, there are white men loading ships with barrels and crates, and Africans in bondage. All are looking out to the ocean to witness one lone ship being engulfed by a great white light. The light is emitted from around a massive flying disc. The disc has a flat top with a short-skirted rim, and what looks like little black spikes coming out from the bottom.

"This is a Rembrandt?" asks Joseph. "What makes you so sure this is a Rembrandt."

"Look at how he uses light and shadow, the poses and faces of the subjects- it's trademark Rembrandt,"

Youssef pitches. "That, and he wrote an inscription on the back," pressing another icon. Popping up in a smaller window, a detail of the back of the canvas. A message written in Italian was inked on the wooden frame.

Youssef leans in to read it. "It says… '*A story told to me by a man whose father told him. From the Bight of Benin, a ship holding a cargo of Negroes bound for the New World, swallowed by the light of a flying metal beast.*' This was from his private collection, donated to The Holy See by his family about two hundred years ago."

Joseph is nearly catatonic.

"I told you," smiles Youssef.

"So…" Joseph stammers, "aliens did this? Those people were brought through time by aliens?"

"That would explain the flying saucers," Youssef shrugs. "How about this army down here in the Tiepolo painting? This African army down here. They're not aliens."

Joseph's mind is spinning, but his inner skeptic is pumping the brakes on this information. "These are all just stories that they heard about- they didn't see any of these things happen. Rembrandt painted a lot of religious scenes, and he wasn't around for any of those things. Could someone have actually seen these paintings and got inspiration to make this happen in real life?"

"That would make this a little on-the-nose, wouldn't it?" shrugs Youssef. "These paintings are older than anyone living today and were locked away in storage for hundreds of years. I mean it—you're the only living person outside of this building that has ever seen this."

"So what…are you suggesting that aliens abducted these Africans from another time, and dropped them hundreds of years in the future off the coast of New York and New Jersey either by accident or…for what possible purpose?" Joseph rubs his eyes hard. "This is…fucking insane! Sorry."

"I grew up in South Jersey," Youssef smiles. "Don't mistake it, I'm not suggesting anything. I just believe that there's either coincidence, or there's a connection. This smells like a connection to me."

"This explains the non-disclosure agreement you had me sign before I came out here."

"We have to be very protective of the materials stored here. Over two thousand years of world history is entrusted to us. Much of what you'd find here is pedestrian, maybe not that interesting. There are other things that happen to be…disruptive. Just that people couldn't handle it."

"It's a lot to handle," Joseph sighs. "To be honest, I don't know who would even be receptive to this. You know how people are- they want the truth, you tell them the truth, then they think you're lying."

Youssef laughs. "You know, I think sometimes…maybe humankind was raised the wrong way, you know what I mean? We don't take care of each other enough. We certainly don't take care of the planet. We're getting dumber as a whole. It's easier to take advantage of dumb people, right? So few of our societies are mature enough to absorb real truth."

"America has had that problem for a long time," Joseph says shaking his head slowly. "The wealthy keep them desperate and stupid."

"America," Youseef sighs. "You know, I haven't been stateside since 2017."

"That's a long time ago."

"It's not the same country I grew up in. And who wants to expose their children to anger and ignorance on that scale. It's been depressing watching my homeland come apart, you know?"

"Being there hasn't been any better. It's just frustrating. Centuries and centuries of the same garbage and it just won't stop. It doesn't seem like anything will stop it."

"Only time will tell. You know, America was made to adapt and evolve, but it's never a painless process. Sometimes, it takes a war to cleanse our way to a better future. Our country was divided by war before, and it looks to me as if it's headed for another."

19

January 18th, 2648
1:21 pm
Nueva New York

"This is Floor 444," announces the voice from the speaker.

The elevator slows to a stop and drifts horizontally to the right, coasting along the face of the building. Maximilian continues to be mesmerized by the futuristic scene as it plays out in front of him. The flying saucer he watched detach itself from the building had floated away so weightlessly that it hardly seems real. Nothing about anything that he has seen since he first stepped into that portal back at his apartment has been believable. Even though he has only been gone for about thirty-five minutes, it feels like days or even weeks have gone by.

"Now I just have to find a way back home," he blurts out loud.

Suddenly, his vision blurs momentarily. He rubs his eyes and shakes his head, then looks to his left.

"Shit!" he says as he spots the stream he just passed through. It's bending through into the wall of the building. And the elevator is moving further away from it.

Maximilian quickly turns to the control panel.

"How do you stop? Stop!"

The elevator slows. "Next stop, Floor 444, Section 12."

The elevator eases into a full stop, and the elevator door opens.

"Floor 444, Section 12. Have a great day!" says the voice from the speaker.

The hallway reminds Maximilian of something that he's seen in a spaceship from a science fiction movie. The walls are pale white. The floor is light gray. The ceiling looks as if it is made up of square light panels, which spread flat light all around. About 40 feet ahead, there is an intersection.

He steps forward, walking slowly. The squeaking of his shoes, still wet from his water-drenched pass through that flooded hotel, overpowers the sound of his footsteps on the smooth, plastic-like floor. He reaches the intersection, looking left then right. Everything is identical on either side; white walls, gray ceilings. This time, there are doors. Maximilian takes a right, towards the direction of the stream.

The doors are the same gray as the floor and recessed into the walls. Next to each door is a digital screen displaying some branding for each location. One of the displays shows an animation of a bird flying over a mountain, which then freezes and forms a graphic version of the image, with the name "Systech" appearing at the bottom. Another display simply reads "Bripann Inc." with white letters on a blue background. Another shows a dome-shaped structure sitting on grey ground with a dark sky and star field behind it; the moon. The caption read "Altar Industries: Meeting Your Lunar Needs."

Maximilian stops in front of the next one, which is further down the hallway. It shows a hand enter the frame, with a pointed finger drawing an "O." As the "O" moves towards the viewer, the inside reveals space, and planets, and spaceships flying past the screen, a flash to white, and ending with black type reads:

O

Oroko Industries

Maximilian feels a swelling in his chest. "What the hell?"

He reaches out and touches the screen, which opens the door next to it. He slowly steps inside.

The reception area is slick and luxurious, with furniture that looks familiar but is completely alien in design to Maximilian. On the right side, a very cute, well-dressed woman sits behind a glass-topped desk that levitates in front of her. The woman casually gestures over the holographic images in front of her while talking into a tiny headset and mouthpiece that hovers in front of her full, red-glossed lips.

"I already told him I wasn't interested," she says. "It's more trouble than it's worth. I mean yeah, he's rich…yeah, okay, he's wealthy, so what!"

Without looking up, she holds up her finger to Maximilian; the universal sign for 'I'll be right with you.' She continues to gesture at the hologram, then turns to a super thin display next to her. She touches a few things on the screen then swipes her hand to move whatever was on the screen into the hologram.

"Not that he's not cute, either," she continues. "He's cute! But I mean, the profiles just didn't match. You have to pay attention to profiles. Okay listen, I've gotta jet. Chat later."

She looks up at Maximilian and says, "Can I help yo…" she freezes, staring at him as if he has twelve heads.

"Are you okay?" asks Maximilian, not sure what she is reacting to.

She moves her mouth slightly but is unable to speak. At that moment, two more people in mid conversation enter the reception area. As soon as they see Maximilian they stop cold, staring at him.

He wonders if maybe it's his clothes they're responding to. They are wearing very different clothing than he is used to seeing, and he's sure that comparatively speaking he may look as if he stole his clothes from a museum exhibit.

"I am sorry, I do not know if any of you can help me," he says. "I am looking for someone."

At that moment, another person enters the room.

"You!" says Maximilian.

It's the time traveler, finally! This time, he is not wearing the jumpsuit. He's wearing the same sort of unrecognizable fashion that everyone else is.

He looks at Maximilian and smiles warmly.

"You tried to leave me at the police station, and I followed you", barks Maximilian. "I went through those…wormholes or whatever they are, and followed the streams- some voice said 'follow the stream, ' and I did, and ended up here! What the hell is this place? And who the hell are you? And why is my name on the door of this place?"

"It's my name, too," the time traveler says. "It's the name I got from you."

The time traveler points past Maximilian. He turns around and looks at the wall behind him. It's a large painting of an older man, possibly in his 80s, standing in front of a wall of books. At first, Maximilian doesn't know why he has been directed to look at a painting of some old guy until he realizes that the old guy in the painting is him.

"Welcome to the 27th Century, Maximilian Oroko."

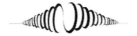

Davis Oroko is 38 years old. He is the great-great-great-great-great-great-grandson of Maximilian Oroko, who is also one of his most inspiring role models.

Davis has been anticipating this day for a long time. Ever since he began his first experiments in time travel, his one goal was to arrange some way to meet his 6th Grandfather—the man that would one day author a great manifesto that would change the course of the world forever. However, due to a series of unforeseen incidents and missteps, the meeting he always dreamed of was awkwardly realized.

Davis' father, Pierre Oroko, used to tell him stories of the first teleportation rings built in the late 2570s. His grandfather, Bellame Oroko, developed the world's first teleportation technology in 2561. He risked the entire family fortune on the equipment and a workforce, devoting thousands of research and experimentation hours into what Davis was eventually able to convert into his time travel technology.

It took fifteen years and hundreds of billions of dollars for a crew of four hundred men to set out to construct the first teleportation ring in space; an accomplishment that would make the Oroko Family one of the wealthiest in the solar system.

It was built 50 miles from the Earth's orbit. Massive metallic rings, at least half mile wide in diameter, built big enough to accommodate the massive star freighters that were accustomed to making two-and-a-half-year-long trips to Mars. With the rings, that trip's time would be reduced to mere seconds. The plan was to build the first ring, load the components to the second ring into a star freighter, and pilot the freighter through the ring to other side.

Pierre was fifteen years old when he accompanied his father on that first trip. Davis remembers that his father would tell him about how scared they all were. Everyone, that is, but his grandfather. "There wasn't a dry pair of pants on that ship!" he would always say. "But your grandfather, he just knew it would work. And it did!"

It is said that Davis takes after Bellame's mastery and obsession with science and technology. He is known to have said the same words as his grandfather when asked to explain how he got to be as good as he is: "It speaks to me."

At 19, Davis started experimenting with shrinking the teleportation technology, making it more portable. His plan was to be able to teleport back and forth without the use of rings.

He began his experiments with an orange, throwing it into a miniature portal, which would emerge from the other portal set up in the adjacent room. But one day, there was a power surge, and the orange disappeared. Three weeks later, while sitting in his office, the orange appeared out of thin air, still in flight, and hit the wall. At the time, Davis was not considering the possibilities of time travel at all. Even in the 27th Century, the very notion seemed like a long shot, at best. But this startling revelation proved to be the greatest lead he ever imagined. Davis immediately combed through the programming logs and upon discovering the data, he found that the power surge inadvertently produced a time-based wormhole.

"...and nearly ten years later, here we are," Davis says.

"I had to take several wormholes to get here. Why is that?"

"Yes, the layovers," Davis begins. "When I first started mapping World/Time, it was very difficult to find a direct line to a specific point. The problem is that the universe is always expanding; everything is in constant motion. The Earth is not in the same place it was a year ago, a month ago, an hour ago, a second ago- constant motion. It took us three years to write the code to track the movement of the universe and find the best locations for worm holes. You have no idea how many probes I sent out that came back frozen, banged up, wet, you name it. Lots of trial and error, as you could imagine."

"You lost me at World/Time," says Maximilian, thoroughly perplexed.

Davis laughs. "Well, World/Time means exactly what it says. 'World,' meaning any number of the given dimensions or universes in existence. And time meaning...well, time. It's a unit of measurement that I use to label locations."

"I see," says Maximilian. "Your method aside, because I could never in a million years understand the science behind what it is that you are doing, I must ask why you are doing this? What are you trying to do with the slave ships?"

"In the simplest terms, I am righting the wrongs of our history," says Davis.

"What does that mean?" Maximilian asks.

"To be honest, I was never really interested in history. I just figured that those were times long gone and have no significance to me or the world around me. So much of what happened in the past is just mistakes and malicious behavior, and one fuck-up after another. It bored me. But then I learned about the Middle Passage."

"Ah," says Maximilian, nodding. "That will do it."

"Whenever I take an interest in something, I devour whatever I can find. What I was finding was frustrating me. It's like our people...we lost our way. Africa is the Cradle of Civilization. Mathematics, science, architecture, metallurgy, language, all of it was born in Africa. Dynasties thrived for millennium after millennium. And then, within the last couple of thousand years, it was all taken away. Taken away, given away, there are many ways that we forfeited the power of our land, our intellect, our bodies and our souls. To put it lightly, we fucked up."

"That is an interesting interpretation," says Maximilian.

Davis walks to a bookshelf on the other side of the room. Maximilian had not even noticed it there, being so distracted by everything else. It's kind of odd to him to see something that appeared to be so antique in a room full of futuristic technology. He watches Davis take a book from the shelf, one of a row of duplicates, and bring it to him. As Maximilian takes the book, he immediately sees his name, printed in a slender blue serif font underneath the title, larger in point size, and reads "The Maximilian Emancipation."

"Six years from your present, you release this book," begins Davis. "This book, your book, will become the foundation for improving race relations not only in America but internationally as well."

Maximilian looks at Davis as if he's said something in German.

"It's true," Davis continues. "I studied this book in school—we all did. Generations of children do. It changes everything. Sure, by the time that I had read it, the world I was living in was nothing like the world you lived in or the world that came before you. Our ancestors, our people, suffered so greatly, and for what? Greed, religion, disease, Europeanism. These things destroyed us as a people, and stunted our growth by thousands of years. I find that to be unacceptable. But that was our history. It was our past. And for most of my life, I was angry about it. Then I discovered time travel.

"You see, now these things that you've written about don't have to be. Can you imagine a world like that? A world where we are not victims? Where we are allowed to thrive and evolve the way we should have been able to—before European colonialism. It's a world that should have been, and now it is."

"You're trying to change the past," says Max. "You want to alter history?"

"Not alter history," says Davis. "Create it. Let me show you."

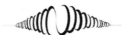

Down a flight of stairs, in a room directly below Davis' office, sits the machine. It's not the image that Maximilian has in his mind when he thinks of a "time machine." It doesn't look as smooth or as sleek as the other technology in the room. It has that made-in-the-garage look to it, with exposed wires and cables snaking to the machine from the floor and around the edges.

The machine itself consists of a large cylinder sitting on its side, about 10 feet long by 7 feet high. At the mouth of the cylinder sits a multi-layered circular platform that looks like a vinyl record turntable. At the rim of the platform is a handrail with what looks like a touchscreen control panel.

"She's beautiful, isn't she?" says Davis, smiling. He steps behind a glass-topped counter and places his HOLOCOM[12] on the surface. The holographic display pops up over the counter.

"I can control the machine from here," Davis begins. "As I was saying earlier, we were able to map out a series of wormholes, making tunnels or paths to different World/Times."

Gesturing over the image, he brings up a world/time map. It's a decahedron with labyrinthine curves and lines swirling and winding in, out and around each other, like a star map with lines connecting the white dots. Another gesture zooms in on the map, which opens up the cluster into more defined paths. With his palms up, and twisting his wrists, he rotates the map allowing for three dimensional viewing that provides a more thorough examination.

"This is just a sampling of what's out there. There are still many undiscovered, uncharted portals that are yet to be calculated. It's been enough work to build this up. Here…"

Davis reaches out and touches an area of the map. Everything but one path disappears.

"This is the path leading to your apartment. This is what I took when we met over an hour ago."

He gestures to bring back the map, then selects another path.

---

[12] Portable holographic computing device.

"This is the path that you took to get here. See, you had to go back to the past, back to 1730, then you made the great leap to the year 2387, and finally here to 2648."

"Why did I have to go back to leap forward?" Maximilian asks.

"That's just the way it works right now," says Davis. "It's been difficult to find direct links, so sometimes it's been necessary to leap around. And now…"

Davis brings back the map and selects the next path.

"This is one of the few direct links that I have, including the one that took us from your apartment to New York City. This is where it all begins."

"Where what begins?"

"Africa's rebirth. This is where a new direction will steer the African continent towards the greatness it deserves for future millennia. I've seen it. I've seen what will result from the work being done here. And I tell you, Maximilian, it is the most glorious thing I have ever seen. You think all of this is impressive, this world outside this building…you have no idea what lies in store for our people. We finally live up the greatness that was taken away from us!"

Maximilian stares at the hologram of what just looks to him like a squiggly light blue line, but turns out to represent more than his mind can conceive.

"You cannot do this," he says. "You cannot alter history like this. You should not."

"Nothing is changing in your World/Time Max," says Davis. "That's what World/Time means. You can't think about this in terms of what you've seen in 21st Century movies and books. Whatever I've changed in the past…it splits from that point into another path. In other words, once a change is made, that change exists in its own world, in its own time."

"What are you saying? You are creating a parallel universe?"

"Exactly! That's exactly what this is! Everything that I'm doing in the past, your present will never know!"

"But what about the slave ships?" Maximilian asks.

"That is your World/Time. And there is a World/Time right next to yours where those ships never appeared."

"So you did alter the timeline!"

"I didn't alter anything! If we had never met, you wouldn't have known anything about this. It doesn't affect anything that has been done to you, or will be done."

"I have been having dreams," Maximilian says. He doesn't understand why he feels compelled to discuss his dreams at this moment.

"They are," he continues, "About this man who lives somewhere in Africa, but not the Africa that I know or remember. He is a history teacher; he teaches eight-year-olds and teenagers. He has a wife named Nyah, and she's…"

Maximilian trails off as he has been watching Davis' expression morph from passive interest to masked anxiety.

"Is his name Masomokali Kébé?" asks Davis.

Maximilian's chest explodes in a wave of shock that ripples through his body at lightning speed. After a few moments, he starts to breathe again, and can muster up: "How did you know that?"

Davis forces himself to internalize any physical response that he has to this news.

"How long have you been having these dreams?" Davis asks.

"Since the first day of the event. The day the ships appeared—the day you made the ships appear, I should say!"

"That must be why he's blacking out," says Davis as he clears the World/Time map, and opens up a new holographic window. Maximilian doesn't recognize what Davis is manipulating. It just looks like a lot of words and random pictograms, surrounded by animated charts and spreadsheets.

"What are you talking about?" asks Maximilian. "What is going on? And how the hell do you know him?"

"It's probably nothing," Davis lies. After rifling through the digital pages, he finds what he is looking for.

"Then what are you doing?" asks Maximilian. When Davis does not answer back, Maximilian steps to him and grabs Davis' arm, spinning him around to stand face to face.

"What the fuck is going on?" Maximilian demands. "How do you know that name? Why do these dreams seem so real? Are they real?"

"Yes, they are," says Davis. "He's your doppelganger. He's you, but…from a different World/Time."

"That you created," Maximilian growls through a clenched jaw. "Oh, that is just great! So much for your theory of nothing going wrong! Why am I experiencing what he is experiencing? Because it should not be happening!"

"Right now they are just dreams," Davis says. "It shouldn't be any more than that. Who's to say that all dreams are merely windows into the consciousness of others?"

"What you are doing is dangerous and wrong! You are messing around with things that you do not completely understand. You are smart and clever enough to build this thing, but you have not thought through the ramifications."

Davis puts his hand on Maximilian's shoulder. "Look, granddad--"

"Do not call me that!" says Maximilian.

"You've been through a lot of the last hour," says Davis. "It's a lot to take in. You're just over-tired. Why don't I just take you home, and we can talk about this later. Okay?"

Maximilian perks up when he hears the word "home." Yes, that's what he wants right now; his living room, his chair, his bed! He is struck with such a strong homesick vibe that he finds himself agreeing with Davis.

"You are right. I am very tired," says Maximilian. "Yes, take me home. Take me home, and then we can discuss this further. I have many more questions."

"I understand," says Davis, as he gestures over the holographic interface, and brings up a new view. After making a few selections, Maximilian is startled by the sound of the time machine powering up. Davis makes a few more selections and a few more gestures. A sound like the crackling of electricity fills the room. The machine's cylinder spins, and levitates from the ground. As it starts to vibrate, a pinpoint of light appears over the platform in front of the machine's cylinder. A sound, as if a match has been struck, precedes a bright burst of light that grows into a vortex.

"Your apartment is on the other side," says Davis. "It's ready when you are."

"That's it?" asks Maximilian. "No layovers, just straight home?"

"Straight home," says Davis.

Maximilian steps up to the vortex. He stares into the light blue swirling lights, moving slowly like a newly stirred soup. He almost can't believe it. This must have been how Dorothy from The Wizard of Oz felt when she found out about clicking her heels.

"Go ahead," says Davis. "I'll see you there soon."

Maximilian nods to Davis, then jumps into the vortex.

20

The time portal opens up, and Maximilian lands on his feet. The first thing he notices is that his feet feel as if they have hit earth, not carpet. Not only earth but grass. Long, golden grass. A field of it extends out in all directions. About 1,000 feet directly in front of him is a jungle wall thick trees.

"What the hell?" he moans. "You asshole. You fucking asshole!" His shouting is absorbed by the great sweep of wind that blows right through him, whipping his clothes, and snapping the grass.

Maximilian searches the air frantically for a stream to follow to get him out of here. He squints his eyes, cranes his neck, cocks his head, trying to see something, but he can find nothing.

He told me too much, that is why I am here, he thinks to himself. *He banished me here, somewhere, because he told me too much.*

Maximilian looks in every direction, taking in everything he sees.

It feels like home, though. It feels like Africa. Where and when, I do not know? Wait. Do I see people?

Maximilian watches five men emerge from the wall of trees. They spot him. One of them points at him. The five move towards him. Maximilian moves towards them. *Should I be moving towards them? Shouldn't I be running away?*

As soon as the men are close enough, Maximilian assumes he is in the past. The men are wearing copper armor plates covering their chest, arms, and shins. Each one is also holding a long, black spear. The crafting is reminiscent of warriors of the Krou people, but he isn't sure.

"*Hello!*" Maximilian yells out in Krou, waving his hand. One of the men waves back. Now less than 50 feet away, he can see their faces. Even though their armor looks to be Krou, their facial features do not. The closer these men get, the more they look as if they are from completely different tribes. He stops in his tracks. The men continue towards him.

"*Do you understand me?*" he calls out, again in Krou. By this point, they are less than 10 feet away. They do not respond. They slow their pace as they approach, coming to a halt face to face with Maximilian.

"Are you Maximilian Oroko?" one of the men asks in perfect English.

Maximilian nods slowly.

"We have been expecting you," the man says.

Maximilian does not mask his confusion. "Where are we? Who are you?"

"We are not to answer any questions," the man says. "We are only to escort you back to the village."

The man reaches up to his ear and taps a communication device.

"We found him," he says.

March 21st, 1223 B.C.
11:11 am
Bahiya, in the Continent of Africa

Maximilian walks down the cobblestone path, which turns into an asphalt road that leads into modern village. Buildings and structures made of wood, stone, and concrete are laid out among the walkways and roads of a bustling mini-metropolis.

The streets are busy with African men, women, and children going about their business—shopping, working, playing, living. The streets are clean. The foliage is neatly manicured. The shops, restaurants, and homes are impeccably designed and furnished. Maximilian cannot pinpoint any one style or design. There are bits and pieces of many African cultures, from the clothing to the tools, the smells of the food, and the music. It's like a melting pot of many African tribes. This is a village unlike anything Maximilian has ever seen before.

He notices more than a few looks and stares from the people that he sees. The looks are more of a curious nature than any fear or animosity.

"This way," the leader says, pointing to a large building to their right. Maximilian assumes he is the leader because he is the only one that has said anything at all. The building he points out looks different from the others, like a police station or a prison of some sort. Whatever it is, it does not look as warm and friendly as the other structures.

Maximilian is led through a reception area and down a hall to a room at the end.

"You may go in," the leader says.

He opens the door and is greeted by the back of a man who is looking down at the computer display embedded in the surface of his desk. When the man turns around, Maximilian does not recognize him at first. But the man recognizes him.

"Stooge!" says Onorede, in English. "We have been waiting for you for many years!"

His unofficial nickname triggers Maximilian's memory. Otherwise, he does not recognize Onorede at first. The man he is looking at now is at least 20 years older than the young man he saw only a few weeks ago.

"How...what the hell are you doing here?" Maximilian blurts out.

Onorede laughs. "This is my home, Dr. Oroko. For all of us, this is our home. We have come a long way since you last saw us."

Maximilian shakes his head. "What is this place? Where are we?"

"Bahiya. That is the name of our village. This is a village that we built with our own hands over many, many years. We are still building, in fact. The city is growing more and more each year. What do you think so far?"

It's all starting to make sense for Maximilian at this point. Davis must have sent him here to show him what he was doing—to illustrate his master plan. Unfortunately, seeing these things in person is not changing his mind.

"Where is Davis?" he asks.

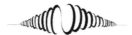

A 68-year-old Davis Oroko stands at the precipice of a large field that spreads out for several acres in front of a mountain range. Embedded in the mountain is a massive steel mill that overlooks the mighty and productive city he created. Laid out in the field in an assembly-line arrangement are huge saucer-shaped structures in various states of completion.

Usually, there would be dozens of people working in the field and the factory. But today there are no people working; it's a day of rest. For everyone but Davis, that is. Today has been a full day for him. When he hears the fuel-cell powered all-terrain vehicle pulling up behind him, he sighs deeply and smiles; it's almost over.

He turns around with great anticipation. And there he is; Maximilian Oroko, who climbs out of the vehicle ahead of Onorede.

"What the fuck, Davis! Davis?" The closer Maximilian gets to Davis, the more his face seems to change; as if Davis aged 30 years as he approaches him.

"What the hell is going on?" Maximilian demands. "Are we in the future, or in the past?"

"We're in the past," says Davis, "But you're seeing a future me. The me you saw an hour ago was me from 30 years ago. However, we are currently in the calendar year 1223 BC the dawn of a new age in African history; our New Destiny."

"1223 BC?" asks Maximilian. "Why?"

"A new start," says Davis. "A fair start, without interference. An opportunity for our people to be who they are."

"I did not know we were this far away from ourselves," quips Maximilian.

This makes Davis smile. "Don't get me wrong- I'm a product of that history as much as you and these people are. This isn't for us- this is for the future of our people. A chance to live beyond the glory that led us for thousands of years in our World/Time. This, cosmically speaking, is a second chance."

Davis pats Maximilian's shoulder, directing him to the field in front of the mountain. "Those are flying machines, Max. Built with materials harvested here." He watches his 6th grandfather's face contort as if he has been punched in the gut.

"You are building flying saucers in the year 1223 BC?"

"I didn't want to go back too far," Davis shrugs, "but I figured a couple of thousand years would work. That's assuming we stick with the Gregorian calendar. I'm considering switching to the Akan calendar, but that's another story. Anyway, it's the saucer-shape itself that's more practical to apply the time travel technology to; the cylindrical shape. It wasn't easy, though— it took over eight years to build the first one. These I'll have done in about five. And that's when the real work begins."

"Flying time machines," says Maximilian. "That is how you got the slave ships out."

"That's right." Davis points towards the village. "To

them, that was 20 years ago. For you, it was what…three weeks ago?"

"I…I don't know what to think about this," Maximilian says. "This is all very overwhelming. It's too much, I…"

Davis watches as his flabbergasted 6th grandfather looks out at the landscape in front of them.

"I'm sorry, Max," says Davis. "I'm sorry that I brought you here this way. I thought this would be the only way for me to show you what I was doing, and what I was thinking. I read those three books of yours every summer, every year. You talk about how exceptional we are, as a people. You talk about what strengthens us, and what poisons us…it made me think about what we could have done differently."

"Nothing," Maximlian says. We missed the glory of our people. We missed it by about 5 thousand years! And we…we are the fire that has risen from the ashes of our ancestors. We have an obligation to burn brighter that we ever had before."

Davis smiles. "Yes! That is exactly what I am doing here!"

"Are you?" Maximilian asks. "You're right—we got a raw deal. No matter how we got there, stolen or rejected, it's true—those who inherited those circumstances have suffered. I always had the notion that it was up to us to pick ourselves up and rise again. That's what I wanted from us. But I was always disappointed. I grew up with people that constantly disappointed me."

"People do that sometimes, don't they?" smirks Davis. "I have news for you; not much has changed in the 25th Century. People still let you down—especially the way things are these days. Do you know that there are 4 billion people living in Nueva New York? Nearly 65% of them are poor. That was after the Appalachian Migration. These days most people don't think about race the way they did in the 21st. When the Multination Coalition took on America's debts, that was the end of the empire. All of the suffering and anguish that we had to bear as a people was all for what? A couple of thousand years of so-called leadership. If you ask me, it wasn't worth it.

"The American Experiment was a failure," Davis continues. "It couldn't stand under the weight of using the white supremacy myth as an excuse to wield and maintain power. The only way that America can work is if all people have an equal opportunity. That was never going to happen with a mythical ethnonationalist mentality. There were Caucasians that would rather see the country burn than share it with others. That's how we are where we are today.

Davis shakes his head. "Talk about a waste of time and energy, for ego, narcissism, pride…what's to be proud of? Because their skin is melanin-deficient? It makes no sense. It makes no sense for our people to suffer under such nonsense. Now, we can do something about it."

"Not everyone," says Maximilian, shaking his head. "Not everyone can do something about it. You've saved a relative few, it's true. But why them? Why these people?"

"These people were going to die," says Davis. "That's why I picked doomed slave ships. The Henrietta-Marie, the Trouvadore, the Coureur, the Desire, the Leusden, the Hannibal, the Fredensborg. They were doomed, fated to horrible deaths, so they were of no longer of any use to our World/Time. Whether they died or were removed by some other means, they were not meant to be there. That's why I brought them here. It's sad to say, but these are people that our world did not miss. So to take them and bring them here didn't disrupt a thing."

"I remember many of them believed that they were in the afterlife," says Maximilian. "It's almost true. "

Davis grins and nods. "You get it. You know, Max…there's something that you wrote, and I don't…I don't know if I should say anything, but you talked about this philosophy of looking within to live with all."

"Looking within to live with all?" Maximilian considers. "That does not sound like me."

Davis laughs. "You say that we can't love others until we love ourselves. It's true with all relationships, right? You said that it takes more effort to love someone than to hate them. It's easy to hate, it's hard to love. You talked about the kids that used to pick on you in school…and how you felt that you finally understood why they behaved the way they did; they were the product of a society that barely considers their worth. We had always been taught that we had no culture, and we foolishly believed that."

Maximilian nods. "That is correct. That is true. Ever since those slave ships arrived, I have been thinking of these things. Even before Joseph called me, I was thinking about it. There was this one time in the 8th grade. I asked Stephanie Tracey to the Winter Dance. She was really pretty- light brown skin, a curly and beautiful afro… I asked her to the dance, and she said 'Ew! I can't go out with you, you're too dark!' She said that right to my face. When I ran track in high school, they called me "National Geographic." Things like that, shit like that. And it is true- it made me so angry, even to this day. I said some terrible things to Joseph a few weeks ago. I told him that I owed nothing."

Davis smiles. "You talked about that in the book."

"What did I say?"

"You said 'Don't condemn when empathy can heal the confusion.' You refer to ignorance as 'confusion.' You also say 'when they're ready, they'll listen. If they're not, they're missin'.'"

Maximilian bursts out laughing. "I can say for certain that there is no way that I said or wrote anything like that!"

"Page 236, line thirty-two," Davis recites. He puts his hand on Maximilian's shoulder. "This is my life's work. I've seen your future, my past. Frankly, I'd rather spend my remaining 63½ years watching humankind evolve."

Maximilian is tired and too emotionally and physically drained to respond.

"Come on," Davis says, "Let's get you something to eat and drink. Then we'll get you home."

As Davis, Maximilian, and Onorede return to the village, they are greeted by a homecoming celebration.

"What is happening?" asks Maximilian.

"They are all very excited to see you again," says Onorede. "You are loved and admired by everyone here, Maximilian Oroko."

As soon as the vehicle parks, men, women, and children surround it. Maximilian looks out at hundreds of African faces, young and old, smiling and beaming with delight at him; the man that helped them and gave them comfort in their greatest time of confusion and despair. From the moment he climbs out of the vehicle, he is hugged and kissed. His hands are held and shaken. Voices in various tongues, including a surprising amount of English, thank him.

A swarm of grateful citizens guides him through their village, taking him on a tour of the place they now call home; Bahiya. They explain to Maximilian how when they were brought here, it was nothing but an empty prairie. But with Davis' guidance, and with their individual expertise, they were able to build up the entire village. Among them are teachers, carpenters, metallurgists, musicians, cooks, scientists, warriors, herbalists, gardeners, enough people to share their knowledge to form a productive and thriving society.

Maximilian marvels at how much growth and comfort has culminated into a society that is very prosperous and productive. He is amazed at how well the people that he had seen just two weeks ago, who had been traumatized and wrecked, had completely turned their lives around. He sees that these people are not only happy but thriving and at peace. *What a difference two decades makes.*

There is a large feast waiting. He had been wondering what smells so good, and his excitement builds as he is led to an outdoor dining area. It is a picnic-style arrangement, with beautiful place settings of flowers, printed cloth napkins, and large copper plates with glass cups. He cannot believe the wonderful food brought to the table: fish, meat, vegetables, fruit, and carafes of wine. For the first time since this journey through time began, Maximilian feels comfortable. He eats, he talks, he listens, he laughs. These are good people, healthy, strong, and delightful. He feels relieved.

After the meal, the group thins out. It's a work night, after all. Many have to get up early in the morning. This leaves a small core of about forty people, who all decide to start a music circle. They ask Maximilian to participate, and he agrees; he will agree to just about anything after a glass of wine, and seeing as how he's had three, he's more than agreeable.

Maximilian has always been jealous of musicians and regrets not having an interest in music at a younger age. He had this fantasy for years, of himself fronting a jazz quartet, playing piano or trumpet. He wanted to take lessons, but there is never enough time. So when they offer him an instrument, he admits to not being able to play. He is given what looks at first like a short wooden tube, with an opening on both ends. "It's a kazoo," he delightfully discovers. Surely, he could play kazoo!

The kazoo had a way of sounding a little like a horn section to Maximilian. He remembers seeing a group of street performers playing in unison, and it sounded like a small brass band. When they ask him to play something, only one song pops into his mind.

Maximilian performs his song in its entirety, clapping out the beat and doing his best to fill in for as many instruments as he could. They other musicians are very excited and want to learn this new song. He guides the others with their instruments. He plays a phrase, and they repeat it. And after about an hour, they play it very, very well. It is at this point, as they continued to play their newly-learned song, that the fatigue begins its assault. Davis sidles up next to Maximilian, patting him on the shoulder.

"Let's get you home," he says. Maximilian nods.

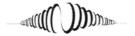

December 3rd, 1794
Morning
Mozambique, Africa

Yumna is kneeling over by the river, washing her clothes with a large wooden board. Her eight-month-old baby is sleeping in a sling on her side.

They come out of nowhere. Four men, African slavers, grab her. They hold her down and take her baby; she will never see him again. Her wrists are bound, her neck enclosed in a steel collar, fastened with a lock and connected to a leather leash. She is forced to walk.

It takes two days to get to the coast. Dozens of ships are docked there. Hundreds of people move around negotiating, loading ships, catching up with old friends and business associates. Barrels full of gunpowder and rum, sacks of spices, piles of pelts, queues of chained and shackled African men, women, and children.

Yumna is even more frightened than she was before. She pulls away. The leash yanks her. She pulls harder, trying to move the other way. The leash is yanked even harder. She screams. Her hair is grabbed. She stops. She is being scolded verbally, his face close to hers; her eyes are closed shut. He pulls her by the hair; she scurries along on the tips of her toes. They stop. She opens her eyes and sees a pale-faced man in front of her. He is looking at her and speaking a language she does not understand. She thinks of her baby. She wants to die.

Suddenly all the speaking stops. Like a ripple in a lake, everyone seems to stop what they are doing. There is a sound in the distance. A deep, thumping sound, hard and rhythmic. It is getting louder, slowly overtaking the din the noise at the dock.

Several curious men run in the direction of the thumping drumbeat, towards a rocky hill that leads to the shore. When they reach the top, they see something that is beyond the scope of anything they could ever imagine; they are frozen in shock and fear.

It's only 2,000 feet away. It looks like a massive ball of light as bright as the sun. A mass of people emerging from the light; hundreds of them, in military formation. Men and women, warriors, in full body armor, holding long, serrated spears. Symbolic banners wave on posts held at their flanks. They march full stride towards the coast.

The men from the coast are not standing on the hill for very long when their shock-induced malaise is interrupted by a blast of the sound from a chorus of horns. The sound takes the form of a procession of notes and chords that, to someone in the know, has a familiar melody. A melody that would not be heard for another three hundred years. A melody that was passed down to them, taught to their ancestors by a man from another World/Time, who spoke of a musical collective with a name that embodied the three elements of nature: Earth, Wind, and Fire. The opening fanfare of the song "In the Stone."

With a power and sound never heard before, a wave of horror spreads among the sailors, traders, slavers, and the enslaved on the coast. The men on the hill sprint back to coast, yelling things like "Run!" and "There's millions of them!" and "Get back to the ships!"

21

August 27th, 2041
10:12 am
West Chester, PA

Maximilian wakes up, in his bed, still dressed from the day before. He is a bit surprised, seeing as how he usually falls asleep in his chair in front of the television. He can't remember getting up in the middle of the night to get in the bed. He doesn't remember much about last night. He feels a bit groggy, as if he has slept for a year.

After a refreshing forty-minute shower, and brewing a pot of his favorite coffee, he sits in his favorite chair and begins to enjoy his day off. Before he can truly settle in, he has to do what he normally does on his days off; shut off his NAVI. It's his way to unplug from the world so that he can enjoy some time to himself fully and completely. No calls, no texts, no email, no video messages, no contact with anyone, unless it's an emergency. If it's an emergency, the people who need to reach him know how. Everyone else can go to hell. As he reaches for the NAVI sitting on the side table next to his chair, deactivates the telephone feature, and switches to television mode.

He doesn't remember watching last night's episode of a show that he never thought in a million years he would start watching. He would never admit it in certain company, but he has come to enjoy The Gerry Baines Exchange. Of course, being that Baines' reputation among intellectuals is that of a circus clown, Maximilian has found that Baines has grown on him a bit. He still does not agree with many of Baines' policy views, and he is certainly not interested in his religious slant, but he is still engaged.

"Play last night's Gerry Baines' Exchange," he says out loud

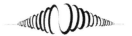

August 26th, 2041
9:02 pm
Furious Studios, New York City

"Ladies and Gentlemen," Gerry says to the camera, "I have really had to struggle with saying what I'm about to say to you right now. I don't want to sound fake, and I don't want to sound like I'm full of myself, or any of those things. But you know what? I can't think that way. I can't think that way because it does you all a disservice. God spoke to me again. And no, this time it wasn't in my kitchen. This time, well, this time it happened twenty minutes ago, in this studio, in my office."

Gerry's producer Tom, sitting in a chair staring at monitor holding a styrofoam container of Chinese food, swallows whatever he had in his mouth hard.

"Jesus fucking Christ," he says, "Not this shit again..."

He and Gerry had this conversation three days ago, about his so-called proclamations about speaking to God. Tom thinks that Gerry got lucky in these recent weeks with this religious narrative. It's true that it helped Gerry secure more ratings than either of them had ever seen, but he thinks Gerry may be taking things a bit too far. He thinks Gerry might be letting this stuff go to his head. *No,* Tom thought, *he's not that crazy—he would never, ever go any further than this*. And yet, here he is listening to this.

Gerry Baines steps to the camera, right hand over his heart, and left hand held up.

"I swear to you She did. And this time, everyone…" says Gerry, as he chokes up. "This time She told me something that outright scared me. It scares me because it involves me," he says, looking up into the air. "I don't know how to say these things without sounding like a crazy person, or some arrogant fool! So many of us are called on by God, and so many of us ignore the call because we're afraid of how it may make us look or sound to others. It's not always the crazy homeless guy on the street that can own communication with the divine! She talks to us, the regular people, too. And we're ashamed to say it. But I'm not ashamed anymore!

"I was in my office, preparing for the show, as I always do. I'm looking over my notes…and I hear this voice, just like before. The voice said…'Lead through me.'"

Gerry flinches, acting out the confusion of that moment. "That's what the voice said—it said 'lead through me.' I just sat there in silence for a moment, just letting those words, those three simple words, sink in. What could that possibly mean? Well, ladies and gentlemen…I think I know what it means."

Gerry lets out a big sigh. "I can't begin to tell you how much I appreciate the attention that you, the audience, the concerned American citizen, has given to my show. It lets me know that there are still large groups of us out there that are on the same page. We all have a common vision of what this country should be. We love liberty, we love freedom, we love moral values, the strength of our convictions, and a love of God, above all the pettiness and arrogance of the elites and the right wingers.

"Because of you, in the last few weeks, this show— the Gerry Baines Exchange—has become the most watched news commentary program in America. In just three weeks, more and more people have joined us here, united by our love of God, and values and the good will She has bestowed on America! And if you are uncomfortable with lies and corruption from our government, and the right wing stench it has left on our society…that is what has brought so many of you here, in numbers that continue to amaze us here at the Exchange.

"You see the news, you know what's going on. The number of so-called hate groups is on the rise. The NeoConfederates held a major multi-state protest against the proposed microchip implant initiative. They're upset because they say it unfairly targets them. No, it doesn't *unfairly* target anyone. If it targets anyone, it would be those committing criminal or terrorist behavior. Let's take a look- Jimmy, give us the first map."

On the screen behind Gerry, a map of the United States appears. There are red blotches on the map covering most of Oregon and Washington, along with Alabama, Texas, Florida, Mississippi, Tennessee, Wisconsin, West Virginia, Maryland, and New Jersey.

"These are the areas where people have been protesting. Now, can we add the next layer?"

A layer of white blotches appears, almost in the exact areas as the previous layer.

"These are areas that have seen high levels of criminal and terrorist activity. Next layer?"

The final layer of blue blotches appears, also occupying the same areas as the previous layers.

"And you guessed it. These are the areas that will be impacted the most by implanting. Yes, we need to monitor these areas. That is correct! So what, now we're supposed to feel sorry for the very people that are causing all of the problems in our country? We should have pity for these people? I see your video streams and media feeds, and I agree with you-- these anti-American insurgents need to be called out, sought out and jailed. They are terrorists, plain and simple.

"Ask the liberals- they'll want to protect their right to privacy. What? Are we giving terrorists privacy rights

now? These are the same people that will tell you that
prisons are not the answer. The death penalty is not the
answer. I wonder what question they're <u>really</u> asking if
the answers seem always to elude them.

"The liberals have always lied to us. It's the liberals,
non-believers and the fakers on the right fringe that are
shoving their beliefs down our throats! For example, they
refuse to acknowledge the hand of God in the African
Slave Event. Their racism and false political correctness
don't even want us to acknowledge the fact that those
men, women, and children were brought here to be
slaves, so much so that they will only call it 'The Event.'
What 'event' are you referring to? Oh...the 'African
Slave Event.' They don't want you thinking in terms of
slavery—they can't. Because, just like those enslaved
Africans that She brought here, and the millions of
Africans brought here during the slave era, the slave will
eventually try to get free.

"These are troubling times for us. Our nation is
falling apart. We are getting killed in the global markets.
Every year, more and more people lose their jobs to
China, Russia, and India. Many of our nation's once-
beautiful suburbs have become ghettos and slums.
Violent hate groups like the Neo-Nazi Confederates and
The Black Fist are running through our streets, recruiting
and inspiring the weak minded of us to become things
that are antithetical to what the founders have instilled in
all of us.

"The rich are...beyond rich. The Middle Class has
been gone for over a decade now. That leaves the rest. Do
you see what you have brought on us, President Lopez?
Do you see what liberalism has done to our nation? I
cannot stand here every night and just *report* on what is
going on here! I've got an obligation, as we all do...to do
something! God said 'lead through me,' and that's what I
intend to do. So tonight, I am announcing my candidacy
to become the next President of the United States of
America in 2044."

Tom rises from his chair so quickly that his food drops onto the floor. His mouth is open wide, showing the half-chewed food and saliva mush, as he shakes his head wildly at Gerry.

"You should see my producer's face right now!" Gerry says to the camera. "Don't worry, Tom—I still have another year before I can start campaigning! I won't be going anywhere until then. But it's true, ladies and gentlemen. After receiving such positive responses from all of you, and after getting the greatest endorsement of them all," Gerry says while pointing upwards. "I think it's time that we took America back.

"Coming up after the break, we'll talk more about this, and people are living much longer these days, so we're talking to Dr. Griscom about a new diet that we should all be on so that we can live even longer, he says. I wonder what that is—we'll be back after this…"

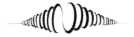

August 27th, 2041
3:23 pm
The White House, Washington DC

Secretary of State Lucy Fender sits behind her desk watching the thousands of protesters beyond the Great Lawn, behind the fence, beyond the barricade, and in front of the line of police officers dressed in riot gear. They have been protesting every single day for nearly two weeks now, from dusk 'til dawn, and there is no sign that they will stop anytime soon.

Lucy reaches into her desk drawer and pulls out her flask, but she doesn't get even get the chance to twist the lid off before her NAVI rings.

"Goddamn it," she says, answering the call. "Hello?"

"What are you doing?" says the deep voice on the other end.

"Trying to swallow our problems," Fender says.

"Did you do what I had asked you to do?" asks the voice.

"Yes, I did," she says, standing up from her desk and walking to the window. "It's not going to help, you know that right? We've got another two years before we can make this happen."

"As long as you do what you're told, you won't have to worry about that," the voice says.

"I hate this. I hate all of this. We ruined this country, you know. Hundreds of years of progress, and millions of people tossed away to appease the few." Fender shakes her head. "It's a goddamn shame."

"Are you lecturing me?" asks the voice.

Lucy closes her eyes and sighs deeply. "No, I'm not," she says. "I'm scared."

There is a long pause before the voice speaks again. "Circumstances have changed. Alterations are required. Your hard work has not gone unnoticed."

"Thank you," sighs Fender.

"There are other ways."

"I'm listening," she says.

"Soon."

Click.

January 13th, 2648
2:57 pm
Nueva New York

Davis Oroko just watched his 6th grandfather Maximilian Oroko enter the time portal, sending him back to the year 1223.

As soon as the portal closes, he manipulates the holographic interface, setting a course for two trips. The portal reopens. Davis grabs his HOLOCOM and two other smaller instruments. One of them is a quarter-sized black disk that he sticks onto the back of his head, over the stem near the cerebral cortex. The other is a homemade device, a black box the size of a bar of soap, with a small touch screen and two LED lights on the end. If activated, these two small pieces of equipment would land him in prison for ten years or more, no questions asked. Good thing he has no intention of activating them here. He steps into the portal…

…and steps out into an empty briefing room inside of a police station.

He looks at his HOLOCOM to double-check his location:

August 27th, 2041
2:53 pm
13th Precinct, New York

Just as he pockets the HOLOCOM, the room lights flicker momentarily. It's time.

Davis removes the soap-sized black box from his pocket. He taps the touch screen rhythmically, as if to the beat of a song, which is a haptic combination key to turn on the device. The red LED at the top lights up. He reaches behind his head and taps the black disk using the same rhythmic combination. The red LED flashes four times. He then holds his thumb down on the touchscreen. The green LED light flashes three times, then stays on; the red LED turns off. Davis keeps his thumb depressed on the screen. The longer he keeps it down, the more area he can cover.

To affect everyone on the floor, he needs to hold for about 45 seconds. He could cover about 2000 feet with this one device, but he only needs to target the few people who encountered Maximilian and his earlier self. After this, no one in reach of this device would have any memory of anything that occurred in the last two hours. Except for Davis, of course, who is wearing a signal blocker on the back of his head.

When 45 seconds has passed, he removes his hand from the touch screen. When the green light shuts off, he pockets the device. On his HOLOCOM, he calls up a map of the police precinct. A red dot marks his current location, and the red 'X' marks his destination; the interrogation room. Davis notes his path, pockets the HOLOCOM, and opens the door of the briefing room, entering the hallway.

As Davis turns a corner that leads to the interrogation room, he accidentally bumps into a woman also turning the corner.

"I'm so sorry, excuse me," she says, in a bit of a preoccupied daze.

"It's all right," says Davis. As she walks away, an aroma of fresh baked cinnamon buns follows her. Davis watches her for a moment and smiles.

He opens the door to the interrogation room and sees Maximilian's NAVI sitting on the table. He picks it up and surfs through the interface to find the incriminating video clip documenting the last time he was in this room.

"So archaic," he says.

He finally finds the file and deletes.

"Next stop," he says as he takes out his portable computer, and taps the screen, opening up a new portal. He steps inside…

August 13th, 2041
2:22 am
West Chester, PA

…and walks out into the living room of Maximilian's apartment, which is dark except for the multicolored glow of the television. He is asleep in the chair in front of the TV. On the table next to his chair is a bottle with about 3 ounces of rum left inside, a half-empty glass filled with watered down rum and coke, and his NAVI.

"Shit," Davis says quietly.

He checks his computer and sees that his calculations are off by three weeks. He is supposed to be here on the 28th of August, not the 13th. Precision has been a difficult hurdle for Davis to conquer. Relatively speaking, Davis' time travel method is still in its infancy. Fortunately for him, recovery and improvisation have been his saving grace.

"Hey…!"

Davis turns to see Maximilian's eyes open. He looks very drunk. Too drunk to do anything but sit there.

"You're dreaming again," says Davis.

"Who are you?" Maximilian drunkenly asks.

"I am not the issue," says Davis, as he summons up the sound of a match being struck, which opens up a time portal.

"She likes you, you know. You should ask her out."

"Who…?" asks Maximilian, as his eyes roll back into his head. He's out.

Davis smiles, and steps into the portal…

August 28th, 2041

3:18 am
West Chester, PA

...and reappears in Maximilian's apartment. It is dark. The television is off, and Maximilian's chair is empty. Davis steps quietly to the back of the apartment and peeks into the bedroom. He is there. Sound asleep, exactly where his older self left him. *Perfect.*

Davis walks back into the living room and places Maximilian's NAVI on the table next to his chair. He taps on his computer, opens up a portal, steps in...

January 13th, 2648

2:58 pm
Nueva New York

...and steps into his lab.

Davis sighs deeply. Six hundred years, in about three minutes time. No matter how often he makes these trips, he's still amazed by it all. Built with his own hands, conceived by a master in the field of time travel theory, who would never live to see this miracle.

He steps to the machine to conduct the ritual that has brought him luck since he began his first experiments. He kisses his hand and places it on the name plate he had embossed on the steel plaque on the side of the machine's cylindrical body. He rubs his hand over each of the four letters and the version number next to it; KIKI3.

"Thanks, 6th Grandma," he says.

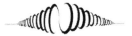

Ramadan 3, 1463

(August 29th, 2041)

1:37 am

Masomakali Kébé wakes up. No dream this time, or none that he could remember. In fact, he hasn't had a dream in the last few nights. He's been sleeping very well lately. After a few moments of lying still, he decides to pull himself up from the bed.

The view from his bedroom window is still as beautiful as it's always been. The fresh smell of flowers from the garden below is just as fragrant as it's always been. And every star in the sky is just as luminous as always. He breathes in deeply and exhales soothingly. He loves this house. He loves this village. He loves his life.

And he loves the woman who slides her arms around his waist. Nyah squeezes him tightly from behind, hugging up close to him.

"Dreams again?" she asks.

"No dreams," he says. "Just up, admiring everything we have."

She smiles and moves next to him to share the view.

"There's a storm coming," she says. "You can smell the moisture in the air. I love that."

"I love you," he says.

"Prove it," she says, taking his hand, and gently pulling him back to the bed.

August 29th, 2041
1:37 am
Manhattan, NY

Kiki can't sleep. Her brain has been running at full speed, non-stop, for several hours now, and it won't let up anytime soon.

Earlier in the day, she found herself wandering the halls of the 13th Precinct of the New York City Police Department. She has absolutely no idea how she got there. The last thing that she remembers before the police station is having a late breakfast with her boyfriend, Michael. After that, there are nearly two hours that are completely unaccounted for. That is until she made two discoveries.

The first is the text message on her NAVI from Dr. Oroko, which read: "CANT TALK—HAVE ANSWERS—MEET ME AT 13th PRECINCT ASAP." She called Maximilian twice, and left messages, but has not heard back from him. She is very worried that he may be in some danger. She didn't know what to think until she made her second discovery.

She received an email from Maximilian which contained a video clip. In the video, she sees Maximilian, another man, and three people that look as if they were part of the group of African refugees. There was an odd light in the room, out of view of the camera. She watches the Africans walk towards the light, with Maximilian and the man watching. The man uses some device that appeared to have summoned what Kiki immediately recognized as a portal of light which after a heated exchange, Maximilian and the man disappeared into. After a few moments, she watches herself entering the room and picking up the NAVI. Both the email and the text message were sent in that lost two hours period.

Other than the video evidence, she has no memory of entering the police station, or that room, or picking up the NAVI. Something happened between the moments when she sent the video to herself, and when she exited the room—something, or someone, blanked her memory. But who? Or what?

There is only one thing at the moment that is clear to her. After seeing what she saw in that video, watching Maximilian and that other man enter that portal, and the clear link between that and the African refugee event from three weeks ago, all the doubt, the ridicule, the condescension, all of it…it turns out that she was right!

Now, she has to prove it.

Thank you for reading!

If you are reading this, you have completed Book one of the three in what I call the World/Time Diaspora. I hope you enjoyed reading this book as much as I enjoyed writing it. This is one of those stories that I have had in my head since high school and has taken on various forms over the years until I finally decided to try writing it as my first novel.

I love science fiction. The very first show I fell in love with (outside of Batman '66) was called The Space Giants. It was the story of a young Japanese boy who befriends a family of robots that live in a volcano, could transform into rockets, and fought bad guys. Then came the obvious stuff: Star Wars, Star Trek, Space 1999, Alien, Battlestar Galactica, Buck Rogers, Blade Runner, Brazil & Time Bandits, RoboCop...and then came Back to the Future.

Now I had been familiar with time travel stories before—I was a fan of H.G. Wells' Time Machine, and my dad was a Whovian before I had ever heard that term. I always liked time travel stories, but there was something about Back to the Future that struck a chord. That 'something' is pretty obvious- and subject to plenty of stand-up comedy routines: how far could Black people go back in time until it wasn't a problem? Certainly not the 1950s, 40s, 30s, 20, and forget the 1800s-1600s, especially if you're talking about America!

There was a popular thought experiment that I would hear people discuss often; if you could go back in time, would you kill Adolph Hitler? Everyone has a story of what they would do to stop Hitler. I went to predominately white schools from 3rd – 12th grade. We spent a lot of time learning about the horrors of the Holocaust and the pain of the people who survived what is universally accepted as an abomination of humankind. It's important to learn these things with the hope that the more we know, the less we could be inclined to repeat those.

We talked about slavery, as well. In February, and as briefly as possible. The Middle Passage was mentioned. The institution of slavery was mentioned. Then it's Harriet Tubman to Martin Luther King and the next thing you know it's March! Traditionally speaking, there doesn't seem to be a lot of time and energy devoted to discussing Black history beyond slavery. As if we were just born on the boats on the way over. As if thousands of years of history and culture, which predated the first encounters with Europeans, had never existed. The most I got out of those lessons (as they were the same every year) was which of my white classmates gave me uncomfortable looks.

One day I was looking at my dad's vinyl records (he had a side-gig as a DJ on weekends). I love album covers from the 60s, 70s, and 80s, and I would stare at them for hours. The most substantial of these covers, which you know from reading this book, was from Earth, Wind and Fire's album "I Am," illustrated by Shusei Nagaoka. I would stare at the back cover, looking at that Nubian army emerging from this storm of light and fire, with spaceships behind them…that's when this thought hit me: What if you could go back in time and prevent African slavery from happening at all? That was the question that would haunt me for nearly 20 years. That's two decades of gestating, thinking, plotting, replotting, rethinking, and overthinking until I had the entire story in front of me.

It's widely known that science fiction is the best way to tackle sensitive social issues. Using allegory is far more gentle than being blunt. Stories like District 9 and the Alien Nation movie and series do a great job of telling the Middle Passage slave story in a modern setting. Each also had an interesting way of integrating their alien refugees into society. I thought it would be interesting to explore what our modern, frenzied, volatile and media-obsessed society would do if forced to look at its shame in front of the entire world, without the crutch of aliens from outer space.

At first I tried to write a screenplay, but after about 35 pages I was thinking, "This is turning into a 6-hour movie!" No way that could happen. I even thought of turning the entire thing into a comic book that I would illustrate. That was going to take a tremendous amount of time that I knew I didn't have. It didn't occur to me until nine years ago, when thinking about this story out of the blue, that I just said, "Fuck it. I've never written a novel, so…let's try it." After plotting out the entire story, I decided to break it up into 3 books.

I am currently sitting on the train on the way home from work. This is my daily 90-minute commute to and from Manhattan. Five days a week, about 40 minutes a day, 20 minutes in the morning and 20 minutes in the evening, is the time that I have available to devote to writing. It's almost exactly nine years to the day that I began committing this story to Microsoft Word, then Apple Pages, then Google Docs, and finally back to Microsoft Word; two laptops and an iPad, with an occasional iPhone.

Baby steps were what it took to get this book written. We all have busy lives, and it can seem like an impossibility to make the time to do the things that we love or want to try. If you want it and need it bad enough, you'll make it happen. With a family and a full-time job/career, it's difficult enough to make time for extra stuff, let alone dreams or desires. You may not have a huge chunk of time to devote to those dreams…but you can take little bits of time to make things happen. That's what this book is—little bites of time strung together.

I want to thank a few people for helping me out over the last several years. To Jonathan Gunning, your extensive historical notes were eye-opening and insightful- thank you, sir! To Mr. José Zulueta, who is one of my most honest and faithful sounding boards for all things related to story and the craft of storytelling- I referred to your notes often, they are always helpful to me! I would also like to thank Natalie N. Caro for her political insight- we'll need to talk about the next two books!

Next, I want to thank Jennifer Mishler, the invaluable eyes, and brain that helped me transform my caterpillar into a butterfly. Jennifer, you gave me FANTASTIC notes (yes, I just used caps- don't judge me) and helped me to see all of the pieces that I needed to chip away to see the statue. Metaphors aside, you rule! I can only hope that I live up to your feedback.

Mardie Millit is a dear friend of mine, and a multitalented hurricane of smarts and wit. Thank you Mardie for your notes and your edits. You are one of the great influences in making the final version of this book what it is- you gave me a lot to think about, and a couple of things to reconsider. Your eyes and brain are required for the next two books!

Lastly, I want to thank my lady, my partner, my love, Christina Cabot. I started writing this book two months before we met. Both the experience of writing my first novel and embarking on this journey with you have been two of the most fulfilling things in my life. I love you and I'm lucky to have you, and I'm lucky to have the babies—Ravi Alexander and Maya Eloise, my little dreamlets.

And to you, thank you for reading The Maximilian Emancipation. Be sure to look out for the next installment, Book 2: World/Time.

To be continued…

Gasp!

CHARLES A. CONYERS, JR.

Breathe!

CHARLES A. CONYERS, JR.

Jacob Morgan pushes his upper body up through the wave that crashes over his head. He coughs and struggles to breathe as he pulls himself up to his knees. He spits the salty sea water out of his mouth, crawling away. He collapses, panting and gripping the dry, warm sand.

After several minutes he pulls himself together. He rolls over on his back. He opens his eyes, expecting to see a crystal blue sky with fluffy white clouds- which he does. He also sees a silhouette of a person standing over him.

"Hello," the person says.

Jacob crab walks back in a panic, trying to pick himself up, but he is still a bit too weak. This person is still there, standing in the same spot, looking right at him. He is oddly dressed to Jacob, wearing a skin-tight suit of pure white that projected a ghost-like black aura. As Jacobs eyes adjusted to the light, he could see this person's face. His most striking features are his blonde hair and dark blue eyes and smooth light peach skin. To a certain type, he is the epitome of handsome.

"Excuse me," the man asks. "Mr. Morgan?"

The man steps towards Jacob, who flinches and moves back.

"Hold! Not a step closer, please!" demands Jacob. He reaches for his holster and pulls out his father's pistol.

The man stops. "I'm not here to hurt you, Mr. Morgan," he says. That's when Jacob notices the helmet the man is holding, as he slowly lowers it to the ground. The man also removes a large duffle bag strapped to his back. His equipment is made with a material similar to his suit- white with an eerie black glow.

"I'm here to help you," the man smiles.

"Who says I need help?" Jacob barks. "Who are you?" Jacob looks around, for the first time taking in his environment. He is on a beach. He sees grass, plants, and flowers that blend into fields that seem to spread out for miles until it hits the mountains. "Where in hell am I?"

"Allow me…" the man offers as he reaches into a pack mounted to his belt. He pulls out a thin sheet of glass. He taps on the surface and shows Jacob the display:

May 8th, 1768
2:19 pm
Benin, Africa

Jacob shakes his head. "Africa? What am I doing in Africa?"

"I believe you were rounding up niggers to take back to Virginia, correct?"

Jacob looks up at the man. "Who are you?"

The man laughs. "Yes, of course- my apologies! My name is Green. Alistair Green."

Alistair extends his hand. Jacob stares at it for a moment. He then lowers his gun and accepts the shake. Alistair smiles.

"My, I'm getting goose bumps!" he giggles. "I'm sorry, I don't mean to be so odd…I am a huge fan of yours. It's taken me six years, four months, three weeks, two days and a little over 13 hours to find you. I will tell you, sir, that every moment was well spent!"

Jacob, soggy with patches of sand stuck to his face and caked on his wet clothes, is baffled by everything Alistair said.

"I've been looking for you because I want to help you," Alistair insists. "I know what you have just been through. It must have been very confusing and frightening, seeing niggers acting like white men as if it was their God-given right! It must have been sickening, sir."

"What in Jesus' name are you talking about?" asks Jacob. "The only niggers I know about are the ones I sold, and the ones I own."

"Well, shit," Alistair says, shaking his head. "He wiped your memory. I still don't know how he does that. We're working on it. No matter. We've got to get you back home!"

Alistair reaches into his bag and pulls out a 2nd suit and helmet.

"Put this on, please," he asks with a smile.

"What?"

"Could you please put this suit on, sir?" asks Alistair in the most earnest tone. "It won't hurt if you put it on."

"What won't hurt?" asks Jacob.

Alistair smiles. "The fastest trip you've ever taken! Please, sir—you can put it on right over your clothes. It will stretch to fit."

Jacob reluctantly takes the suit. As he pulls it over his limbs, Alistair fiddles with his glass sheet device.

"Yorktown, correct sir?"

"Yes. Yes—how do you know all of this? How do you know me?"

Alistair smiles sheepishly, still tapping away on his device. "I don't want to say too much, sir—I can't say too much. I can only say that seeing you, and being in your presence...you represent all that is right and good with the White race, sir. Your leadership, your vision, your words...I keep saying you're an inspiration, but you're much more than that. You're...you're like a god to me, sir."

A few more taps and Alistair gives a thumb up. "All set! Now please, sir...don't be startled."

With a single tap, Alistair summons a sound reminiscent of a struggling hydraulic squealing into motion, followed by a high-pitched tearing sound and the blocky appearance of a bright pink rectangular door-shaped portal.

Jacob watches in astonishment as Alistair steps to the portal. He looks back and smiles at Jacob, extending his hand.

"Come with me, sir," Alistair offers. "Let's get you home. Let's make history."

Made in United States
Orlando, FL
25 June 2023